The Adventures of

Claire *Never* Ending

To Beatricé
and Eric,
Enjoy CarieB

Sponsors of Big Dreams

In your hands (or on your tablet) you are holding a dream come true. Along with 113 other outstanding backers, these folks helped this book come into the world, and gave support that will help with much more to come. Many thanks to:

Shannon Kehoe
Jennifer Hilliard
Ben Curran
Todd Ellis
Yin Zhou
J'Lynn Wheeler
Mark Wheeler
Marcelle Forget
Tony Brunelle
Nadia Fisher-Plum
Eric Plum
Don Kerr
Kate Kerr
Mary Larkin
Kate Foster
Alistair Downes
Luc Paradis
Lynn Townsend
Nicole Chryssicas
Roy Lalonde
Françoise Hinca
Szilárd Bárdosi
Anne Waters
Derrick Cooper
Linda Sabourin
Mark Armstrong
Shannon Kealey
Becca Brunelle
Jane Bidgood
Nicole Scobie
Judy Brunelle
Mike Brunelle
Louise Cheung
Michael Cheung
Anna Sámson
László Sámson
AnneMarie

THE ADVENTURES OF

Claire *Never* Ending

Catherine Brunelle

a.k.a. Ms. Brunelle, Mrs. Sámson,
Bumyboobs, Babe, The Girl,
Caterina, a fellow Claire

CC BRUNELLE

First Published in 2013

Published by Catherine Brunelle
www.CatherineBrunelle.com
www.facebook.com/CatherineBrunelleWrites
Ottawa, Ontario
Canada

For any orders or enquiries please send an email to ClaireNeverEnding@gmail.com.

Printed in the United States of America.

Cover text by Ian Kirkpatrick.
Author photograph by Lou Truss.

ISBN 978-0-9737525-2-6

This book is dedicated to my Zsolt.

You are *my* beginning, middle and end. I'll love you forever.

The Claires

Amelia Claire Earl
Elizabeth Claire Earl-Grey
Mrs. Brennan
The Witch of Arnprior
The Miss Pierres
Mrs. Anna Claire
Mrs. Aliza Claire Angyal
Mrs. Marianne Claire Rivers née Stives
Miss Amelia Claire Stives

Amelia Claire Earl, 2011

Amelia Claire Earl gazed over the rim of her basket that hung suspended from the massive yellow SunGro hot air balloon. Hundreds of meters below, farm houses with their rusted tin roofs sunk into the faded autumn fields, and in the distance the circle of a Ferris wheel was captured against the horizon of midday sky.

She was listening for her cue.

And suddenly, there it was—the faint but rhythmic thumping of a marching band drum.

Amelia launched into action. She checked the calibration of the wind and lowered the temperature of the flame to almost nothing, allowing the balloon to drop toward the ground at a safe but increasing speed. Ducking into her tiny cabin, she ripped off her puffy arctic jacket, grabbed at the leather coat with the sheep skin collar folded beneath the cot, and took one last gulp of her now cool chicken soup from her favourite "I heart NY" mug. She slammed the empty mug back down on the switched-off hot-plate. Amelia tugged off her woolly hat and neck warmer while simultaneously reaching into her jacket pocket and pulling out a white cashmere scarf. She tied it loosely around her neck as she stepped outside the cabin.

Amelia chewed on her thumbnail and she checked the wind direction again. "One more for SunGro, then this gets real," she told herself. "You'll be the first woman balloonist to circle the world solo. All we gotta do is catch that southerly swish."

Amelia thought back to her first meeting when she'd secured the sponsorship meant to send her around the world. She blushed at her recollected naivety.

***

"You're gonna be our star," Tony Dante had said while shaking her hand in the long-table board room of 342 Burke Plaza in downtown Calgary. "Or rather, you'll be our sun," laughed Tony, while his shoulders rose and fell like blue-blazer mountains.

"The sky's the limit," said Amelia. She nodded her head to the rhythm of his shake.

"And your budget, let's remember that limit too," reminded Harriet Wilson as she tapped her pen upon the rim of her glasses.

Tony was all charm, Harriet all business: they came as a set. Harriet was a smallish woman with a neat bun atop her head. She wore that knot of hair so tight it lifted her expression to one of constant shock. Like a sharpened pencil, Amelia had always thought.

That was nearly three years ago and it felt like an entirely different life, one overflowing with excitement and anticipation. Since then Amelia had only managed to circle North America, getting stuck in the Westerlies and North East Trade Winds and doing one promotional SunGro event after another. Then, last year, Hurricane Rita happened. Amelia had been blown so far off course there wasn't a chance of catching the southerly shift of currents before winter descended in full force.

But this year she'd catch it—she *had* to catch it. Nothing would stop her this time.

Amelia tidied up her bunk, rinsing out her mug and gathering scattered socks and panties into a small suitcase.

The fair would have clowns with bouquets of yellow balloons reading 'LIVE LIFE BRIGHTER;' children whose cheeks were fat with fried mini-donuts; parents wrapped in autumn fleeces; hobbyists looking up into the sky with magnified eyes; rows of cars parked in makeshift lines upon the field; a small Ferris wheel and rigged games; and a merry-go-round with gold painted ponies, cranking out a whimsical tune through its air pump organ.

There'd be cameras. There'd be reporters. There'd be a mayor. There'd be SunGro representatives handing out pens and pamphlets to promote their new 'Bright Living' plan to help save the environment. And, of course, there would be Walter, with another homemade sign waving above his head.

Amelia glanced in the small mirror on the cabin wall and plucked at her mess of red curls before putting on the leather aviator cap, which, according to SunGro Energies, was the standard uniform of a balloonist. They had presented her with the cap and its additional goggles when she had won the commission.

The air balloon was sinking closer to the fair. The marching band's thumping grew louder. This was it. One last stop. She checked the high-o-meter again; everything looked on track for a nearby landing. Her thoughts lingered and wavered with the shifting breeze as she and her balloon drifted closer to the SunGro fair.

"I can do this."

As her balloon passed above a plot of freshly laid earth, she suddenly felt overcome with an urge for buttered popcorn dripping with yellow salty goodness. Amelia stepped outside her cabin and stuck her head over the rim, sucking in the country smell, hoping to taste mouth-watering wafts of carnival popcorn. Instead, she inhaled a long, thick pull of cow shit.

"Ugh!" Amelia shouted as a wave of nausea punched her in the gut. "Oh my G—" she vomited a stream of chicken soup that dispersed over the side like rain.

Amelia heaved once more and when the spasms were over, she slid down to the bottom of the basket. "Oh no," she whispered. On her fingers, she began to trace back time and count the days of the calendar. "Oh no. It can't be."

Amelia wiped off her mouth. She crawled into her cabin doorway and sat on the floor, chewing on her thumbnail. Suddenly she stopped, spitting a piece of fingernail into the air.

"Get yourself together, girl!" she commanded. Amelia pointed toward the sky, and began shaking her finger to the rhythm of the increasingly loud marching band drum.

"Okay," she replied to herself.

"You can do this."

"I can do this," she replied again.

"Nothing is going to stop us," she stated.

"Not a damn thing," she agreed.

"All right!"

She meant it, *all* of her meant it. Nothing was going to stop her. Besides, even the best adventurers had hiccups along the way.

Amelia would touchdown, say hello, restock, and wave goodbye.

Mingling with farming manure, the scents of the carnival floated into her cabin doorway: sweet cotton candy, deep-fried corn dogs, and mountains of popcorn. Amelia stifled her urge to gag, because even more grasping than the smell was the sound of the crowd. People were cheering over the marching band's persistent playing.

"One more stop, and then goodbye," she promised herself.

Amelia would touchdown, say hello, take some photos, find some mouthwash, and then get on with her adventure. Oh, and restock as well; that was essential. Restock and get her mail, and appear in that television spot. Have a hot shower as well, send a postcard, do some laundry, have a nap, visit the pharmacy, grab some Chinese take-out *and then* goodbye everyone!

Hola, Mexico and the south east trades. Bye, bye, North America with its stubborn wind streams. And then, *and then,* upwards and onward to Africa, India, Asia, and success.

According to her plans pinned to the make-shift camper table beneath her large black cookie tin, today was her last chance to make the shift. Birds were already passing her in flocks, but they didn't have the obstacle of a pushy sponsor who insisted on 45 promotional stops within Canada and the US per spring/summer season, before proceeding to the next region.

Amelia stood up and left the cabin. She checked the flame; it was burning low. The balloon was descending nicely.

They were most likely watching her, watching and waiting, cameras and phones posed, necks craned upwards. Amelia slapped her cheeks and shook her fingers to work out the cold.

The high-o-meter slowly counted the distance between her and the ground. Seventy feet. Too far up for a good photo. Sixty feet. Fifty-five feet. Thirty-five feet—not a bad shot for a good lens.

Amelia once again leaned over the basket edge (*taking a deep breath before doing so*) and smiled at the crowd below. She shouted: "Hello!" and waved an arm high.

Clapping, shouts, and laughter greeted her smile. "Hello," she called again and pointed up to her balloon. "*Live life brighter!*" she called down to the upturned faces. There were the expected balloons, children and parents, SunGro promoters, Ferris wheel, marching band, cars, and ... oh, yes, she'd forgotten about the red carpet. A team of yellow-clad roadies were circling beneath her basket with a long red carpet, trying to match the exact place she'd touchdown.

Twenty feet. Ten feet.

People were moving forward. Amelia scanned the crowd. Harriet Wilson and Tony Dante walked up to the front of the group. They'd flown down to Alliance, Nebraska, for her last touchdown of the season in their North American market. Amelia's parents were *not* in the crowd. They were going to meet her somewhere in South America once she managed to catch the next current stream. Her dad had bought SPF 40, and her mother was waiting to buy a last minute deal on flights for wherever Amelia landed. But there *were* the Bakers, Chuck and Lindsey, who'd been at the last six touchdown spots. They were balloon hobbyists and followed every landing and festival within five states of their home. Amelia had already signed a page of their scrapbook that contained over 437 different air balloons with pictures of the pilots and the couple.

Amelia smiled to the Bakers before squatting in her stance and bracing for impact. After a few bumps, the basket scraped to an eventual stop. Cheers erupted as the roadies rushed through the crowd with the red carpet. Amelia's balloon was staked to the ground.

She did the big arm wave, as expected, and pointed above her head at her yellow balloon with the big red sun.

"Live life brighter!" she shouted with a grin that attested to the statement. Every month she applied whitening strips. Like the red hair and leather goggles, white teeth were written into her contract.

Through the parting crowd stepped Tony and Harriet. Tony, in his long, dark wool jacket, swaggered toward her. Harriet scurried after him, clipboard held by gloved hands and knot tight upon her head. They proceeded up the red carpet as the band launched into a hyper speed rendition of 'When the Saints Go Marching In'.

Amelia's eyes kept scanning the crowd, looking past rows of kids, yellow balloons, tired parents, flash bulb reporters, waving promoters, and clashing of symbols. Looking, looking, until... Ah, yes, there he was. Up above the crowd popped the sign of Walter D. Pouring, president and sole member of the Anti-Air Balloon society. In big black letters he had spelled out: *Bye, Bye, Balloons. Keep American Skies Clean.*

Walter D. Pouring had been at every single one of her touchdowns since she'd first stepped into a basket under the SunGro logo. He was always at the back of the crowd, always holding up a fresh sign with a new and ridiculous statement. The press loved him almost as much as they loved Amelia.

She gave Walter her trademark 'arm-over-head' wave. Walter raised his sign into the air and shook it more frantically. It was their standard greeting.

Tony and Harriet approached the basket as the music settled down; Amelia knew the routine. Standing inside her basket, she flashed a wide grin for the reporters. Tony and Harriet moved into position on either side, and Amelia put her hands upon their shoulders.

"Here!" "Here, Amelia." "Smile for the camera." *Flash—pop—click—snap.* Cameras shuttered around them. Tomorrow's headlines: *'Balloon girl greets SunGro suits.' 'SunGro's Sunshine.' 'Live Life Brighter.'*

"So you made it, finally," Harriet hissed between her teeth.

"Live life brighter," Amelia shouted to the crowd.

Tony cleared his throat. It was their cue. All three reduced their smiles to a look of solemn attentiveness.

"Welcome ladies and gentleman, boys and girls," boomed Tony. In another life he was probably a ring master. "SunGro Energies is proud to welcome Amelia to her last North American touchdown before sailing off to warmer skies."

"And I'm proud to be here in beautiful Nebraska!" called Amelia.

Cheers broke forth and the three of them smiled.

Flash—pop—click—snap.

"SunGro Energies is dedicated to efficient energy use, and Amelia is our messenger who will travel the world." Tony laid a giant hand upon her shoulder. "On behalf of SunGro, we'd like to welcome you to the last carnival of the autumn season. Amelia will be here to answer questions and take pictures, and then tonight we'll be hosting a massive fireworks display to send her off in good form."

Amelia swallowed a grimace. Fireworks meant explosions. Explosions meant smoke. Smoke meant all hell's worth of confusion in her balloon as she sailed away.

A petite woman began to walk up the red carpet and Tony welcomed her with his free hand. Harriet said nothing, as always, but eyed Tony's hand resting on Amelia's sheepskin jacket.

"Your very own Mayor Bloombridge!" shouted the ring master.

Cheers. Claps. Hyper-speed brass section.

Tony and Harriet shook the mayor's hand. The mayor looked very mayorish with her conservative blonde bob and dress suit of navy blue. Yet, turning to Amelia—there was nothing for it—Amelia had to bite the inside of her cheek to keep from laughing. Severely cross-eyed and smiling, Mayor Bloombridge shook Amelia's hand.

"Welcome to Alliance. We're proud to have you," said the mayor.

Mayor Lindsey Bloombridge had not always been cross-eyed. After two terms on the council listening to the complaints of Mr. Akeridge, a local man with little better to do than nit-pick and petition for more bylaws, she'd woken up one morning with a permanent case of the cross-eye.

Turning toward the crowd, the mayor cleared her throat. "On behalf of the citizens of Alliance, and the county of Osten, and Farmer Frank Richard whose field this is, we'd like to welcome Amelia, and hope she enjoys our fine hospitalities before embarking on her flight around the world."

Snap—flash—cheers—claps.

And because no event feels right without its expected motions, a large red ribbon was placed before Amelia, along with a cardboard set of giant, spray-painted-silver scissors.

Amelia climbed over the edge and accepted the scissors.

"Keep American skies clean!" shouted Walter from the back before the band launched into the Alliance County College "Fight-Fight-Fight" football song. People burst into cheers and reporters were ready to swarm with their barrage of questions.

Amelia closed shut the cardboard scissors upon the silky ribbon as Tony and Harriet pulled each end of the pre-sliced material; the red pieces fell to the ground.

The ground...

Amelia was on the ground with SunGro, and the Mayor, and the press, and the children, and their parents, and the balloonists, and the clowns, and the band. On the ground for now.

And the group closed in on her.

One hour later Amelia had posed for a photo with nearly everyone at the fair.

"Get to the station in time for your interview. The driver will know where to go," Harriet reminded her as she and Tony stepped into their black SUV with tinted windows. Off they sped over the muddy roads towards the city.

Amelia turned from the road and headed back toward the fairground. Already, she was itemizing her to-do list.

The lead roadie, Chris, ran up to her in his yellow T-shirt. He was appointed by Harriet to assist with all things air balloon: restocking necessities, checking the equipment, changing the linens, stocking thermals, and scanning the basket's cabin roof for leaks. Amelia had passed him a list of problems after cutting the pre-sliced ribbon.

"Getting there, Amelia," Chris told her. "But that Mr. Pouring is causing a problem. He's standing in front of the balloon waving that sign of his and marching back and forth around us."

Amelia looked over at the yellow balloon. "I don't see him," she said, squinting.

"I told him you were coming and he ran away."

"Of course."

"He was leaning over your basket at one point, looking at the new supplies."

Amelia shook her head. Again, Walter was interfering where he shouldn't.

"I'll come and check on the equipment once more. There's just something I need to do before that."

Chris the roadie ran off toward the balloon. SunGro roadies, by nature, always ran.

Amelia walked off towards the fair. She could already taste the popcorn.

***

With buttery fingers, Amelia slammed the door of her private car and pulled off her costume. "Finally!"

"Ma'am?" asked the driver, looking back.

"Into town, please. Harriet said you knew where the TV station was?"

"That's right."

"I'll just need to make one stop before we get there."

"The hotel, ma'am?"

Amelia glanced over at the old suitcase beside her. It was a beat-up hand-me-down, and inside was her cookie tin with the orange grove lid, a week's worth of dirty underwear, and all the other laundry she couldn't stand having the roadies clean for her.

"Not the hotel yet, though I'm dying for it. Ah, any pharmacy will be fine, thanks. My allergies are killing me."

"Could be decay this time of year. My wife's allergy to mould keeps her up all night sniffling."

Amelia nodded. "She should try steam; it helps me sometimes. You just pour a bowl of hot water, add fresh mint and stick your head over it with a towel. If nothing else, it's refreshing."

They bumped over the country road as the driver veered right and left to avoid the massive puddles of mud.

"Sorry, I didn't get your name," said Amelia.

"Curtis."

"Good to meet you Curtis."

"And you, miss?"

"Amelia."

"Amelia," he repeated.

Stretched out on either side of the road were flattened fields of pale gold, wheat and corn now harvested. The sky was a good one, full of blue. Crows flitted up and down with black blurring wings as they moved from field to field. And sometimes, in the far off, Amelia spotted deer amongst the old trees that stood as wooden guardians from the wind. It would have made a nice postcard.

"Pretty area," said Amelia.

"We like it," replied Curtis.

There was a jovial horn honking behind them. The Bakers' four-by-four SUV pulled up beside Amelia's car. Lindsey was waving as Chuck pounded on the gas and went skidding ahead of them. Amelia waved back. They seemed nice enough, the Bakers. Maybe a little *too* crazy for balloons, if that were possible.

"Fools," grumbled Curtis as the mud sprayed against his window and he flipped the wipers on.

Amelia sat back and relaxed as Curtis navigated onto better roads. She stared out the window as the fields slipped away, replaced by suburban homes and four-way lights. She watched it all, yet saw none of it.

Curtis pulled into a strip mall and pointed towards the far corner. "Pharmashare, right there, biggest pharmacy in town. They'll have your medicine."

Amelia slipped on her jacket. "Thanks; I'll just be a minute."

"No worries, miss."

It was a big pharmacy with bright lights and an open layout. Amelia passed through the cosmetics section and glanced around cautiously. It was already 11:45 a.m., and she was meant to be on television at 12:30. Harriet would start calling the driver any moment, and the driver would say they'd stopped at a pharmacy for allergy medicine. Harriet, always the sharp one, might realize she'd never seen Amelia with allergies before. But, then again, this close to show time she might be too busy panicking.

A mother with three kids swarmed around Amelia as the family marched towards the grocery section. The youngest, zipped up in a puffy blue jacket, turned to her and stuck out his tongue.

"Danny!" cried his mom, shrugging an apology towards Amelia.

Amelia flashed her bright, white smile, and immediately felt embarrassed. This wasn't the stage, or her balloon. Time to stop over-acting.

Looking above the aisles, she scanned the signs. Fluorescent lights lit up glossy white floors that reflected beige steel shelves, on which sat colourful products lined up in neat rows. The shop *was* huge; it had everything. Allergy medicine was aisle three.

Amelia grabbed a box of *Sinuflex*: good for congestion, itchy pallet and runny eyes.

Next was the hard part. Flipping up her collar, she leaned against the shelf of allergy medicine and checked whether anyone was around.

No one. Good.

Glancing up at the aisle signs, she moved row to row. A man stood by the prescription desk leaning on his cane. *No good.* She turned around and lingered, picking at a loofah that hung upon a rack.

Peeking back, the man and his cane were being addressed by a pharmacist. Doctor-patient confidentiality, figured Amelia; she was safe. Back to walking by the aisles, scanning the signs above.

'Family Planning.'

Here we go.

She dove into the aisle, stopping by the cardboard baby display.

Four feet away a young, tall and skinny fellow with a case of acne hovered by the condoms. Amelia hovered by the pregnancy tests.

Each glanced at the other. Each tried to act natural.

It was awkward.

Turning away, she faced the opposite row, this one was lined with tampons and sanitary pads. *No better.* She turned back to the tests. The boy snatched at a red condom box and hoofed it. Amelia wished she'd been so quick.

There were options, lots of options: *ClearLine; BabyBlue; Pregnancy Predict; Pregnascare; Pharmashare's Own; First Detector; Early Word; Stork Pen; Babyator; Initial Response; Oopsies; Am I Stick; Pregnant Pause; Ovula; Early Detection; First Trimester; SensiStream; Clinicare.*

Amelia grabbed the most expensive box and tucked it beneath her arm. Walking toward the cash desk, she also snatched a bottle of apple juice from the grocery section. She'd take the test after the interview. That would be that, and then she'd get on with life.

Nothing was going to stop her from flying around the world.

Nothing, nothing, nothing.

Not a thing except herself.

***

"Okay, and five, four, three," the director stepped back while signalling two, then one.

"Whatcha eating, Alliance? Good afternoon from us at Studio 24 in the heart of Alliance town centre."

"What are *you* eating, Alliance? Welcome back for another show, and Trudy, what's going on this afternoon?"

"Well Bob, big things are happening in our small town today. And by big, I mean huge!"

"Ha ha, that's right, Trudy. We have a growing star with us here in Studio 24: Amelia Claire Earl."

"Not that you're huge, Amelia," said Trudy, grinning.

"Ha ha, no, that's right, but her hot air balloon is!"

"Oh ho, that's right, Bob. Today we'll be talking with Amelia of SunGro Energies about living life brighter."

"And after that, John from the Crossroad Café will be dropping by to announce next week's specials—"

"*And* he'll be showing us his secret recipe for meringue puffs, Bob."

"That's right, Trudy, I hope you're ready to eat dessert this morning."

"I sure am. And finally we'll have..."

They were like two idiotic parrots perched on a ledge chattering to one another. Amelia couldn't peel her eyes away. Maybe they were Siamese twins separated at birth, or maybe they were robots programmed to talk in synchronization, or maybe they just felt as ridiculous as her with their over-eager smiles, blown out hair, freshly pressed jackets, and bleached white teeth.

Tony and Harriet watched by the side, sitting in high folding chairs and nodding towards her. Tony winked and smiled. Harriet chewed her lip; live television made her nervous.

During the last community television interview, Amelia had slipped into a thoughtful haze. In the middle of the host's question, she mumbled that she would "like to be naked all the time," which resulted in about five seconds dead-air because the interviewer, Jake Hardgrove, had actually dispelled his nerves by picturing Amelia naked, as he did for all of his guests, and thought that maybe she'd read his mind.

"Are you naked often?" had been his next question, which almost killed Harriet who was all about company image and staying on message.

Amelia had said no, because it was too cold in her balloon, but otherwise she'd have considered the idea.

"Psst," hissed Harriet, waving her hands as Bob and Trudy jabbered back and forth. Amelia blinked and caught her eye. Harriet shook her pointed head and mouthed, "Wake up," which was just as well, because the questions started pouring in.

"Where are you from?"

"Smallstream, Alberta; that's up in Canada."

"Oh! I have an aunt in Canada."

"Is it cold up there?"

"In the balloon?" asked Amelia

"No, in Canada!"

"Oh ho, Bob!"

"It's cold in the winter."

"Well, miss, it must be freezing in that balloon of yours."

"That's why I'm catching the southerly swish."

"Southerly swish, sounds like a dance move."

"Ha ha, Trudy!"

"Oh ho, Bob!"

"It's a change in the wind stream."

Amelia normally tried to shine during her interviews, but today was too difficult for her. Something about television people put a bad taste in her mouth, and today of all days the taste was beyond bitter. Everyone was paid by someone, she supposed They were all little circus dogs with bow ties. Jump, sit, smile, laugh; it was like looking in a warped mirror, because she was one of them too, wasn't she?

"... by living life brighter?"

"Sorry?" asked Amelia.

Harriet snapped up from the side and waved her hands.

"Right," Amelia recovered. "SunGro Energies is encouraging everyone to live life brighter by opting to reduce their carbon footprint. Everywhere I go, I spread their message, and I'll have gone almost everywhere soon, at least in North America; hopefully the rest of the world too, in time."

"You're on a mission to balloon around the world solo?"

"That's right. I'll be the first woman."

"Well, you sure look the part, very Amelia Earhart."

"That's the idea. Red hair is part of my job, but it's from a box to be honest."

"Oh ho!" laughed Trudy.

"All women have their secrets," added Bob with a wink.

"Yep," replied Amelia.

"Just don't go getting lost without a trace like that other Amelia!"

"Bob!"

"Ha ha, sorry, Trudy!"

"I'm named after my—" Amelia held out her fingers and counted, "great-great-great-great-great-great grandmother, Amelia Claire Stives, not Amelia Earhart."

"Well then, you'll be fine."

"Just fine."

"Totally fine."

"Alliance wishes you loads of luck."

"Loads of luck!"

"Lots of luck."

"Best of luck!"

"Thanks," replied Amelia.

"You can catch Amelia and her air balloon at Farmer Richard's field just 10 minutes out of town. She'll be launching tonight in a blaze of fireworks, so don't miss it!"

"I know I'll be there, Trudy."

"Me too, Bob!"

"Me three."

"Oh ho, Amelia!"

"Ha, ha. Next up: John from the Crossroad Café will be coming round ..."

Fade to commercial. Two-minute change around: out with Amelia, on with John and his chalk board of specials.

Rising from their chairs, Tony and Harriet guided Amelia away from the studio.

"You did good, kid," said Tony. He winked down at her.

"I can't stand interviews," replied Amelia.

"How are your allergies?" asked Harriet. "You didn't sniff once."

"*Sinuflex*; nothing beats it."

"I'll have it stocked on the balloon." But Harriet didn't write it on her notepad, and she wrote *everything* on her notepad.

"I just need rest," said Amelia.

Stepping through the back door to the studio, they came out onto the side street crammed between the buildings of downtown Alliance. There were rows of dumpsters, hidden from the main street, yet conveniently beside the exit. The smell of trash lingered in the air. As Amelia opened her mouth to ask why they'd come out the back, she got a mouthful of the sour-sweet decomposing stench.

With a whooping surge of stomach muscles, Amelia vomited over Tony's polished black shoes.

"My shoes!" Tony kicked out his feet and wiped away the corn dog and bile.

"Are you sick, Amelia?" asked Harriet. She clicked her pen as it hovered above her notepad. "We can't send you away sick."

Tony was whimpering over his shoes, now knocking his feet against the station wall and shaking off the last drops of Amelia. "God damn it," he muttered. "These are good leather."

"Sorry, Tony. The nerves just hit me along with the garbage smell," replied Amelia. She was still half bent and trying to stay upright from the nausea. Wiping her mouth, she stood up and flashed a weak smile at Harriet and Tony (who was now using Harriet's handkerchief to polish away the last traces of vomit), and prayed there were no bits between her teeth. "I'm fine, it's just nerves. Today's a big day, lots riding on this."

"Lots," replied Harriet. She tucked away her pen.

Amelia walked towards Curtis's car as Harriet and Tony stepped into their SUV and drove away. Sometimes Amelia couldn't stand the pair of them.

Stepping into the car, she asked the driver to take her to her hotel. As he pulled away from the studio parking lot, she opened the bottle of apple juice, despite having just thrown up, and drank it all in several long gulps.

***

A dark hotel room with fresh pressed linen rumpled on the bed, the duvet pulled back, pillows askew, and a hint of Lysol in the air. There were the expected sterile objects: a desk with a wooden chair, radiator beneath the window, bedside table with a bible in the drawer, and Amelia on the bed sheets spread over the duvet in a long, white T-shirt and panties. Lights out, curtains pulled, opened black cookie tin beside her, its lid with the faded image of an orange blossom tossed onto the floor.

All around her were the postcards, those many postcards she'd flipped through since childhood. The middle-named Claires and their countless notes: *"Arrived safely in Bytown, bought some fish from that market I'd mentioned. Not as fresh as home.""We miss you here, come back soon." "Apple pie needs at least ten dashes of cinnamon, otherwise there's no point." "Making do with what we can, thanks for the tea leaves. Love to all." "It's kicking now. She'll be a strong one."*

In the dim light they were difficult to read; certainly, the older ones were impossible with their faded ink, but Amelia couldn't handle any more brightness. She'd been going over the postcards, feeling the bumps on their surface, looking at their browning spots, dropping age-old glitter onto the sheets. One by one, the Claires, her mother, and her grandmother, and her great-grandmothers all the way to her name-sake. They had all managed to survive these moments, and Amelia would too. Though it wasn't survival that scared her, it was sacrifice.

Between her fingers Amelia flipped over a postcard of the Alliance County balloon festival. She had grabbed it at the pharmacy while being rung through as the clerk, name-tagged Dotty and well near retirement, looked Amelia up and down, passing the pregnancy test, apple juice, and postcard over the scanner.

Dotty Ann Brown had tried to have children since turning eighteen and marrying her sweetheart Aaron Brown, of Brown and Son Tailors in Alliance. Aaron was the 'Son' back then, not the 'Brown'. They'd tried for a baby for 35 years until the menopause got her. When Aaron's father finally passed, they'd taken down the 'Son.' It was simply 'Brown Tailors' now.

But Amelia didn't know any of that; she paid in cash and took off to the car.

She turned the postcard over and over in her fingers. There was a picture of Alliance with hundreds of air balloons filling its sky: red ones, yellow ones, blue ones, rainbows, beer mugs, clovers, logos, symbols, all clustered above the town.

Flipping it over, the postcard was bare except for the single message 'I'm pregnant' scrawled in Amelia's hand across the back.

She turned it over again, then again and again. One day it'd be in the old black cookie tin. One day, some day, her daughter, and her daughter's daughter, and her daughter's daughter's daughter would read it and wonder.

Knock, knock.

"Who's there?" called Amelia. But she knew already. Sliding off the king-sized bed, she pulled at the bottom of her shirt and shuffled towards the door. A ray of light shone through the peephole. Looking through, she unhooked the latch and let him in.

"I thought you'd never come," she mumbled, retreating to her bed.

"Why no lights?" Walter reached for the bed lamp.

"Just leave it." Amelia picked up the postcard again, flipping it over in her fingers. "Anyone see you come in?"

"No, don't worry. No one's watching."

"Harriet's watching."

"She's too busy with Tony."

Amelia smirked, "Tony's too busy with himself."

She didn't feel like being big and bold right then. She felt like being spiteful and hurtful and curled up in the dark. "It was *his* idea to have the fireworks. I told him over the radio, "no fireworks, Tony." I said it explicitly, you know that? But there you go, he announces to everyone that I'll fly off in a display of bangs, bursts and, Technicolor fire. Those two..."

"I've already got another sign made: Only jerks use fireworks—"

"Keep American skies clean?" guessed Amelia.

"Exactly."

Walter put down his signs and took off his costume. SunGro Energies had hired him based on his booming voice and ability to look like a non-threatening crazy man. But really it was just a red flannel hunting hat and thick glasses wrapped in cello-tape that did it. Once he took those off, he was just good old Walter with the proud face, messy hair, and smile that melted Amelia.

At first she'd believed the show. He'd appear with a new slogan, raise a protest, settle quietly, and then the press would flock to question him and, in turn, they'd always side with Amelia against the mad man in the flannel hat.

He never missed one of her touchdowns.

And she'd wave, she'd always wave and he'd shake his sign. But earlier this year, during her third tour of North America, one day when no one else was paying attention as she touched down in St. Jovite, Quebec (on a landing where Amelia had attracted only two pressmen and a bus-load of Japanese tourists who seemed genuinely thrilled to meet her), one day—that very day—Walter had smiled.

Then she had learned everything. *Everything.*

Walter pulled back a curtain, light poured into the hotel room. "What is it? SunGro?" he asked.

"No, not SunGro; I can deal with Harriet and Tony." SunGro, the press, the selling of her dignity, and all the crap she agreed to for the sponsorship, it all dissipated the moment she took her balloon into the air. That was her real life; that was where Amelia Claire Earl came alive. Down here, it was business; up there, nothing but pleasure.

"So what is it?"

"Oh, Walt..."

Walter moved aside the postcards and climbed upon the bed sheets. His fingers were still cold as he laid them upon her bare thigh. "Are you worried about going south?"

Despite his stupid signs, he really did support her.

"You wanna come with me, Walter? Just for one ride? I'll stuff you in the laundry hamper, no one will know. We can make love at three thousand feet."

Amelia wanted to do everything in her balloon. She'd been flying since she'd turned sixteen and was hired at the Great Big Balloon Company outside Calgary in Beaverbrook. Ever since then she'd slept in balloons, eaten in balloons, played in balloons, found love in balloons.

Walter just smiled and shook his head. He was afraid of heights.

"You'll be lonely, is that the problem?" he asked.

Amelia almost laughed. Lonely, no, more like crowded. She had more company now than she'd anticipated.

"Well, I don't know what I'm going to do, but I guess you ought to know." Sighing, Amelia pointed toward the bathroom. "Check out what's in there."

Walter's fingers slid down her leg as he moved towards the bathroom. She picked up her postcard again, reading the message over and over. He flipped on the light switch and a fluorescent glow flooded through the doorway.

"Underwear?" asked Walter. Amelia had soaked and hung her laundry. The shower curtain was decorated with dripping bras and panties.

"No," called Amelia. "Look by the taps." She began scooping up the postcards into the cookie tin, all except for the Alliance County balloon festival, that was either headed for the garbage or the post box; she hadn't decided yet.

"Amelia?" called Walter.

"Yes."

"Does a pink happy face mean what I think it means?"

"Yes."

"Because the box here says it means that you're—"

"Yes, Walter."

There came a long pause from the bathroom.

Amelia stared at her postcard, flipping it over and over. Balloons or babies. *Balloons or babies?*

"Amelia?" Walter was standing in the bathroom doorway.

"Yes, Walt?"

He came over to her and climbed onto the bed. Carefully he placed his cold fingers upon her stomach. "Will you marry me?"

"Dear Lord, Walter, too soon!" She laughed and smiled at his large, shocked expression. "You're such a sweet fellow and I love you, but no, I won't marry you. Not yet."

"But it's my baby!"

"I don't even know if I'll keep it." As she said it aloud, it became obvious. She had to keep the baby. Maybe if it'd been a one-night stand, or if she'd been younger, or if he hadn't been there on her bed, looking at her like that.

"You have to keep it," whispered Walter, pushing up beside her so that they were face to face.

"Walt, babies aren't my dream. It's the ballooning. I can almost taste it I'm so close; first woman around the world solo. I can't stop now. I can't, okay? And what would I *do* with a baby? I fly air balloons, not storks. I've never even held a baby for God's sake, and now one's *inside* of me!"

She wouldn't cry. Amelia would not cry. *No, no, no.* Not even with all the self-pity in the world, she wouldn't cry.

"Don't be stupid, Amelia," Walter stroked her stomach. "No one will make you stop flying. I'm here, too, you know. We'll manage this together."

Whether he was right or wrong, she wanted to believe him. She wasn't ready to *marry him*, but she was ready to believe him. Flipping the postcard, she wrote her parents' address. She'd mail the note, and one day her daughter's daughter's daughter would read it, and wonder, and make her own decision.

***

Flash—pop—click—snap.

Drum roll, please, trumpets up, and one, two, three: ready!

When the saints, go marching in,

Oh, when the saints go marching in!

The band stood before the stage lifting their feet in time with the music, dressed for the occasion in full band uniform and yellow SunGro badges. In place they marched, up down, up down, until mud churned beneath their feet. *One-two-three-four!* The conductor waved them on.

"Amelia!" "Amelia over here!" "Smile, honey!" "Amelia, here!" "Jerks, jerks—fireworks!" "One last shot, here, here!" "Amelia!"

Up the red carpet she walked, pale and disoriented. Today's carpet stretched from the Ferris wheel all the way to the stage at the edge of the fair. Her balloon was sitting picturesque in the background, lit up by spotlights in the dark Alliance sky.

For the sake of photographic opportunity, she, Tony, and Harriet had just attempted to board the Ferris wheel, except that Tony was a massive man and the two women could barely squeeze beside him. So, left on the ground while the girls took a spin, Tony charmed the journalists with how they'd discovered Amelia, all the while waving and winking at them both.

Sitting there, waving back and smiling, Amelia and Harriett had lifted off the ground. Slowly, slowly the Ferris wheel turned. Amelia, the thick-haired redhead with the achingly wide smile and forever drifting eyes, and Harriet, the thin-haired pencil pusher who was not made for publicity but was sharp as a tack. Together they rose, paused, swung, and rose a little higher.

Against the carnival lights Amelia watched traces of her breath. Around them everything glowed, flashed, rang, and whirled; the fairground was alive at night, and they were thick in the middle. The merry-go-round played its crank organ music; children shouted as they won toy dogs; and the cameras *snapped-snapped-snapped* as the women rose upwards. Manure, mud, and fairground scents floated through the cool Alliance air of Farmer Richard's field.

Amelia wrapped her white scarf tighter and adjusted her aviator cap. On the balloon a proper thermal jacket was waiting, along with long johns and head gear that could hold off -40 degree weather.

She waved to the lights and sounds. Walter was out there too, watching her from afar. They'd had their goodbye, but he'd be watching and shaking his sign; it was his job, after all.

And the band struck up in the distance.

SunGro Energies truly knew how to send a girl off. Send her off and impress, impress that 'living life brighter' meant doing so with SunGro Energies. *SunGro Energies: living life brighter.* God, Amelia was tired of it; the stupid slogan didn't even make sense if you were talking about energy conservation. Regardless, there'd be less direct promotion in the future, once she caught the swish. Amelia would no longer be flying over their target nations.

Harriet pressed her clip-board into her body. "Having a good time?" she asked Amelia.

Amelia smiled, sighed, and waved down to the cameras. The Ferris wheel paused, swung, and Tony blew them a kiss.

"As good as ever," replied Amelia. Her cold cheeks spread with warmth; she could never control her blush. "It's a big day."

"A big day," repeated Harriet. She released one hand from the clipboard, took out a pen from her breast pocket, and clicked it.

The Ferris wheel rose, paused, and swung. They were at the top now, the very top. From here Amelia could see the make-shift stage, her lit-up balloon, and the roofs of each pigeon crap-covered stall. It was less glamorous from the higher up, though the sounds softened here.

Harriet clicked her pen again.

Amelia felt an urge to fill the silence with conversation. "Well, with the swish and everything, if I miss the swish it's all over for this year, again. If I don't leave tonight I may not leave at all."

"Of course, the swish, but I didn't mean that, no. I meant your pregnancy."

The wheel descended, paused and swung in the air.

"What are you talking about?"

Harriet pulled back the papers of her clip board and revealed Amelia's Alliance Balloon Festival postcard. Clearing her throat, she read: "'Hey Mom and Dad, I'm pregnant!' They'll love this, won't they? Who won't love the fact that 'dream girl, Amelia Claire Earl' is with child? A little baby! But wait: 'Oh no, no, no,' they'll all say, 'Isn't *she* the girl in the balloon, the one flying into unknown territory—'"

"Unknown territory?" Amelia interjected. "South America is not unknown terri—"

"Unknown territory!" insisted Harriet. "'Isn't she the one flying into unknown territory? Oh, that poor baby!'"

Amelia grabbed her postcard and tucked it into her jacket pocket. "You're a pencil-headed bitch, Harriet."

"And you're a box-dyed slut, Amelia, but the point *here* is that I have the power to cut your purse strings." Harriet raised her long pale fingers and snipped in the air. (When she was much younger, Harriet had played the piano and her favourite song was "Silent Night", which she would perform on the piano in her comatose grandmother's room every morning until the old woman finally woke and told little Harriet to 'shut up with the racket already,' right before flat-lining and dying in bed.)

Amelia watched her imaginary purse strings fall to the ground. "Tony won't stand for this."

"Tony's a monkey."

"A monkey who won't be impressed."

"I'll buy him a new toy, maybe a blonde this time, someone younger. We'll get another girl to replace you. He'll forget. He's forgotten before."

"This isn't fair. I can't be more than four weeks—"

"Fair? SunGro Energies cannot be held liable for the potential risk of a delicately pregnant woman embarking on a dangerous journey at our insistence."

"Have you told anyone?" asked Amelia.

The Ferris wheel lowered, paused and swung. *Snap—snap—snap*, she could hear the cameras again. The band was kicking into their millionth rendition of "When the Saints Go Marching In." Tony was shouting a grand 'hello.' Harriet leaned over and waved.

"No, Amelia, you can do that yourself, right now on the stage. Tell everyone you're not flying tonight; tell Tony he's a father; tell the world to live life brighter."

Harriet clicked her pen.

Amelia almost threw up.

The Ferris wheel turned, stopped, rocked. Then the bar was lifted and they were both set free.

Flash—pop—click—snap.

"Amelia!" roared Tony, the large-suited monkey, "Your audience awaits!" He held out his hand for Amelia as Harriet slid unassisted from the seat. Amelia took his support and began walking down her red carpet. It was no wonder Harriet assumed he was the father. Harriet and Tony were the only people Amelia had spent any substantial time with during the SunGro tour, or at least as far as they knew. Even now, Amelia clung tightly to his arm. If she let go for just one second, she would most certainly collapse.

"Amelia!" "Amelia over here!" "This way, here!" "Amelia, here!"

"Smile, honey; this is good news not bad." Tony slapped his hand upon her shoulder. "You're finally gonna fly around the world."

Roadies ran, people clapped, the band played, and Mayor Bloombridge smiled as she gave a warm Alliance County welcome to Amelia and SunGro Energies. Onto the stage they walked. Up, up, up the stairs, and the band kept marching in their place.

Amelia stood beside Harriet as Tony accepted the microphone and began to charm the crowd. There were the Bakers front and centre with their binoculars at the ready. Chuck Baker waved a photograph past the line of roadies and bodyguards. Amelia bent down to sign his picture.

"Good luck!" said Lindsay Baker, raising her arms as a cheer sprang from the audience.

Standing up, Amelia was given the stage. Tony moved back, "Say something to your fans," and he passed her the microphone. Amelia looked across the crowd. She saw frosted breaths, running noses, rubbing palms, and glowing eyes, hundreds of glowing eyes, all of which were glued to her, glued to Amelia Claire Earl who was going to fly around the world in her giant yellow balloon.

Flash—pop—click—snap.

Amelia didn't know what came next. Not until she heard the click of Harriet's pen.

Click, click. Click, click. 'Get on with it; get on with it,' Harriet was saying through her Biro Morris code.

Amelia put on her best game face. She refused to disengage, even if about to disappoint. "Hello, everyone! How are you this evening? On behalf of SunGro Energies, I'd like to welcome you here tonight!"

Cheers, claps, whistles, shouts.

Her eyes scanned the crowd, scanned and scanned, but she couldn't find Walter. This would have been easier if she could see him watching.

"Flying around the world has been my dream. And dreams, as you well know, are worth chasing, *always* worth chasing."

Here she faltered. An enveloping silence buzzed between her ears as she glanced down at the stage with its masking tape place-marker and took a deep breath.

"But I guess there's not much to say now..."

Click click, Click click.

"...except the very truth. I have loved flying, and I will love flying again, but today I have to announce that I won't—"

BANG.

An explosion detonated above her head.

BANG BANG BANG.

Green trails of light coloured the sky.

"Damn it!" shouted Tony, "They weren't meant to fire till takeoff!" Tony ran from the stage, followed by a yellow stream of roadies and a few snapping, clicking cameras.

CRACK! BANG! Trails of purple, red, pink, blue spiralled out around them. The crowd clapped and cheered as the fireworks exploded one after another, *BANG BANG BANG* like the brass band's cymbals.

Amelia put down the microphone and turned to the night sky. Pink screamers were twisting above the fairground, then orange poppers and purple implosions. They crackled and sizzled and sprinkled to the ground. Harriet was frantically flipping through her clipboard papers.

All around her people roared with each new burst. Amelia looked down again, towards the people, towards the ground. There were no signs above the crowd, no cleverly crafted protests. Walter was nowhere to be seen, her lovely, wonderful Walter. Amelia stepped away from the microphone.

Click, click.

Amelia turned towards Harriet. "Harriet Wilson, you listen to me right now, and put *down* that damned pen."

Harriet looked up from her board, but she kept the pen in hand.

"I *am* going up in that balloon. And I *am* leaving the second these explosions clear. *How?* With your precious SunGro endorsement. *Why?* Because Tony isn't the father. Walter D. Pouring is the father of this baby, and unless you want every single media agent to know within the next five seconds that you've hired him to kick up attention, you'd better keep this little secret to yourself, at least for now. And besides," snapped Amelia, "why can't I fly pregnant? What age are we living in anyhow?"

CRACK. BANG. FIZZ. SWIRL.

Harriet's mouth hung open in a perfect, thin-lipped 'O'. She blinked and tucked away her pen.

"Tony's not the father?"

***

At exactly 21:46 that night, Amelia Claire Earl lifted from the Alliance County farmlands of Farmer Richard's field. Up, up, up she rose into the dark, smoke-cleared sky. Down below people clapped, cameras clicked, and Walter waved his protest sign. Earlier, as Amelia was walking toward the stage, he had temporarily donned a yellow roadie T-shirt and sternly instructed the fireworks to be shot off early; it had been too late to stop things as Tony ran toward the pyrotechnics.

The high-o-meter measured her ascent: twenty, forty, sixty, eighty, a hundred feet above the ground. The band sound began to fade. The carnival's smell lingered, but was soon replaced with the sharp scent of ozone and frost. Higher and higher, until, with a slight twist in the breeze and a slow turn of the balloon, the winds changed their gentle direction and carried her away.

Amelia zipped up her thermal jacket, placing a mitten-covered hand above her stomach, and sipped on a warm cup of chicken soup. All around her were quiet honks, chirps, and rustling feathers. Birds flew in streams that turned with the breeze. It was the current's caress, the southerly swish.

Elizabeth Earl-Grey, 1980

Imagine a woman who appears normal. Her hair is a mass of soft brown curls that are resting upon a red knit scarf tied around her neck. Her overalls are plain blue, under which she wears a light red sweater with the sleeves pushed up. There are gold bangles on her wrists, plain studs in her earlobes, a silver ring on her finger, and when she smiles at you and introduces herself, "I'm Elizabeth Claire, my friends call me Liz," you smile back and say 'hello' and don't suspect she's anyone special; certainly, no more special than the other women around campus.

But have you looked inside her pocket? Have you asked about that envelope?

Go on, ask her now.

"Oh, this?" she'll say, patting her hip. "It's something I carry. Postcards from my mom, her mom and our family. That's all. It's just a few of them, most are at home." And suddenly she'll become quiet. Words will form in her mouth and you'll see her tasting them, sucking them, swallowing them whole. She won't speak again, *not* once you ask about the postcards. Not until a new idea springs to mind.

"I'm pregnant, you know" she'll suddenly say. She'll tell you how far, "Six weeks"; about the father, "My husband Eddie, he's a caretaker here"; and the gender, "A girl, I think. Of course we don't know yet but all the women in my family have girls first." She'll even tell you the baby's name, "If she's a girl, then Claire will be the middle name. Eddie and I are still thinking of a first, and Earl will be her last. I'm not worried about the Grey; my brothers, Alan and Joseph, can pass that on."

And then she'll go quiet again because she isn't a natural talker.

Eventually, when it's most polite, she'll say, "Nice to have met you," and slip away because, right now, at this very moment, she's late for an appointment and only stopped because you asked.

Off walks Elizabeth C. Earl-Grey, twenty-three-year-old mother-to-be, known to her friends as Liz. She slips on her Walkman (a wedding present) and cranks up the music. Blondie trails behind her as she crosses the lawn and disappears between the impressive stone buildings. It's 1980, November 2nd, and the weather's fine in downtown Toronto. She's just a normal girl, floating about like any other.

***

The smell of roasted duck was on the autumn breeze as Liz hurried down College Street toward Mrs. Wong's apartment.

She was already late. Mrs. Wong would have laid the tea, let out the cats and was probably now waiting outside her front door, fanning herself like always despite the autumn cold, with sweat upon her brow and frown lines fixed in place.

Mrs. Wong would be waiting.

But that smell, that wonderful smell of roasted duck with salted skin and dripping hot fat—saliva pinched as it flooded her mouth. It wasn't her, figured Liz, it was the baby. The baby wanted to suck on the wing of a crispy duck.

As she turned the corner onto Spandia Street, signs burst from their buildings in protruding, colourful Chinese characters. Everything around her: people, billboards, flyers all called in Mandarin and Cantonese with hasty English translations. *Happy Lucky Treats, Crispy Duck Buffet, Cheap Purses Cheap, Lily Valley Store, Fresh Fruit and Veg, Fried Noodles Two for One, All You Can Eat.* This was Chinatown—always thriving, always ready to make a deal. Liz switched off her Walkman and wove between the sidewalk shoppers; she passed vendors holding prawns, watches, apples, bags, scarves, dumplings, paper fans, carrots, peas and more to be snapped up.

From the windows above came a drumbeat and children shouting

Sie-Sie-Sie-Sie! in unison. Red bits of paper, decomposing leaves, and leftover crackers littered the gutters from last Saturday's parade; the dragons had come out and thrown lettuce to the crowd.

It was her favourite part of town, excepting the university campus.

Slowing ever further, Liz studied the restaurant windows. Red, dead, and hanging ducks were roasting behind glass after glass. The cooks lounged inside, watching her as she watched them, as the fat dripped off and sizzled. *Yummy yummy! Half duck half price* only *three dollars!*

Liz was late. But this—she breathed deeply and imagined the salt on her tongue—*this* was for her baby.

With greasy fingers Elizabeth now ran along the back allies of Spandia Street. Blondie's "Sunday Girl" blasted through Liz's Walkman as her feet hurried and her brown hair shook into a curly mess. Humming along, she jumped over boxes, ran around trash cans, and avoided cats skulking ledge to ledge, curb to curb. Her mother had advised her to stop running, for the baby's sake, but Liz couldn't help herself. She loved to run. There was a passion in her legs that demanded to go quickly, to almost fly off the ground. And so, in her second-hand shop red Adidas, she ran.

Mrs. Wong's home was at the turn in the alley. Liz cut back onto the road and came through onto Shine Street. Her feet slowed down and she turned off the music. Before her was a row of old red brick apartments. Glancing up towards the doorway, Liz noted that her client was absent from the porch. Two by two, Liz mounted the black-painted fire escape steps, finally knocking upon Mrs. Wong's door.

Knock, knock.

She listened carefully for footsteps. There was nothing.

Knock, knock.

Liz removed her headphones and pressed an ear against the door. "Mrs. Wong?" she called out. "It's me, Elizabeth, Elizabeth Grey, Earl-Grey, ha-ha?" Mrs. Wong loved ridiculing Liz's marital name.

"Hello?" she called once more.

Still nothing.

Tucking her Walkman into an over-sized pocket, Liz tested the door. It was unlocked. She cracked it open; the smell of jasmine tea and cat dandruff poured from the apartment.

"Mrs. Wong?" she whispered and crept in further. Beneath her long-sleeved shirt rose goose bumps. Maybe Mrs. Wong was in the washroom, or fixing her hair, or wiping her face? Maybe, or *maybe* she was dead and slumped over a pot of tea. Liz was getting the vibe.

"Mrs. Wong?" she whispered again.

"Girl!"

The old woman lay sprawled on the orange rug of her one-room apartment. Her floral muumuu was spread out like a fan and the Asian woman's large, angry face was fixed upon the ceiling. "You call me ambulance. I'm broken. Because you late, I'm broken! I had bad luck: no fortune, no luck. I never walk again!"

Liz blinked as Mrs. Wong kept on shouting. A moment ago she'd expected to find her dead. How did she read it so wrong?

"You call ambulance, right now!"

"Right now," replied Liz.

"Right now!"

"Okay, I'm calling." Liz picked up Mrs. Wong's phone and dialled 911. "What's wrong?" she asked as the phone rang.

"You no see? I got no fortune and choose unlucky shoes. No fortune, no luck!"

"Can you move?"

"Yeah, no problem, I just here on ground because it's better. What you think?"

The operator picked up the line and Liz provided the address and condition of Mrs. Ling-Shi Wong. She put the phone back down.

"They'll be here in twenty minutes."

"Twenty minutes!"

"You're not priority."

"Not priority! Did you say my name? Did you say I'm on floor? I can't move. I no walk again! This is priority!"

Liz moved around to the old brown couch, taking off her scarf. She'd have to stay, she supposed, at least until the ambulance arrived. "I was hungry," she said. "The baby was hungry for crispy duck."

"Duck?" Mrs. Wong's face turned from red to maroon. "You late because of duck?"

"The baby was hungry."

"I get no fortune today. I unlucky today. It's your fault."

"I can tell your fortune now." Liz slipped off her bangles and held them over the horizontal woman. "Here, just throw them. It's on the house."

"It's *my* house!"

Liz smiled.

"You think it is funny? It is funny, Earl-Grey? You the one who funny. I'm innocent woman here, but you the one who late for duck!"

"Crispy duck."

"Oh! Cheeky now, Earl-Grey? You think I'm just old woman, I no matter, I not powerful? But you don't know. You tell fortune, but you no see." Mrs. Wong spat onto the carpet, grazing her chin. "I curse you. I curse you and your duck!"

Liz slipped the bangles back onto her wrist. "Now, Mrs. Wong, don't say things like that. It was for the baby."

"I curse you and your baby! You no gonna forget."

"Really, I'm sorry I was late."

"Doesn't matter." She spat again. "I curse you! I curse—" That was when Mrs. Wong had an aneurysm and died right there on the carpet.

At first, Liz was confused and whispered, "Mrs. Wong?" over and over. But then, after several pokes, prods, and a compact mirror held beneath the woman's nose, she concluded expiration. "Oh, Mrs. Wong."

Twenty minutes and one cup of green tea later, the ambulance arrived and took Mrs. Ling-Shi Wong away.

***

Mrs. Wong wasn't her only client for the day. She still had to visit Professor Alexandra Zubkin on campus, Lisa McCartney at the hair salon, and Tanya Bergman, journalist at the *Toronto Times*, but Liz couldn't shake off the image of Mrs. Wong lying there, staring blankly at the ceiling.

And the duck was stirring in her belly. She, or the baby, wasn't reacting very well.

But she had a duty to her other clients. She left contact details with the ambulance driver, Mike Watte, originally from Pembroke, and she ran from the row of brick apartments back towards the university grounds. This time she didn't listen to her Walkman; it felt wrong to be too light hearted. Instead, she quietly sang to herself as each footstep hit the ground, "Call me, callll me, yeah, call me yeah yeah, any time, call me. Ohhh, call me, yeah." Death was a shame, but it wasn't an ending. Mrs. Wong was probably before the gates of heaven, the tall red Chinatown gates of heaven, infuriated to see rows and rows of roasted duck vendors waving to her amongst the clouds.

Death had to be taken lightly, particularly in her business. Liz shook her head, curls flying, and tried to dislodge the image of Mrs. Wong's slack face. Suddenly, the autumn air felt too cold for just overalls and a light sweater. Inside her, the duck churned.

Finally, Liz turned onto the campus and crossed the leaf-covered green. With her every stride the brown withered leaves crunched on the ground. *Crunch—crunch—crunch—snap,* on she ran, off to Alisa Zubkin's office. Two months ago, Liz had been passed a note from Tamara Colville (a secretary in Student Services), who'd received it from her husband Vincent Colville (post doc), who'd received it from Professor Alisa Zubkin (full professor of physical sciences) after her divorce had been finalized. The professor had been found drunk in the clean room shouting about "confounding bastard variables." When she'd flung a microscope past Vincent's head and wailed that she had no future, he quickly recommended his wife's psychic.

People often thought Liz could somehow shape the future, but that wasn't true. She was near sighted, not far; a psychic, not a witch. To Liz, it was a difference that mattered.

Word had long ago spread around campus about Liz's talent. Embarrassed men and women quietly emerged from the academic halls, passing along notes and casually stopping her on the green to ask for a reading. Professor Alisa Zubkin believed in Liz's sight, but would deny it to her grave should anyone have asked. "So unsubstantial," she often quipped as Liz threw the bangles. "Without method, without evidence," but then she'd flip open her notepad and scribble away as Liz explained the reading.

Professor A. Zubkin, Director of the Physical Science Department at the University of Toronto gave a muffled "*Da*?" as Liz knocked upon her mahogany office door on the top level of the Stanton Building.

"It's Liz."

"Come in." The professor's Russian accent rolled like marbles.

Liz went in.

With thick curtains drawn over the windows, the professor's glowing stained-glass lamps were casting long shadows here, there, and all around the room; each had thin scarves draped across them, giving off a rich red light. It tingled with psychic activity, or at least the professor's anticipation of it.

The Professor stood up and directed Liz into the overstuffed leather chair opposite her desk. "Water?" she asked.

Liz nodded and accepted a tumbler of lemon water poured from a crystal pitcher. Today Alisa's hair was piled high into a round black bun with shots of white scattered through it. The style accentuated her cheekbones and jaw, while exposing the professor's large, weary eyes. Alisa must have royal blood, assumed Liz, the way she was always so erect yet graceful. Eddie said it was the stick up her ass. Liz disagreed.

"You don't need to do this every time," said Liz. "The room looks nice but, really it's—"

"Nonsense, this is appropriate," Alisa cut in. She spun round in her high-backed chair, then spun back with a bottle of vodka. Gesturing towards Liz, who shook her head, the woman poured herself a double shot. "To wake the blood," she said, swirling the spirits around her glass, shooting it down her throat.

"I've had enough waking blood today," replied Liz. She squirmed and sank further into the chair.

"And your baby?"

"She's fine."

"My oldest sister, Alexandra, threw a party when she became pregnant." Alisa peered through her glass. "She invited everyone to our *dacha*. We had bowls of daisies, rapeseed blossoms, those pink and yellow scabious, too; our yard became a spring meadow. My brother, Mikhail, pulled the tables out. We prepared a mountain of food—an entire month's ration. We even had a band. I was fifteen, then." Alisa laughed and stared long into her empty tumbler. She often suggested Liz should use a crystal ball, but it seemed, for Professor Zubkin, the shot glass was enough. "Dmitri kissed me that night. He sang and I noticed him then. It was our first kiss." She waved a hand dismissively and poured herself another drink. "It was a night of illusion. For Alexandra, it was not a baby, only a fibroid. She never did have children."

"I'm sorry."

Alisa shrugged towards Liz. "That was long ago. Now she has many cats and travels with her husband."

Mrs. Wong has cats, thought Liz. The woman's dead eyes flashed through her mind. Who would collect the cats? At least four belonged to the small apartment.

Liz burped. It tasted of duck. "Excuse me."

Alisa put down her glass. "Today, you explain your methods."

"How come?" asked Liz. She slipped off her bangles and moved to the front of her chair, elbows rising onto the wooden desk.

Alisa pulled out a tape recorder and pressed the little red button:

"Today we deconstruct. I will watch; you explain. We will learn."

Click—click, click—click, the tape recorder listened.

"It's not a science."

"Everything is science, Earl-Grey."

"Eh?"

"Scientific method!"

Liz shook her head. She had to stop thinking of Mrs. Wong. It was interrupting her reading. Alisa pulled out her notepad and raised the recorder to her mouth. The Russian scientist mumbled into her microphone: "Subject appears slightly distracted. Circular objects are made ready from her wrist—*check body heat to reliability factor*—and held for the experimental condition—*me*—to proceed."

"*Rrrr*eady?" asked Liz. Eddie always said that after her visits with the professor, Liz's 'R's came like drum rolls.

Professor Zubkin observed.

Liz passed the bangles to Alisa and burped again. "Sorry, it's the baby. So, I hand you the bangles and you just play with them a little and think about how you've been feeling, what you want from life. Stuff like that."

"'Stuff like that'?" The professor wasn't impressed.

Today, apparently, Liz was expected to give a show. The bangles were mostly meaningless anyhow; but they helped her clients focus. "Think about what you most want. What do you want *most*, Alisa?"

The professor put down her pen and tapped the smooth, metal rings. "It's time for a man."

"Good," Liz replied.

Alisa closed her eyes and rubbed the bangles between her fingers. The red light of the lamps made them glow and the professor slouched forward slightly. Maybe the vodka had kicked in. Suddenly Alisa looked almost ghostly as she leaned back in her chair and held the bangles in the air, turning them methodically. Dark strands fell from her bun as she slumped down and rolled her head back and forth. "I want a man, a tall man, a tall man who's handsome but stupid. A very stupid man. One I can keep like a pet."

"Okay." Liz tried not to judge.

Alisa's voice lost its dreamy whisper: "Subject imposes state of hallucination within experimental condition through use of visualization techniques."

"And vodka."

"What next, Earl-Grey?"

"What?" asked Liz. Her stomach grumbled.

"What's the next step in the procedure?"

"You know, just throw the bangles."

"How exactly? What angle? Should I roll the bracelets or bounce them, or toss them a little?"

"Whatever you want."

"No standard method is evident. This is to be noted and reviewed later."

Click—click, click—click.

"It's subjective," said Liz. "With variables and stuff."

"Subject seems unaware of own methods, claiming factors vary within conditions. Only conclusion: reliability is not to be found in experimental methodology. Results, though possibly accurate, may not be valid."

"If I'm accurate, why can't I be valid?"

Alisa opened her eyes and leaned forward. "That's science, darrrling."

"Well this *isn't* science." Liz snatched the bangles from Alisa's hand and tossed them onto the desktop. "There, let's read your fortune."

Alisa tsk-tsked but looked down across her writing mat at the sprawled metal circles. Liz too leaned over the results and scanned the arrangement. Six brass bangles were scattered across the brown mat. Liz closed her eyes. *Concentrate. Concentrate.* Finally, she opened them and looked again.

"Okay." Liz held a palm above the closest arrangement. The wedding ring on her finger reflected redness from the light. "You see these piled bands? That's a joining ... umm, like two people who are one."

"Promising?" The professor's steady nod reminded Liz of Eddie's wiener dog bobble head. More of the professor's dark hairs slipped from her bun.

"Yeah, like it's a significant closeness. Two who are one. You're not pregnant, are you?"

"Definitely not."

"Okay, well I think something in your life is more intimate than you realize. You may already know the man who's your 'two in one.'"

The Russian professor considered her Rolodex. "It'd better not be Dimitri, the bastard."

"I don't think so," replied Liz. "Feels almost feminine."

"Feminine?"

Liz continued the reading. She scanned the other bangles one by one, then the rings as a whole. "Okay ... you see these three here, in the shape of the arch?" Three bangles were lined up like a crescent moon. "That can mean a few things, but because it's almost 'hanging' over the joined pair below, I'd say it's the Scythe."

"The scythe?"

"Like Grim Reaper in Tarot cards. It represents death."

Alisa raised the tape recorder again: "Subject invokes sense of fear in experimental condition. Possible explanation: create hysteria in order to heighten desperation for belief."

"It doesn't mean you're going to die ... not necessarily."

Click—click, click—click.

Professor Zubkin's eyes were the size of dinner plates; she relinquished the recorder, resting it on the table between them. She may have been a scientist. She may have objectivity in theory, but in reality Alisa Zubkin was like anyone else: ruled by their emotions.

'It represents a threat, right?" continued Liz. "So, death's part of this threat, but I think ..." She rolled her head and shook her hair again. *Concentrate. Concentrate.* "I think it's not a threat to *you*, but more to your 'two as one' relationship. Like, that joining will be broken if you're not careful."

Liz's eyes grew larger: "And here!" She pointed to the last bangle that hung near the scythe and the pair. "This is the threat. This is the person, or thing, or something—I can't quite tell. It doesn't feel right. Like it's almost here but it isn't, and it's trying to inflict the Scythe on your pair. It's the threat; it wields the Scythe, but it's not *quite* a person, it's more like—oh!" Liz gasped and sat straight in her chair.

"Like the Grim Reaper?" asked Alisa.

"No, like an angry ghost," replied Liz. Then she burped duck.

Alisa Zubkin had called to her as Liz sprang from the chair and escaped the professor's apartment. "Earl-Grey!" she'd shouted. And Liz ran faster, bangles abandoned, tape left running.

She was running now, running down the steps of the Stanton Building, running through the tour group of international students, running past the cannons, past the petitions, past the mid-day Frisbee players. With every step her stomach wanted to revolt, burping, burping, burping. She couldn't stop burping duck. Through the grounds, through the park, around back streets, past the cluster of student housing, past the rows of Victorian homes, past the hobos and the demonstrations, down the street where families settled, around the old, sturdy trees and purpose-built apartments. She ran and ran. No music. No bangles. No ease.

She burped duck again. This time, as she turned onto her street, nausea spread within her. *Run, run, run* to the front steps of their apartment. She wouldn't make it.

Liz turned back to the curb, to the sewer, and her body convulsed until every bit of ducky pulp was spewed between the grates of a Toronto Municipal sewer. But still, between the bile and physical exhaustion, she could taste the duck. The fat-dripping, red-roasted duck.

It was getting colder. Every day was getting colder. She shouldn't be running around in just her overalls and long T-shirt despite the Indian summer. She shivered now. It felt as though the temperature had dropped ten degrees. She closed her eyes and rolled her head, kneeling on the sidewalk, face suspended above the curb, hair falling forwards. Cars drove by and people followed their routine.

Dogs were walked, groceries carried, sunshine enjoyed, and leaves were raked. Someone high up played *Rapper's Delight* and it blasted through their open window. Across the street, students hooted and sang along. Liz rolled her head more violently and let her hair swoosh back and forth. *Concentrate. Concentrate.*

Eddie was home.

Liz and Eddie had known about the pregnancy for just over two weeks. And immediately after they had found out and settled down to adult conversation, the question arose: "What are we doing here?"

Here. Toronto. Cherron Street. The apartment with splintered floors and neighbours smoking pot. How could they stay here?

Eddie was writing a novel while working night shifts as a custodian for the university; Liz was earning under the table with her readings. It was a living for two young ex-students, but not for an about-to-be family, or it shouldn't be at least.

Her mother, Dorothy, had been pushing them to move to Montreal: "*It's a great idea*!" she exclaimed over the phone. It was a good idea for Liz's mother, but not for them. Liz and Edward couldn't move to Quebec, wonderful as it was. Edward had bare bones French, and Liz needed space from her mother. "*No mom, thank you but no.*" They were less close since the divorce had gone through and everything changed overnight. Her Dad had stayed in Arnprior, while her mom fled to Quebec with Lulu, the mayor's ex-wife. It was an unexpected arrangement, and Liz wasn't yet sure how she felt about her mother's new choices.

But that didn't mean she and her mother weren't connected. They were, of course. She had received a postcard from her that very morning, one in a string of many they sent back and forth. Neither woman was good with letters or phone calls, but postcards—postcards ran deep in her family. They meant more than a simple hello.

Legging it up the stairs to their fourth-floor apartment, Liz pulled a key from her pocket and unlocked the brown front door.

"Eddie?" she whispered, stepping over a bag of garbage that needed taking downstairs. "Ed?"

No reply. He was probably sleeping. She pulled out her Walkman and laid it down next to the pile of keys and unopened mail on her parents' old end table. When her parents had divorced, she, Alan, and Joseph had gotten a lot of their discarded furniture.

Liz walked down the bare-walled hall, through the lounge and into the kitchen. Last night's dishes were piled in the sink, waiting for someone to claim responsibility. Liz ducked down beside the ancient oven and pulled out the bottom drawer. "Just the thing," she said, standing back up with the kettle in her hands.

A few minutes later, she was carrying two mugs of mint tea as she walked carefully back towards the bedroom. Eddie had left the windows open and swirls of cool air cut a chill through her.

Earl-Grey. You no gonna forget. You and your baby no gonna forget.

Liz burped. How could there be any duck left to burp?

"You can't haunt me," whispered Liz in the foyer. She glanced at the garbage then over to the laundry hamper piled high with T-shirts and sweaters and month-old towels. "Look at this place. What else can you do to me?"

She wasn't unhappy in her home. She was, instead, uncomfortably happy, precociously balanced between disgust and contentment in their mess, with pinches of pleasure reserved for the intimate moments. She and Eddie, she and the city, she and her fortune-telling. But more and more, looking around her, she was beginning to realize that maybe, possibly, she wasn't ready to cope with the life of a small, unpredictable baby. She couldn't even look after an apartment properly.

You no gonna forget.

"It's just morning sickness." Liz sipped her tea and kicked off her tennis shoes.

I curse you, Earl-Grey.

"Curse me," muttered Liz. "Why not curse everyone who abandoned you to that cramped cat-piss apartment?"

You no gonna forget.

Liz wasn't sure if she was going crazy. The memory of Mrs. Wong was vivid—her splayed-out floral dress, the woman's spitting mouth, her shaking black hair with pure white roots, and her fists pounding on the carpet. The scent of jasmine in the air, then clocks ticking empty moments, and finally, eventually, sirens shrieking down the street. Poor Mrs. Wong.

You no sorry for me! I no cursed.

"Well, I'm not cursed either." Liz was sure she wasn't; it wasn't possible. Always when dealing with psychic forces, Liz carried protection. While her clients believed in the bangles, she believed in the postcards. Generations and generations of the *Middle-Named-Claires* had passed along their postcards. Liz kept her favourites in her pocket. They were her talismans, her deep-rooted protection. So long as they were with her, nothing could get through.

Earl-Grey...

Mrs. Wong couldn't curse her, even *if* she had the know-how. Liz had protection.

She pushed open the bedroom door with her foot. "Eddie," she whispered, walking into the room with its pulled blinds. "Sweetheart?"

From the mass of blankets stirred a man, her man. He lifted his head and squinted. "Tea?"

"Your favourite," she replied.

"How you doing?" he asked.

Liz stepped up onto the bed and carefully sat down beside him, putting down her mug. Eddie rolled over and rose onto his elbows. This was their routine. Every afternoon she'd stop by to wake him up, and he'd rise onto his elbows to survey the room as though there was something new to see. Eddie proceeded to blink slowly, rhythmically. "What time is it?" he asked.

"Just past noon." She stroked his short brown hair, trying to reduce the bed head.

"It's still early."

"I got sick."

He blinked and rolled towards her. She passed him the cup of tea. "Sick?" he asked.

"Just outside."

"I've been reading about morning sickness." Eddie reached with his free hand for the book on his bedside table. "Let's see here—yeah—'Morning sickness can strike suddenly and often within the first trimester.'" He passed the book to her. "You should read this."

She waved it away. "Not now."

"It's full of advice. I can't do all the reading in this pregnancy."

For the past two weeks, Eddie had been reading baby books voraciously, in the way that Liz ate potato chips: one after the other, after the other, after the other.

Liz sipped her tea, breathing in the spearmint. Eddie launched back into the book. His finger trailed across the page as his lips moved to the words. "You need more light," said Liz. She stood from the bed and opened the blinds, burping loudly as she returned.

"You eat some Chinese food?"

"Jesus," mumbled Liz. "Yeah I had some duck, and haven't felt myself since. And then this woman cursed me today."

"I thought you had your things, you know, the letters—"

"Postcards."

"—postcards, in case you got mean mumbo-jumbo shot at you."

"I *do*, but it's like I'm almost talking to her, you know? Like she's in my head or something, and she just keeps saying I won't forget. 'Earl-Grey, you no forget.' And she won't shut up. The damn woman curses me, and our child, and then dies there on the carpet. She couldn't even take it back." Liz wanted to throw her tea all over Mrs. Wong's big dead face.

"Liz..."

"'I curse you, and your baby!' she spits, and all because I was late ten minutes. A stupid ten minutes. What, she couldn't wait to wear her ugly platform shoes just a little bit longer? And now I *don't* feel myself; instead I hear her all the time, I can't stop burping, the baby is twisting up my guts."

Liz's expression wobbled and threatened to shift into high gear sobs. She whimpered and grasped for her mug of tea. Eddie was prepared; he'd read about the mood swings and was ready to be patient and understanding, as recommended by Doctor Flanders's book of pregnancy concerns. Gently, he lifted the mug from her grasp and stroked back the wet curls on her cheek. "But you have your postcards."

Liz reached into her overall pocket and pulled out the envelope.

It no matter Earl-Grey. You cursed!

"Old bitch," mumbled Liz as she looked over the small collection. They were mainly postcards from the train-line, a few from the circus too. "They should have worked, Eddie. I picked them out just for me."

Edward Grey was a logical man. He liked the world to be in order, to make transparent sense. But he loved his wife even more than his sense, so, when necessary, he applied his logic to the illogical. "You picked them out just for you, but Liz, there's two of you now."

Eddie poked his finger into her belly.

"Oh, my God, she cursed my baby."

You cursed my baby, Mrs. Wong!

You late, I have bad luck and die! You curse yourself *with duck!*

"Forget the duck!" shouted Liz. "Who cares about the damned duck!"

Who care? I care! I dead!

Liz burped and burped and burped. Eddie stood up and went by the open bedroom window. "Here it comes," he mumbled. "Sympathy symptoms; I read about this. I'm gonna be sick."

Eddie leaned out the window and sucked in fresh air. Liz burped a steady stream. Their entire bedroom smelled like a Chinese restaurant.

Eddie called from out the window. "You need to go to the hospital!"

Liz crawled out of the bed with a hand on her stomach, and began ransacking the closet. "Where's the tin Eddy? Have you seen it?"

"I put it in the kitchen."

"The kitchen?"

"It's a cookie tin!"

Liz hurried along the hall, forgetting to put on her slippers, then cursed as she got yet another splinter in her foot. Finally she hopped into the kitchen, opening and slamming cupboard doors until she found the large, black cookie tin with the orange grove on its lid.

"Candles!" shouted Liz. "Eddie where are the—"

"In the dresser, living room dresser!"

"Living room bloody dresser," repeated Liz as she opened the utensil drawer and grabbed the matches. "Eddie! I need a bucket of cold water, use the bathroom tub, the one for my bras."

This no work. You gonna get it.

Bugger off, I'm busy.

How you like duck now, Earl-Grey? Ha!

Mrs. Wong was laughing at her. Liz could hear the thick laughter in her mind, and suddenly her guts began to twist and turn. "God! She's filling me with gas!"

"Let it out, sweetie," called Eddie from the bathroom.

Liz felt as though she were turning into a giant balloon. Any minute she'd float out the window or burst and explode. Floating, cramping, burping, Liz began to set up her arrangement.

Elizabeth Claire Earl-Grey was not a witch. This was an important distinction for her. She was *not* a witch. Liz was simply a psychic. She didn't set intentions; she didn't wave wands; she didn't cast spells; and she didn't ride broomsticks. Herbs and medicines were never her thing either, and not once, not once did she deliver a baby or mend a wound. She was *not* a witch. But sometimes, in extreme moments, moments like when she'd nearly been hit by a bus, or when her brother Joseph had gone through the ice, or when an uptight unlucky grouch of a woman placed a curse upon her unborn child, she appeared more occult than not.

The air swirled around her, lifting her hair and making her eyes water as Liz struck match after match, trying to light the army of candles set up around their coffee table. Eddie came in with the bucket of water, set it down beside the television and began shutting the windows.

"Leave them open," Liz instructed.

"Here," Eddie took over the matches and began to make headway. Soon, amongst the smell of fat and salt and fried lettuce came wafts of cinnamon apple, vanilla bean, and strawberry rose. From the street outside cars honked and Mrs. Umbridge, one floor up, listened to her daily program of CBC Canada's orchestral arrangement. Beethoven's Fifth charged through the air as did Mrs. Wong's laughter.

You so stupid, girl. You no beat me.

Shut up, Mrs. Wong.

I no Mrs. Wong now. I free! I gonna take over a better body, much, much younger.

"She's gone crazy," said Liz. She opened the tin and shook the mass of postcards onto the table within the semicircle of candles.

"Liz the postcards are gonna fly away."

"Let them fly, I only need the right ones. Just keep them from the windows. Mom would kill me if I lost them."

Eddie took up guard position in front of the windows. Liz held her hands over the pile of cards and closed her eyes. *Concentrate. Concentrate.*

You no concentrate!

Concentrate. Concentrate.

Hey, duck girl. You got stupid name, what kind of name Earl-Grey? You steeped in hot water?

Concentrate. Concentrate. Concentrate. Concentrate.

Earl-Grey!

Liz burped, rumbled, and groaned. She had to clear her mind. She had to think of her baby. Her priority was this baby. That was hers, and no one would take that away.

No one, no one, no one.

Suddenly Liz's hands could feel the charge, it was as though a cord had been plugged in and she suddenly felt alive. Everything dropped away, the noise, the smells, the voices, all of it. Her hands circled the pile, then finally dove into the generations of greetings: postcards passed down mother to daughter, and mother to daughter, and mother to daughter. These were the words of the *Middle-Named-Claires.* Each woman shared that common thread, that common name, and each woman passed along her wisps of knowledge through the postcards.

Elizabeth Claire's fingers touched and sorted through the comments of Anna Claire Pierre, who'd written to say she would be waving from the station, and Mary Claire Elgin who had swam in Horse Shoe Lake and that it had been a crystal blue, Ruby Claire who had written to wish a happy birthday. Elizabeth touched, sensed, and pushed away the cards that wouldn't do. There was power in each and every rectangle of scribbled cardboard. But her daughter needed the right.power; she needed the right Claire to defend her now.

"Honey!" called Eddie.

Liz opened her eyes. Postcards were everywhere. Candles were burning low. The wind whipped around them, threatening to suck everything out the window. Eddie was running interference, trying to contain the debris. "You started throwing them everywhere, like a woman possessed." Eddie stopped abruptly and turned to his wife, leaning over the coffee table and scrutinizing her face. "Are you still Liz?"

Liz pushed him away, "Of course I am. I have *my* postcards. The better question is, is our baby *still* our baby?" She didn't want Mrs. Wong to get bolder.

"So who's that?" Eddie nodded to Liz's hand. Liz looked down and flipped over the old card. It was withered and yellowed, and the scrawling handwriting was almost impossible to read.

"Oh great." muttered Elizabeth. "It's my great-times-five grandmother. And she's always had attitude."

Liz began to hiccup again.

You in trouble, Earl-Grey.

Liz ignored Mrs. Wong and focused on the postcard. "Eddie, when I say so, pour the water over the candles, and then over me."

"What?"

Liz lifted a candle and breathed in apple cinnamon. She closed her eyes and began to chant slowly at first, then more and more quickly—with strange whispers escaping. Eddie tried to listen. He leaned over and tried to understand the words his wife uttered, but it was a language he'd never heard her use before.

"Liz?"

She didn't answer. Instead her head went limp as the postcard was pressed against her belly, and the wind whipped, raising her hair into a curly cloud, picking up the discarded cards and swirling them around the room. Eddie stopped watching and ran in circles, batting the postcards down and blocking the windows.

You no win, Earl-Grey.

I'm sick of you, Mrs. Wong. Your stupid shoes were your stupid fault.

I unlucky!

That's not my fault.

I no fortune!

That's not my fault.

You late for duck!

Okay, that's my fault, but you had an aneurysm, and that, for sure, would have happened with or without me.

I no leaving! You gonna get a little Ling-Shi Wong baby girl.

Liz's mutterings had become loud, aching moans. Eddie couldn't snap her out of it. He called her name, pulled her hair, and was now standing above his wife with the bucket of water, debating: should he throw it?

There was a new voice in Liz's head. A voice that seemed far away, yet was growing in strength.

What the hell's going on here? Who're you? asked the voice.

I Mrs. Wong!

What are you? Asian? Still? You do know that you're dead, right?

I no leaving! Little Ling-Shi Wong baby up next!

Ling-Shi what?

Eddie jumped back as his wife stood up and began thrashing back and forth standing on her tiptoes. It was as though she was fighting with herself. She stopped moaning, and started spitting, hissing instead. It looked like an all-out battle. "This can't be good for the baby," said Eddie. His foot tapped and his arms swished the water in the bucket. All he had to do was throw it. His wife held the postcard, her rigid arm dipped up and down over the flames, threatening to catch and burn the ancestral card.

Stop that biting! demanded the voice, now with the edges of a woman's tone. There was an English accent creeping through.

Who you? You no mess this up!

That's it. I've been nice. I'm the nicest woman in the whole damn world.

You no woman!

Not now, but you should have seen me when I was this girl's ancestor. Lord, my chest was beautiful. Bloody hell, stop all that biting!

I Mrs. Wong!

I'm Amelia Claire Stives! And I don't need to bite, not when I can punch.

Liz was hopping up and down on the spot, burping, hissing, snapping, dodging.

"Liz!" called Eddie. "Liz, I'm throwing this water now. Liz?"

Liz watched as Amelia began laughing and having fun, slapping around the ghost of Mrs. Wong. She would enjoy this, figured Liz. This was her type of thing; Liz's pilgrim ancestor was always the crazy one, the reckless one. She had been a survivor, and a true witch, no doubt.

Not a witch, girl! said the voice of Amelia Stives. *Just a woman connected, is all. A woman connected to all parts of herself, all parts around herself, before, after, and even in you.*

But despite the beating, the crispy duck still tasted on Liz's tongue.

I Mrs. Wong!

Not anymore you're not. Now get your hands off our youngest Claire; not even out of the womb. How's that for a fair fight? Picking on a child, you should feel ashamed. Go on, then, get out. No? Not going? Then enjoy some more of this!

Liz rose higher on her feet, thrashing side to side, rocking forwards and backwards at impossible angles.

'Liz! What the hell is happening? I'm going to throw it this time, really!" yelled Eddie.

Suddenly, she dropped onto the couch and sat still, perfectly still. No more escaping gas, no more weird sounds.

But she was the one, wasn't she? thought Liz. *Amelia was the one for my little girl.*

And don't you forget it, sweetheart.

Mrs. Wong is gone?

Long gone.

Not coming back.

Never coming back.

Good. Thanks.

And...

And?

What's my reward for saving your daughter?

Liz sighed.

Eddie couldn't wait any longer. He doused the candles and then drenched his wife with the leftover water. Liz leaned back on the wet couch and looked at the yellow postcard in her hand.

"She gone?" asked Eddie.

"They're both gone."

"That was fucking crazy."

Liz nodded. "I've thought of a name for our baby girl."

Eddie sat down beside her and put his head to Liz's stomach.

"How about Amelia?" asked Liz.

"Amelia ... Amelia..." Eddie rolled it around. "I could like Amelia."

"Good, because that's the only way she'd leave."

"Mrs. Wong?"

"No, my great-great-great-great-great grandmother." Liz counted the greats on her fingers. "Amelia Stives, she's a stubborn pain in the ass."

"Family always is."

Liz turned onto her side and shivered into her husband. They lay there, yin and yang, on the couch and stared up at the ceiling. "What are we doing here, Eddie?"

"Our thing."

"Our thing?"

"Our new family thing."

Liz smiled and snuggled further into her husband. Eddie propped himself up onto his elbow and rubbed her stomach. "What do you think about Alberta? I've got an uncle there who offered me a job a while back. He's got a farm but no kids to help run it. It'd be a change."

Liz imagined them on a farm—slopping muck and rising at dawn. "It'd be a change."

"A big change."

"A big family change."

The breeze crept in and brushed against their faces. They lay together, side by side, the three of them—her family. Liz's family. She glanced out the open windows—at the buildings, electrical lines, and the bricks. "Maybe we could do with a little more sky," she whispered. And she smiled, and lay there, and felt perfectly content.

Mrs. Brennan, 1958

You'd never notice her behind the frosted post office window, sitting alone and lost in her thoughts. She's the sort of person others don't notice. Many people don't notice much at all, which is a shame. Her name is Dorothy, like Dorothy in *The Wizard of Oz*, though she looks nothing like the ruby-slippered Judy Garland. She's far too dark skinned, with black hair and mud coloured eyes, but she does imagine that perhaps one day she'll be carried away by a twister to somewhere full of adventure. Life in a Technicolor adventure like they show at the theatre would be a thrill for our Dorothy behind the window, sitting at the post office counter. Of course, what she doesn't realize (because, like many people, she often doesn't realize many things) is that life is made of Technicolor dreams—with blues and greens and purples and reds. And there are Technicolor smells and Technicolor tastes and Technicolor touches as well. There's even a Technicolor Dorothy, though she doesn't know it yet. But let's stop by and pay her some attention, which is often all a person needs. Let's park our 1958 Buick and slide along the icy sidewalk, press our faces to the frozen post office window, and take a look inside. I want you to meet Dorothy, not because she's famous or wise, but because today is a special sort of day—today, Dorothy Claire Brennan wakes up to the world.

Dorothy examined the paper chain that she'd been constructing over the past week while minding the counter during the post-lunch lull. Paper strips of red, yellow, and green were strung together; it seemed just fine, nearly long enough for the entire tree. She dropped the chain on the polished counter and picked at her chicken sandwich, contemplating how best to return the second-hand cradle. It was her fault, after all, for making up the reckless lie.

Toward the end of the noontime rush at the post office, Father Connell had stopped in to collect a package from Ottawa, and Dorothy's husband Patrick had thanked him for his considerate gift of the beautiful cradle. It was upstairs waiting for the baby to arrive.

Father Connell, despite Dorothy's gasp as she clutched her bundle of letters more tightly, replied that he hadn't given any such gift, though he was sure it was a fine cradle, and wished them both a good day, excusing himself politely and quickly leaving the shop.

Patrick Brennan had turned on his wife and exploded into a redheaded huff. What had she been doing telling him that the priest had given them the cradle?

Dorothy admitted she'd gotten the cradle from Mrs. O'Bannon as a gift.

Spiralling even further into shame with thought of charity from the mayor's new wife, Patrick bit his fist and abandoned his pre-lunch tallying. As he stormed from the post office, leaving Dorothy to herself, he promised to make her confess all upon his return from the diner.

Dorothy hadn't dared point out to Patrick that he'd accepted Mr. Albert's old fishing lure just that morning, and was planning to chop a hole in the ice once the freeze had deepened so he could try out the squirrelly twister, which was reported to have caught a twelve-pound pike the previous summer. Why Mr. Albert would want to give away his best lure, Dorothy had no clue, but she didn't ask her husband about that. She was of the curious sort, but she certainly wasn't stupid. Eating wasn't the only pastime that took place over lunch at the diner, but she had no mind to interfere in her husband's gambling, regardless of his wins or losses, though the latter happened far more often. In Dorothy's opinion, it wasn't any business of a wife what her husband did amongst other men.

Patrick's mood was bound to perk up soon; Christmas was fast approaching. Dorothy had gotten all the shopping done, and had that very morning prepared a fruit cake, which was sitting upstairs soaking in rum. She liked the season and took pleasure in decorating the post office. It was, she would say to herself, 'a chance to make things nice.'

Ducking into the back she picked up a small box of spare paper rectangles, and returned to the front to settle down and resume her chain—which is precisely where we find her now, as she mulls over the problem of returning the cradle. But Dorothy didn't have time to get more than five rings completed before the old door chime rang and in blew Mrs. O'Bannon, the mayor's new French- Canadian wife, covered neck to foot in a long fur jacket and her head wearing a raccoon hat. "Dotts!" cried Mrs. O'Bannon. She pulled off her raccoon hat and revealed rollers pinned to her head.

"Mrs. O'Bannon?" replied Dorothy.

Mrs. O'Bannon was like those blue-eyed, blonde women in Pepsi advertisements: all smooth and peachy, but with their hair done up. She was known for her flawlessness. And for being a scandalous divorcée who'd seduced the mayor on his holiday to Montreal and married him within a week of their meeting. But this afternoon Mrs. O'Bannon looked more excited than graceful, with her loose curlers, fur jacket, and an imperfect smear of lipstick across her mouth.

"Dotts, put on your coat! You *must* see this."

Dorothy held onto her paper chain. "I can't leave the shop."

"Close it up!"

"But Patrick will kill..."

"Dotts, we're going to miss it!" Lulu O'Bannon anxiously looked out the window. "And I came here just for you."

"What do you mean?"

Dorothy had met this now frantic woman one year ago in the post office. Mrs. O'Bannon had then been wearing a navy dress that fanned from her hips, pinched in at the waist, and was topped with a scooped neckline. She was by far the most beautiful woman in town, which fitted the expectation everyone had for a wife of the mayor, even if she was a divorcée remarried. Katie Bantry, the bank manager's wife, had been sour for weeks after the Mayor's remarrying, realizing that she was now relegated to second place in the town's unofficial beauty pageant. To top it all, she could never compete with the mayor's wife's charming French accent. She would glare at the new addition to Arnprior society and encourage the other ladies to follow suit, not that Mrs. O'Bannon ever noticed. She didn't give most of the ladies in town more than a second glance—except for Dorothy, whom she seemed to notice almost immediately. It was, for Dorothy, secretly thrilling.

During that first encounter, Mrs. O'Bannon had purchased a postcard that came with a special edition pole-jumping stamp, saying how she liked the river photograph on the card. She wrote a message with Patrick and Dorothy watching her, getting their first look at the latest sensation in Arnprior gossip. Dorothy had a natural curiosity toward postcards, and when she saw that the card was addressed to '*Cher Maman, et ma belle soeur*' in Montreal, well, for some sentimental reason, she instantly liked the mayor's new wife.

Now that Dorothy was three months pregnant, Mrs. O'Bannon was inviting her over for teas, talking about maternity fashion, and asking 'Dotts' to call her Lulu. There was something about this woman that Dorothy found difficult to deny.

"No more questions, just come along. *Vite!*"

"All right," sighed Dorothy. She left the chain and half-finished sandwich. Ducking into the back room, she slipped into a pair of Patrick's hunting boots, threw on her old, beaver-fur coat and grabbed a red flannel hat, tucking her rope of black plaited hair beneath the coat collar. Unlike Lulu, Dorothy failed to look like a porcelain doll against the fur. She merely disappeared into the wrapping.

Ding, ding. Lulu was ringing the front bell. *Ding, ding.*

"Coming," called Dorothy. After one last sigh, she hurried out.

After locking the door, Dorothy was pulled away from the shop by Mrs. O'Bannon's small gloved hand. The morning's fresh snowfall had left the street a landscape of snowdrifts and ice patches. As they stomped down Main Street Dorothy's giant boots swung through the white peaks and kicked powder into the air. Cars risked crashing on a day like this, and twice Mrs. O'Bannon had to save Dorothy from slipping flat onto the road.

"I've got you, Dotts, don't worry so much." Mrs. O'Bannon kept laughing and pulling her along. Dorothy wondered how a person could get away with so much lipstick. The mayor's wife had a deep shade of scarlet painted across her wide, smiling mouth.

"Please slow down, Mrs. O'Bannon."

"It's Lulu, Dotts. Lulu. There's no time for slowing down. It may have already flown off!"

"What is it? A plane?" Dorothy kept a secret list of dreams locked tight in her mind; third on that list was to fly on a plane. She wanted to go up high and look for the halos her father had long-ago pointed out shining around the sun, big golden circles of light. He said that's where Dorothy's mother had gone; and ever since then the sky had held a fascination for her.

"Not a plane, Dotts, it's better than that."

Hurrying down Main Street they crossed the church and kept on moving closer to the river.

"We're going to your house?" asked Dorothy. As the mayor's wife, Lulu had the privilege of living in the biggest house along the Ottawa River in the Prior area. It used to be a convent but had been converted for the sole use of the mayor's family.

"Near there," answered Lulu. Grasping Dorothy's arm, she pulled her off the road. Carefully they trekked among the trees further into the bush, skirting around the back of Mayor O'Bannon's manor home. "Okay," Lulu said, stopping. "He's around here somewhere."

"The mayor?"

Lulu smiled her wide, red smile. "Most certainly not, he's at lunch. Now just look into the trees."

Dorothy peered high into the black branches with their layers of ice and powdered snow. She squinted at the sunlight and sharp blue sky that filled the trees, reflecting off the whiteness. Her eyes clung to dropped needles, twigs, and bark.

"Lulu, what am I looking for?"

"Listen," whispered Lulu, taking Dorothy's arm.

Dorothy closed her eyes to listen. Eventually, she heard.

Birds twittered all year long: the call of the jay, the knock of the woodpecker, the tweet of the sparrow, the taunt of the crow ... the forest was a symphony of constant music. And now, suddenly, a baritone took his solo.

"There!" squealed Lulu into her ear.

A mere ten feet away rose a deep and throaty call. Dorothy squinted through the brightness and spotted eyes, beak, and glimpse of talon.

"I thought they hooted," she whispered, "Like '*hoot-hoot*', not '*ough ough*'."

"Come on Dotts, isn't he something?"

"He is something." It was the largest, whitest bird Dorothy had ever seen. "Best looking fella I've ever met."

Lulu sighed, "*Absolument*. Have you seen one before?" Lulu broke her reverie to glance at Dorothy.

Dorothy looked over and smiled at Lulu. "Never."

The bird must have been a meter high at least, a weightless giant sitting on the frozen maple branch. To think she had nearly missed him, and now he was all she could see in the cold, blinding forest. Pure white feathers plumed across his body; blending him into the snow and trees.

Between her and the owl, the forest listened: *crack, snap, swish, roar,* and the river's current pushed against the nearby frozen riverbank.

Dorothy's feet began to itch. They were always itching; it must have been the baby's doing. Now she quietly lifted one foot out of its hunting boot and leaned against Lulu for support, bending over slowly and scratching her sole. Then, she slid her foot back down and did the same to the other foot.

The owl hooted its unusual growl, and blinked several times. Yellow eyes watching them. Dorothy's eyes watching back.

"Did you know I'm part Métis?" Dorothy whispered to Lulu. "Well I'm a mixture, but at least one quarter Indian."

"I didn't know."

"I've always wondered if it meant I was in tune with things, with nature. Sometimes I can feel a sort of connection. Though Patrick says it's just my fancy. I'm not magical or anything."

"You may be," answered Lulu.

"Patrick figures not."

Dorothy slipped her other foot back into its boot, keeping her eyes upon the owl.

"I'd like to be an owl," she whispered. "I'd fly around the world."

"They're mostly up north," replied Lulu.

"Then I'd fly to the Arctic and meet a penguin."

"Those are down south."

Dorothy glanced at Lulu. The mayor's wife wasn't any younger than her, though clearly she had more education. Dorothy couldn't understand what had drawn a woman like her to the Prior; she was clearly groomed for grand things, grand places.

"Oh!" cried Lulu.

Flap, whoosh. The owl launched from its perch and flew off between the branches.

"Come on!" said Lulu, once again taking Dorothy's arm. "Come on, Dotts!" she exclaimed, pulling.

"What about the post office? Patrick's going to blow if I'm not there!" But already Dorothy was following as Lulu moved into the forest. She'd never been allowed to wander too far from Main Street without Patrick along, except to visit her father's apple orchard, but that was way back when her father, Old Jesiah, still owned that bit of land. He'd lost it to debts and soon after drank himself to death. She had already been married to Patrick before that scandal had set in, though the loss of the land had upturned their plans.

Dorothy shook her head. Too often she was filled with memories like that, memories that weighed her down and rounded her shoulders. Lulu was hopping ahead, turning back and waving her arms. "Come on Dotts!"

"At least slow down. I'm three months pregnant!"

"That's nothing," called the mayor's wife, taking them along a path of bushes, pointing her free hand in the air as the owl soared above. "When I was five months along with Jacquelyn, I ran half of *Le Marathon de Montréal* and it covers the whole island!"

"That's crazy!"

"My mother agrees with you!"

The creeks had frozen and were easy to pass as Dorothy hurried after the owl, arm in arm with Lulu. And as for the path, well, they left it behind when the owl dived to the left and they'd had to start running through the drifts of snow between the trees. It wasn't long after that the owl had disappeared from sight.

"Do you see him?" asked Dorothy, slowing her run. Her flannel hat was clasped in her hand, the beaver coat unfastened and her long dark braid was coming loose at the end. Lulu looked no better: some of her curlers had fallen out leaving awkward waves, while others resolutely remained pinned—giving her the look of mid styling, but still, to Dorothy's amazement, the mayor's new wife was a beautiful woman, even with curlers on, albeit one in distress.

She began to stumble, causing Lulu to slow down. The women caught their breath.

"Dotty," Lulu said, leaning back against a birch and looking up into the sky with squinting eyes, "it's time you used that intuitive power of yours."

"I was talking fluff when I said that," replied Dorothy.

"Doesn't matter, whether you think it's fluff or not. How often do you get to see a snowy owl, Dotts? Giving it a try won't hurt anything, and I won't make fun."

"I don't even know where we are," replied Dorothy.

But when Lulu turned and gave her a look, a look very similar to what she'd received from her husband on nights Dorothy wasn't up for trying, she figured it couldn't hurt to play along, which was much the same way that she'd eventually gotten pregnant.

Closing her eyes, Dorothy tried to listen. It was a tricky thing, listening. First there came the beats of Dorothy's heart—*thump, thump, thump*—and her breathing, none of that would stop. She passed over them; she passed over Lulu's fidgets too.

Tweet-flap-chirp. Crack-snap-hiss. The birds calling for each other, and squirrels, still fat, running limb to limb. *Whispering, whispering* came the wind like dropping sugar; light powder lifting and blown high into the sky. And the river, in the distance, gently gushing.

'*Shh, shh,*' Dorothy whispered to her mind.

Layer upon layer, she listened. Dorothy opened her eyes to the forest light. Nearly blinded, she pointed toward the sun. "That way, maybe."

"Maybe?"

Dorothy shrugged. "Maybe that way."

And off she and Lulu went, walking slow and careful, scanning the trees for the Snowy Owl.

"I can't see anything, Lulu. It's too bright." The sun's reflection off the white blanket of snow was blinding.

"Look through your fingers, Dotty. Jacquelyn and I do it all the time."

They held their hands before their eyes and peered through the cracks. Again Dorothy's eyes flitted back and forth, clinging to the dark spots—twigs, bark, and branches above. And as she kept scanning the forest, finding nothing, a feeling began to grow inside her, began to percolate and gain intensity.

"Lulu, I have to go back. It's past lunch, Patrick will be home any second."

"He'll be fine without you."

Dorothy bit into her loosening braid with its frozen tip. She hadn't left a note or anything to stop his worrying. He would walk into the shop and see the coloured paper rings (which were meant to be a surprise), the fire, the empty stool, and then he'd call her name. But she wasn't there to answer. He'd call, and there'd be no one but himself to notice. And that is when he'd start getting angry. Dorothy knew it far too well. His face would turn red, and he'd start storming about the place, calling her over and over again. But she wasn't there to answer.

"I'm going to be sick if I don't sit down." Dorothy dropped Lulu's hand and crouched into a snow bank.

"I thought you were made of tougher stuff," said Lulu, looking down at Dorothy.

"Don't go bullying me." Dorothy grabbed a fallen twig and began to snap it into pieces. "Everyone bullies me."

Lulu crouched beside her. She smiled her red, wide smile and put a hand on Dorothy's shoulder. "That's what I mean. Why can you tell me to stop bullying you, but not old Patty red puff?"

"Patrick?"

"The man himself."

"He's better than, than that 'I'm the Mayor' husband of yours."

"Now, now, I meant no harm to you, Dorothy," replied Lulu.

Dorothy sat back onto the snow drift and looked away from Lulu. Her eyes were watering in the brightness of the light, her feet were itching again, and to top it all, she realized a growing hunger in her belly alongside the panic. "Patrick was meant to bring me back three dill pickles and one of those little toothpick flags he always saves from his smoked meat sandwiches. But he'll just throw it all away now, on top of getting upset with me."

She punched a fist into the snow bank.

"I was hoping for France or maybe Italy," Dorothy said. That was number three on her secret wish list. "You know what I've always wanted to do?" she asked Lulu. Dorothy raised her hands to her face and looked through her fingers at the forest.

"What's that?" Lulu sat back into the snow beside her, picking up Dorothy's discarded twig and snapping it even further.

"Travel. That's number three on my list."

"What list?"

"The list in my head. My list."

"What else is on your list?"

"I'd like to go back in time."

Lulu laughed.

"No really," said Dorothy. "If I could, I'd go back. Maybe visit my mother when she was young, and I'd visit the other women in my family too. Did you know—well, you wouldn't know—but every woman in my family, every first daughter that is, they've all got the middle name of Claire?"

"Why's that?" asked Lulu. She dropped the stick and began to look through the crack between her fingers like Dorothy.

"I don't know. Better than a last name, I guess. Those things keep changing," replied Dorothy.

Again Lulu laughed in her light-hearted way. "Don't need to tell me about that. I've changed my names three times in the past seven years."

"Three times?" Dorothy glanced at the Mayor's wife in amazement; Lulu kept her hands before her eyes.

"Three times. My maiden name is Forget, but that changed with Jacques Boivin. I was Madame Lucienne Boivin for a while. He's Jacquelyn's father, a fairly well-off man too, very kind to us. Then came Richard after Jacques died of fever. I was Madame Trudeau that time, which was a very good thing for me and my Jacquelyn because he was a very rich man who spoiled us rotten, but he only liked young things. Once I hit thirty that was all over. Poor Jacquelyn was getting fond of him too. She's the one who suffers most, not me." Lulu lowered her fingers and shrugged gently. "And now there's Sean—so that's Mrs. O'Bannon for you. Three times married."

"Three times," repeated Dorothy. "Four names."

"Four names," sighed Lulu.

"My mother wrote me a bundle of postcards before she got sick and died after I was born," said Dorothy. "I can't even remember her, but I've got about twenty postcards from when she was pregnant all sent in the mail and addressed to me in particular. I've received a few others too, from my grandparents, though Jesiah had wanted to cut them off after they tried to take me away from him. But Patrick's mom, that's why I came to be with Patrick, his mom had saved my mother's tin of postcards, including the twenty from her directly and she kept those safe from my father—he never did recover from my mother's death, just got angry instead. He was always angry. Mrs. Brennan kept that tin for me until I married Patrick and moved away from the old orchard. Receiving those postcards from my line of family was the best gift I've ever known. It was like receiving news from my mother in heaven. So if I could, I'd go back in time and let her know I'm fine."

The two women hunched quietly in the snow. The cold was

beginning to settle into their boots and freeze through their jackets. Lulu picked up another twig.

"You must still have them, the postcards?" asked Lulu.

"I do. I keep all my family's postcards in a black cookie tin."

"Your cookie tin's a time machine. Each time you read one of those letters, you're going back to their lives and letting them know you're fine. It's like saying hello."

Dorothy smiled and leaned forward, raising herself from the snow drift in which they were sitting. She was getting cold, and Patrick would be just about crazy by now, plus, she was suddenly in the mood to sort through her postcards.

"Come on," she said to Lulu, holding out a hand to help the lady up. "I'm so hungry, I could *eat* an owl. Let's find the river and go home."

"But Dotty—"

"I'm tired, Lulu."

"I'd never seen a snowy owl before, that's all." There were times when Lulu O'Bannon reminded Dorothy of a child: she sulked, pouting her red lips, and suddenly looked ten years younger. But even when Lulu went sour, she was still pretty.

"If I was as good-looking as you," said Dorothy, "I'd have stayed in Montreal."

Lulu laughed and took Dorothy's arm to stand; the two began to walk in awkward steps through the high snow. "I had had enough of big city men breaking my heart."

"Your family miss you?"

"*Absolument*," replied Lucienne. "But it's better this way. I send them money."

Dorothy nodded. "Come on," she said. "We'll head straight for the river then follow the bank."

"Sorry about your pickles."

"They'll be waiting."

"Sorry about Patrick."

Dorothy actually laughed to herself. "Well, I may have to return your cradle."

Again through the forest she and Lulu moved: picking around clumps of frozen bushes buried beneath the snow, following tracks and spotting deer in the distance, and their moods began to lift. Once again, they started jumping into the snowdrifts and kicking through the powder—sinking down, then stepping back up to jump through another, then another, and another. It was exhausting; it was exhilarating.

Just as Dorothy was set for another leap, out from the sky came a blur of white, diving past their noses and landing gently in the upcoming pile of snow. The owl sank down and flapped for just a moment before it flew up into the branches with a field mouse in its grasp.

Dorothy gasped and fell backwards to the ground, pulling Lulu down beside her.

"*Oh! Mon Dieu!*" exclaimed Lulu.

Splatters of blood littered the ground as the mouse squeals stopped. Laying back and looking up, Dorothy and Lulu watched the large bird eat the limp creature.

Turning his face toward them, the owl stared down, then dropped back to the forest floor, settling beside Dorothy's feet and whistling loudly as his small, white head bobbed in half circles.

"Should we move?" asked Dorothy.

"I don't know."

"Maybe it's hungry."

"Don't be stupid, Dotty. We're too big to eat."

"I'm not stupid." Too often people called her stupid. But she wasn't at all. Fourth on her secret list of dreams was a high school diploma. What with caring for her father and marrying Patrick, it'd been impossible to complete her schooling when she was younger. But none of that made her stupid. She'd just lately seen an advertisement in the Eaton's catalogue to earn her degree by correspondence. If she were stupid, she wouldn't even consider sending off for an information packet.

The owl's head circled up and down. With wings spread wide, it flapped toward the women and inched back and forth around the snow drift, whistling ever louder. Dorothy had heard the dangers of an animal that acted bizarrely.

"It must think we're bears," whispered Lulu.

The owl hopped forward, raising its clawed feet up and down. His head swung back and forth while his yellow eyes bore into the women.

"We're not bears," Dorothy said to the owl. "We are just two nice ladies who wanted to follow you a little. Nothing wrong with that, right?"

Again he untucked his wings and spread them wide, hopping forward.

"Jesus, Dotty!" Lulu was hiding behind Dorothy. "He wants to claw us, tell him to stop."

Dorothy wished she *could* talk with the owl—she wished she didn't look like a bear, or a field mouse, or anything worth eating, and she could shrink down, climb onto the owl's back and just make friends. Then he'd take her anywhere and they'd go up real high in the air and maybe never even come down again. If she were to die, right here and right now, she and her little baby would climb as spirits onto this owl's back and fly right up and away from everything, away from Patrick and the cradle and the shop and maybe even Lulu, maybe. Though Dorothy didn't mind having a friend, even one like the mayor's wife.

"Try again, Dotty," said Lulu.

Dorothy cleared her throat. *Concentrate, concentrate.* "Hello, Owl. We just want to go home now. We won't follow you again. Not today, or ever. Okay?" Dorothy pushed back against Lulu and slowly the two women increased their distance from the hopping, bobbing bird. "See, we're leaving."

Carefully Lulu rose from the ground, and then held her hand out for Dorothy. Neither woman bothered to brush off the snow on their backs and arms. Instead they looked around the forest. Now that they were standing, the owl felt less of a threat.

"Well," began Lulu, "he's right in our way. We'll have to go around the bushes and find a shallower spot over this drift."

Slowly backing up, the women waved timid goodbyes to the snowy owl, who continued to bob and whistle and fix its eyes upon their retreating, fur-covered shapes.

Stepping over to the side, around the trees and hopping over a shallow drift that had blown against a clump of naked bushes, they eventually circled the bird. Heading toward the sound of the river, Dorothy dared to turn back toward the owl. She raised her hands and squinted her eyes.

"Lulu!" Dorothy pointed to the watching bird.

Lulu turned around.

"Look, just there in front of him. You see that?"

Lulu blocked the light for a better view.

"*Mon dieu*, Dorothy. Is that a trap?"

"Sure is," replied Dorothy. "Patrick's carrying traps into the office all the time. Someone must have been hoping for a bear by the size of that thing."

"And we were about to run straight through. It could have broken our legs."

"I could have lost the baby." Dorothy placed a hand on her stomach. She couldn't lose this baby. It was the only miracle that had ever happened to her in her entire life. The baby and now the owl, they were the most incredible things.

"*O Seigneur*," Lulu crossed herself. "I'll make church this Sunday."

And Dorothy gave a small wave to the bird, whispering a quiet thank you as they turned away.

"You know Dorothy," said Lulu with a tilt of her head and linking her arm through Dorothy's once again, "with your hair let down and all shook out, I figure you're quite striking, very much like a romantic novel heroine."

"What's a heroine?"

"A woman who is the main character in a novel, and who learns how to be brave. She's striking and clever and the reader always loves her. And in the end, in the end, she will find resolve within herself—one way or another."

Dorothy's feet were itchy, her stomach rumbled, her toes felt numb, and yet she smiled.

"That's about the nicest thing anyone has ever said to me, Mrs. O'Bannon."

"Please, Dorothy, call me Lulu."

And through the white, frozen forest Dorothy walked with Lulu arm in arm, over drifts and pile ups, across streams and around boulders, and finally, with the rising sound of the Ottawa River, back toward the frozen riverbank, past the church's spire, toward the Prior and home—where real life was anxiously awaiting their return.

Door locked; sign flipped to closed. And peering through the dark, frosted window, no Patrick in sight. No fire burning in the pot-belly stove, no mail being sorted, no paper chain on the counter.

Dorothy had left Lulu at her manor house, saying it would only make matters worse if the mayor's own wife came along to witness an outraged Patrick. Standing at the post office, she pulled the silver key from around her neck and inserted it into the lock. She said a small prayer for courage, "Please, please, please," and slipped inside with a ring of the chime.

The post office foyer was chilly. First things first. She opened the cast iron grill and prodded the coals, throwing in a few pieces of kindling and crouching before the hearth as red embers began to smoke and catch the slivers of wood.

Second things second. With her boots, coat and hat still on, Dorothy stomped through the lobby, through the office, and to the kitchen. There, in the garbage as expected, were her three pickles and a flag of England. Dorothy reached into the trash and, carefully wiping off the morning coffee grinds, retrieved her three dill pickles. Sliding down the buzzing white refrigerator onto the chequered vinyl floor, Dorothy softly whimpered with pleasure as her teeth crunched through the cucumbers, an Antrium Diner special.

It was strange. She felt calm. She knew she shouldn't, but that knot in her stomach had, at some point, dissolved.

Dorothy ate like a queen, a queen starved, and licked her fingers, and smacked her lips, and sucked on the juice, loving every last gorging moment of pure uninterrupted dill pickle.

She thought about her day. She ate and she laughed, and she laughed and she ate.

It was only at the finish, at the very last bite, that the shop bell tingled and a cold gust of wind swept along the corridor.

"Dorothy!" he roared.

Dorothy sank lower onto the floor and wiped her wet hands across the short beaver fur.

"You here, girl?"

She could hear his belt sliding from his waist.

"Dorothy Brennan! You come here now."

The fire was rolling, he would know she was back home. There was no avoiding what came next.

Dorothy rose up from the floor and walked slowly into the front shop, stepping out of her wet boots and removing her jacket. She glanced out the front post office window: no one was on the street, no one was watching. Maybe Lulu was with her little Jacquelyn, sitting on their sofa and waiting for their afternoon cocoa. She'd be telling her about the owl. She wouldn't worry about Dorothy because Dorothy had insisted everything would be fine; Patrick would be fine. That, of course, had been a blatant lie.

"Stupid woman!" snapped Patrick.

Patrick was standing near the register with a red face and his belt already folded in his hand. Dorothy quickly removed her flannel hat and shoved it onto the bench by the entrance to the foyer. Her hair had fallen out of its tie and lay in long, tangled streaks across her shoulders.

"No note? No nothing?" He slapped his belt against the counter.

Patrick didn't normally hit Dorothy. Instead he struck objects around them. He had broken lamps, spilt jugs, dented tables and once, just once, smacked himself right between the eyes. That was when Dorothy had dropped the glass vase and it'd smashed into a thousand pieces. Patrick had somehow gotten a tennis ball, and threw it against the kitchen wall. It shot right back into the middle of his face.

In the warming post-office foyer, Dorothy smiled.

"What's so funny? " demanded Patrick.

Slap—his belt hit the register.

"You think this is funny?"

Slap—his belt hit the fire place.

"Not even a note!"

Slap—his belt hit Dorothy across the cheek. She fell back with a sharp cry. But before Patrick could register the welt across her face, before he could react and apologize, Dorothy attacked.

Screeching and swooping across the room, arms fully opened and flapping, head bobbing. She landed square against her husband's chest with fingers clenched like talons, biting—scratching—kicking—doing her worst.

Doorthy shouted and screamed, screamed so loud it nearly broke glass. As any person from the Prior will say, on the day Patrick Brennan's wife began fighting back, the whole town heard her rage.

When she was done, as Patrick lay shocked on the ground.

Dorothy knelt next to her husband and easily collected his belt: "It's time to stop bullying me, Patrick," she said. "Because I want to be happy and we're having a baby. So we are going to be a happy little family, or else I'll fly away forever. I'll fly away and be gone."

Because number one on her list of dreams was to stand up to her husband. And if she could track an owl, go back in time to her mother, hear the forest's voice, and meet a woman who thought that *she,* Dorothy Claire Brennan, was beautiful—then this, the little thing she wanted most of all, was most certainly within her reach.

"No more bullying me, Patrick. I'm not taking it one second longer."

Her life was filled with secret wishes, and finally, right there on that floor, on that cold winter day so soon before Christmas our girl finally found her courage, the courage to chase her dreams. And suddenly for Dorothy, life appeared to be full of miracles—playing in Technicolor, if you will.

The Witch of Arnprior, 1928

The cross-country Canadian Pacific line doesn't stop in Arnprior. The fifteen-carriage steamer passes through the small town station, slows to thirty kilometres an hour while tooting its horn to warn the locals. If you wanted to board the train and chug off to Nova Scotia (since the steamer is currently traveling east) you'd have to take the local crawler up to Ottawa, which stops at every small settlement and logging point along the way. If you didn't bring a lunch you'd be plain out of luck, because the tea service on the local is awful. Stale biscuits and eggy sandwiches.

The Canadian Pacific Trans-Canada train doesn't stop for small towns, that's regulations and they're strictly abided by, but it does slow down at the Arnprior station and its horn shrieks for the locals; or rather for one particular local who, in fact—it could be said—is no more local than the train passing through. She's running beside the first carriage now, despite the snowfall, waving her beaver coat-covered arms. Long black hair streams behind her with twists of braids and snatches of feather tied by leather strips. Ruby Claire Brown, not a Native name yet she's full of Native blood, reaches up toward the two pale women wrapped in blankets in the open doorway of the first carriage, who throw her a package and hand her—just barely, *reaching, reaching, grabbed!*—a postcard from her mothers before the platform ends. And she waves to the women, who wave back, and kisses are blown into the twirl of snow twisting up between them as the family breaks away and stretches further and further apart.

Ruby Claire, or plain 'Ruby' as they call her, buries the package within her fur coat and holds the *Victoria Falls, Victoria* postcard to her face, hair flying as the train cars beside her *click-clicks, click-*

clicks past. Matthew's train is picking up speed and the windows are blurring into one long and fast pane of frosted glass. She breathes in the postcard's scent and revels in hints of cardboard and paste, with a sharpness of ink and a touch of perfume rubbed off from a wrist.

We're all fine here. The date squares were delicious. And how is the baby, Ruby? Is it too soon for kicks? Remember to follow your nose and always be good. Love from all of us until next time. We miss you.

Ruby tucks the card into her pocket and slides back to the station fence. Then, picking up her basket that's hanging from the gate, she slips the package into its wool-lined interior, shutting the flap. In her mind she constructs her response: *My dearest Mary, Lizzy and Matthew, of course the baby's not kicking—it's only been four months.* The snowflakes are falling thick and fast. Her lashes bat away the heavy fragments that land upon her face and tumble to the ground. She felt this storm coming for days, carried on the breeze with a dense aura of atmosphere and humidity, a dark, wet-blue presence in the air. If it were August instead of January, the sky would have crashed and glowed with a god-like force. Horses would have been spooked and the sewers would have flooded. The rivers would have churned and raged.

The blizzard hadn't started to whip. That would soon be coming. Instead the wind rises and falls in strong currents that wrap Ruby's body and send her hair flying and mixing in a whirl. She holds her basket closer and walks along the centre of the road, lifting her laced boots high and trying not to fill them with ground-swirling snow. *Jesiah is doing well, praying for a boy. But no amount of praying will work, as you know, because she's a girl through and through. A proper Claire if I've ever known one.*

Leaving the train station will shortly take you onto Pierre Street, which runs lengthwise through Arnprior, or 'the Prior' as locals call their town, and is lined with several tall and important buildings to the right and, to the left, a line of veranda homes that become more widely spaced as the road carries on toward the countryside. This is where the wives of the bankers, office workers, businessmen and foremen live, with their shovelled lanes and hundred-year-old oaks. This is *not* where Ruby Brown lives. To the right, where she's now turning and bending forward into the wind that is steadily gaining speed—*wind whipping, wind wrapping all around her*—are the tall and important buildings. In the summer and spring the pavement before these giants (Bank of Nova Scotia, Woolworth's department store, Hudson Groceries, Royal Canadian Post) is naturally exposed, and becomes the pride of the Prior. Horses clack along the road with their carriages rumbling behind them, men walk with their canes *tap tap tapping* against the asphalt and say to one another, 'Yes, it really is quite hard.' This is where children will crack eggs onto the warming surface in high summer in hopes that the eggs will cook. And above this wide boulevard, not to be forgotten, are the electricity lines with small birds perched upon the wires—*chirp, chirp, chirping* away in the summer sun.

Now Ruby whispers to the horses who are shivering at their posts and pats them on their shoulders, readjusting their blankets, brushing off the inch of snow. They smell of dried sweat and old manure, and the apples in her orchard. Moving on, she follows a path of disappearing footprints and wheel marks and hops—*runs, jumps, steps*—beside the buildings, looking over their dark brick facades and large curtained windows. It's early in the Prior, behind the curtains are the faint outlines of electric lights, and people standing, sitting, getting ready for business. No one sees the Indian girl still out in the cold, in the dawn, in the snow.

We're settling into the Prior fine. Jesiah has stopped his wildness and is constructing a bassinet for the child. He's a wonderful carpenter, a genius with his hands. Lies smell like mayonnaise, off-white with yellow tinges. Ruby sticks out her pink tongue and icy flakes blow into her mouth. Her hair settles across her shoulders, weighed down by an increasing blanket of snow; only black rebel strands now rise with the wind. She stands against the post office window, catching her breath. The baby is slowing her down and starting to show from beneath her layers. She stands up straight like the mothers taught her, but no matter what Ruby does, no matter how she adjusts and tries, she still looks wild; she will always look wild.

She rings the bell and the post office door is pulled back by the wind; little Patrick Brennen is standing in the doorway, snot bubbling from one nostril but, otherwise quite proud, with his arms crossed in a knitted green sweater.

"Mail here?" his high voice asks.

The boy's mother is standing there, arms also crossed. Mrs. Brennan smells like hot cinnamon hearts, burning but sweet, the colour of fire. No Postmaster then, probably upstairs sleeping till the weather passes.

"Straight from the train," Ruby replies.

Opening her straw basket, she removes the medium-sized parcel from the contents and passes it to the small boy. In his arms it looks much larger.

"What do you say?" calls his mother from within. Hot cinnamon hearts. It's warm inside with that fire burning in the cast iron stove.

"Thank you very much," replies Patrick, who then turns round and slams the door shut behind him. He smells of cap guns, dirt and spit.

Postmaster Brennen sends his regards to Matthew, and asks what it's like to be the head of a legend? I half think he'd rather leave his family and ride the Canadian Pacific with the bunch of you. Mail can be so boring, except for the postcards, of course.

And she sets off again, now crossing the empty street. The wind is racing through the avenue, faster than the river's current, skating up and down along the snow-filled streets and shaking up the electrical lines. *Crash! Smash!* Icicles shatter; only fools walk beneath the electrical lines on a windy day. They smell of danger and excitement, sparking explosions of white against blackness, with translucent tones of blue. The wind is picking up, throwing the flakes of snow faster than before—*fried eggs, coffee, dog shit, sweat, dry toast, popping yellows and deep twirling browns with hints of brittle beige*, they blow past her and are gone as the storm begins to cleanse the stench of morning rituals. Ruby wishes she could skate on the wind, feeling it whip around her. Wildness embraced. She would skate beyond the smells and cut through the air, rising up and down, breaking through the clouds.

Instead, Ruby walks along the sidewalk's deep blanket of snow that threatens to pour into her loosely laced boots. Finally she reaches the small brown building, it's set lower to the ground than the proud giants of the boulevard, and opens the heavy wooden door.

"The heat, girl!" comes a shout from within.

Ruby Claire Brown shuts the door behind her, and the snowflakes melt away.

***

During the sawmill days, when trees could be heard falling and the river ran thick with timber, the Arnprior jail was a bustling place filled with cursing, laughing, and taps on the wrist. Along the river's edge, the makeshift camps had held over eight hundred men at peak capacity—eight hundred fighting, playing, sweating, sawing lumberjacks. Sap and sawdust paved the streets, pouring down from a seemingly never-ending demand to chop, cut, and fell.

But the lumber trade was dying, ships and buildings were turning to steel and the lumberjacks soon found themselves drifting onwards, elsewhere. The large jail of the Prior was storage for parade floats and horse feed and salt. The timber era was at an end, and this town, once so large and grand in the eyes of its residents, was starting to shrink into quiet obscurity. Not even the trains stopped any more.

Sheriff Boyle could remember those times. The log-rolling times. But as the trees stopped falling, his mind began to change, to slide into a quieter state of life. With years settled onto his shoulders, his grey-haired disposition found solace in a calm, quiet reserve, with cups of black coffee and a local paper on his lap. But this morning he'd added salt instead of his scoop of sugar, and had only just realized the mistake. So when he shouted at Ruby, who tucked through the door like a mouse through its crack, and the girl jumped at the sound of his booming voice, there was a slight regret in his mind, as it failed to honour his decided change of pace.

And so he didn't object when she pulled out a flask and passed it to her Jesiah behind the bars. Jesiah the apple farmer, turned train robber, turned midnight brewer of the devil's juice, which figured, black sheep that he was, tolerated only because his family was a legacy in the Prior. His parents had died embarrassed by the boy, and rightly so, but it was a shame since he was the only son that they had managed. And Jesiah was tolerated, only just, and even less when he brought the Indian home—mind you, she did brew a fine scrumpy, though it was against his profession to admit it.

Ruby ignored the Sheriff.

With her hand held through the bars, waiting for the empty flask, her mind drifted like the snow outside.

Have you ever fallen in love? In the literal sense? Head over heels—open the safe and steal the money, jump for your life and break fall with a roll, world spinning as the grass whips round while the train carries on and Matthew toots the horn—that throb in the heart, right from the gut, out of your mind kind of love? Straight off into the arms of the man whom you fancied for less than three minutes before he kissed you, saying with a wink: "Want to have a little fun?" And suddenly he was your world, your whole entire world and you revelled in his eyes, in his chin, in his lips, in his arms, in his touch.

Until the next morning, when the train was long gone, and the smell of dew had settled into your skin, and the man who looked so strong with the gun and the dusk turns out to be little more than a boy? Not more than a boy.

Well, that wasn't love. It was *i-n-f-a-t-u-a-t-i-o-n*. And now Ruby was stuck with him. At least for the time being.

"How long this time, Jesiah?"

"Sheriff said a couple days with the stink we kicked up last night. Guess I'll miss this storm coming through."

In the middle of the station was a large stove that radiated heat. The sheriff was boiling a kettle of water on the top; steam rose into the air as the whistle began to scream. Ruby set her basket onto the dusty floor and stuck one hand across her ear, the other across her stomach as the sheriff searched for his oven mitt to stop the whistling.

Jesiah put down his flask and reached for his wife, bringing her closer. "I asked if you could stay, but you know old Boyle, no women in his cells. Anyhow, Ruby, the hay scratches and the salt stings."

"I wouldn't set a foot in that cell of yours, Jesiah," said Ruby. "Warm and cozy as it seems."

"Have you got firewood?"

"Chopped this morning."

Jesiah nodded and accepted the sandwich wrapped in wax paper that Ruby passed through the bars. He knew about love. Love startled you in the night with how much it mattered, catching you off guard when you weren't ready. It found you on a train going sixty miles an hour, and had dark, wild hair but spoke like a high-minded lady—and made the damn best sandwiches he'd ever tasted. And after being alone for so long, after his parents had died in the house fire and everything had gone so wrong, love saved you from self-destruction and gave you a reason to continue.

Ruby knew it too. She knew it, and that was why she hadn't hopped the next freighter to Toronto. Jesiah with his smell of moulding apples and warm bark, he couldn't be left alone. He *couldn't* be left alone.

So when the Sheriff ran his monthly raid on their still, with ever lessening enthusiasm as prohibition had lost momentum, Ruby didn't mind as the old man's brown hat and flashing badge appeared between the loggers all lined up with their reaching cups. The still was disassembled (with jugs of liquor safely buried in the leaves, or the grass, or the snow, depending on the season. They were running the most popular still in the county, it was always in demand. Ruby used an old recipe she'd found on one of the postcards from her great-great grandmother, Marianne Claire. The men were mad for that drink.) and Jesiah was carted off to prison to rest for a few days, leaving her to rebuild another 'secret' site and have a little peace—well, Ruby didn't mind any of that one bit.

In those days without him, she felt free to be wild, to breathe, to drift. Having grown up on a train, it wasn't in her nature to remain still. In the rail days she'd sit in Matthew's front berth and hang her head out the window breathing in the country, filling up on flashing scents. And the train kept moving; she always kept moving. But now, here in the Prior away from the tracks and the steam and the coal and the wind ... the smell of stagnation was becoming overwhelming, even more so since she'd become pregnant.

Have you ever smelled the Rocky Mountains? *Wet rock with moist moss flashing as glacier lakes suck turquoise colour and breath through churning rapids. Cool and clean with a high altitude finish.* What's the scent of Prairie grass? *Long yellow warming oats of manure stinking sweetness, farm after farm after farm after farm with a red barn in the distance.* Know the breath of endless oceans? *Salt splashing rotting bodies and flashing gills, jumping tips of waves and winding streams that stink of slime yet also, somehow, the endless promise of renewal.* All the while with the train engine *chugging, chugging, chugging,* always moving away.

These are the scents of an ever-changing life. This is the world as it streams through your window. Ruby knows it well. She was the girl who breathed her country, naming towns with only her nose held high and the windows open. Ruby had been in love with the wind. Truly, deeply in love. Until, of course, someone else stole her heart, which is only natural, her being a young woman of flesh and blood. And a new love took over within the blink of an eye. His pressing lips and strong arms; her burning cheeks and mind gone funny. Jump from the train, Ruby! He's the love of your life! Lust of your life. *I-n-f-a-t-u-a-t-i-o-n.* And in three minutes her world had changed. Stopped. Settled. Stank.

Jesiah returned the wax paper.

"You'll be safe with this blizzard, Ruby?"

"I'll be fine."

"Take good care of him."

"Her, Jesiah. She's a girl."

"Just don't freeze."

"Stop worrying, we'll be fine. No blizzard's stumped me yet."

She packed her basket and left the station. Wind rising as she pushed open the door. A rogue gust broke into the station and stole away their heat. She stepped out into the clean, rushing air. Even had the sheriff offered, Ruby wouldn't have taken the cell. There was a storm coming, which could not be missed. It'd be as bad as missing the morning train.

The town was beginning to stir as Ruby walked back onto the blinding white street and buttoned up her jacket; flipping the collar she buried her chin and cheeks. It was slicing cold today, the kind of cold that freezes your skin and makes the nose drip ice. A hard kind of cold.

"You feeling warm?" she asked her middle.

No answer. Instead there came the whinny of horses and the sound of men trying to shout them forward. Not much use driving an automobile on a day like this, the tires were no match for the snow. Ruby peered into her basket and hesitated while standing by the road, unsure which direction to pursue. And as she stood, thinking, smelling—*scents of the pulp mill two towns over, the factory furnace pumping out coal-black smoke, doors opening and closing as slips of heat and clouds of perspiration escape into the storm*—the Prior began to wake. Men in straight black jackets with tall fur hats emerged from the side streets and walked, proud and frozen, to their respective places of work. Some wore snowshoes, taking long jumping steps across the piles of snow, others, like Ruby, picked their way along the footprints and horse tracks of others, shaking their feet with every step, brushing at their ankles. All the buildings, those impressive testaments to the booming days of lumber, one after another they opened their eyes with pulled back curtains and blinked from the illumination of yellow lamps within. She crumpled her nose as the wind blew around her, as the town moved around her; soon the children began to appear, one after another, the young ones wrapped in knitted scarves and toques and hand-me-down jackets. They walked single file through the drifts like diligent little ants, heading away from home and toward the large school house on Bell.

Ruby reached into her pocket and pulled out her postcard, bringing it to her cheek as she thought about her family. They had been so happy when she'd written about her pregnancy. They'd even sent the cookie tin with a note about how Ruby had grown into a fine young woman. "We're so pleased you found love."

The cookie tin meant obligation. She was obliged to pass it forward, to write the letters, to continue the tradition of her Claires.

But family, at least in Jesiah's mind, meant settling down, sticking to one place. Though it was no wonder after all he'd been through. "Don't leave me alone," he'd whisper in the night. "Don't you leave me, Ruby."

It had only been three minutes, just three fleeting minutes of complete and utter love. Was it possible to bind yourself so quickly? And now the baby, and the letters. A little family had sprung up around her, growing like a weed.

Ruby rubbed her stomach. She was hungry. Lately, she was always hungry.

The children streamed around her as she stood on the sidewalk and reached into her basket, unwrapping a goose fat sandwich and chewing on it slowly, enjoying the salt. They stared at her as they passed. This was the Indian witch. Red skin. Half-blood. Adults said she was just another low-class vagabond, but with that hair and the mole on her chin, and the look she shot when you stared too hard. (It was always unexpected, you'd think she hadn't noticed the way she floated by in that dream world of hers, then suddenly –*SNAP*– the witch is staring at you, right into your mind, and she knows, *she knows* about that snowball behind your back.) Until their Jesiah brought her to town, they'd never seen an Indian witch before.

And the passing children wondered: what spell was she casting this time? Standing there chewing her breakfast and holding her head to the sky? Katie Murphy dared Owen Bantry to pull one of the feathers from the witch's hair. She whispered to him as they walked side by side (having left from houses six and seven of Elm Street and coincidently, every morning, walking together to school but never holding hands), saying it'd be a magic feather and would bring them good luck for the rest of their lives. And wouldn't that be something, Owen?

According to Jenny McCree, two years senior to Katie and Owen, and with the reddest pigtails in town, it was a well-known fact that witches carried good luck charms on their person, and these charms were so valuable that people would go crazy and start fighting and pulling and kicking till they got their hands on those bits of luck. And when Katie said to Jenny, "So why don't they do just that?"

Jenny answered: "You don't know? Witches cast protective spells so that adults can't see the charms. Only children can see them, *because witches can't fool children.* But don't try to snatch them, she'll turn you into a toad." And when Owen asked if Jenny could see the lucky charms, because she'd just turned thirteen, Jenny replied, "Not anymore, but I remember them from last week when I was still twelve."

You can understand, of course, why every child in town wanted to steal the witch's lucky feathers. And there she was just eating her sandwich in the middle of a snow storm. But Owen wasn't certain. Last week he'd been thinking about pelting her with a snowball, and sure enough, she'd stared him down. If he reached up and pulled out a feather from her few blowing braids, if he *dared* to even try, wouldn't she just catch him right away?

"I don't know Katie. What if she turns me into a toad?"

Katie and Owen approached the witch from behind, stealthily moving through the footprints, holding their backpacks ever more tightly. She was still chewing, still holding her head up into the sky. Her eyes were closed.

"She'll just think you're the wind," whispered Katie to Owen.

Owen squinted through his coke-bottle glasses and raised a red-mitten hand. Maybe he could do it. And if he *did* steal a feather, he'd be a hero. Or even better, a man. A real man.

Slowly, slowly. Owen stepped ahead of Katie and lifted his hand toward the witch. There weren't too many feathers, just a few braided in. He crept up right behind her as Katie swallowed giggles and bit her fist of mitten. *Inching, inching* closer, right beside the witch's shoulders and reaching out to gra—

"Owen Bantry." Ruby turned around and gave him the look.

Owen turned to ice: frozen solid and ready to crack right through, he couldn't even breathe, he couldn't even think. She'd done worse than a toad. At least toads hopped and swam and blew giant bubbles with their faces. She'd turned him into ice! Soon enough he'd shatter into a thousand pieces like his glasses last year when Billy Tharp had thumped him for no good reason.

"Owen?" asked Ruby as she bent down to look into his tiny face. "Can I help you with something, young man?" Ruby had been raised with the best of manners on the train. Nothing less would do when you represent the Canadian Pacific.

"Feather?" squeaked Owen through frozen lips. Katie's mouth dropped.

Ruby straightened up and tucked her waxed paper into the basket. "Why not?" she replied. And reaching back to a flying braid, she pulled out the ridiculous feather (Jesiah's idea to make her seem 'more Injin' for the liquor sales) and handed it to the boy.

Owen grinned and yelped. He reached back, taking Katie by the hand, and the two ran through the snow drifts toward school. Ruby watched them run along, and wondered if her own daughter would get so excited. So wonderfully excited and free. She hoped so. She hoped her little something Claire wouldn't have to wear chicken feathers to become 'more Injin'. Ruby's daughter would be a normal girl like the rest of them. Jesiah would see to it. Her little Something Claire would fit in just fine.

Reaching into her pocket, Ruby pulled out the postcard and sighed. *And that is what's happening here in the Prior. Same old, same old. Now, please, write back and tell me more. Tell me something. Write a good long one, have Matthew do it if you're unable. Tell me about the train, please. Tell me something. The wind is carrying away your perfume.* Cardboard smells like ink and mulch and traces, just the last hints, of perfumed wrists. The mothers were being sucked away into the storm.

Ruby's toes were starting to burn from standing still too long in the cold, and her fingers were starting to ache as they clutched the frozen cardboard. Stupid of her not to bring the sealskin gloves on a day like this, but she'd run so quickly out the door this morning to meet the train, now she'd have to settle for deep pockets and a stinging tingle. Driving down the street northward, a huge gust of wind pushed against her and wrestled for her postcard as she struggled to get it back into her pocket. Pushing and pushing, the wind was insistent. Standing and waiting, Ruby was equally stubborn. She remained rooted to the same uncertain place outside the police station, and she watched as the street began to lift in white waves and plunge in short dives. Cyclones of snow twisted down Pierre Street, between the hitching posts, over the abandoned carriages and automobiles, and up the sidewalks after the stragglers to work. Shouting children were blown away as the last one ran to class, men huddled into themselves as they reached for their doors, icicles crashed from the cables and the horses were being rescued, one by one, and led towards the nearest stable. As another gust pushed against her, pushing, pushing, always pushing and sucking away her warmth, Ruby cursed the town of Arnprior and shook her head.

"No, no, no. It's a horrible idea," mumbled Ruby. Guilt smells likes like burnt sugar, turning quickly into smoke.

The streets were emptying as people filtered away. Cold air was a contradiction, virginal yet full, smelling of atmosphere, ice blocks and blank slates. But the wind carried flavours, hints of this and that, passing scents like a chugging train. It was a kaleidoscope of smells, except for today, today it blew so hard and so fast—these sporadic gusts of force that fought against Ruby's rigid stance, shooting scents faster than her nose could follow. All she sensed were flashes of grease, sugar, burning, mould, blood, ice, dirt, oil, cedars, maples, feathers, sky. It was amazing. It was dizzying. It was tempting.

Gusts of air along the giant corridor pushing her, pushing her. She would always be pushed. Jesiah had had a hard life, young as he was, but he needed the Prior, that was for certain. A fellow like him couldn't live without stability, without the steady constant characters who were part of this town's history. He needed to stay, and he'd been through enough. She couldn't leave him alone. She wouldn't leave him alone. And what about her little Something Claire?

On the train it was easier, with the rolling of the wheels and the ever-changing landscape. But even there she was getting unsettled, rebelling against the noon-time tea service and white apron she was instructed to wear, getting restless with the lady-like manners of the Pacific rail. All she really wanted was to ride with her head out the window and shout into the wind. Jesiah had been the perfect excuse for change. She had jumped from the train and promised to herself she'd be strong, she'd succeed in her new life. But now,

now that she knew better, Ruby struggled to imagine herself with the baby, cradling it in her arms as she and Jesiah rode into town for the early-morning market. She tried to imagine pointing out to the child all the farming scents mixed within the scene: the steaming horses, the damp hay, the fresh pumpkins and corn. And, of course, there would be Jesiah with his bushels of apples, grinning at his neighbours and tipping his hat.

In that hazy imaginary moment, Ruby was both a mother and a wife.

The only problem was that she had no desire for either.

All she wanted to do was jump from a train, roll down the hill, and runaway forever.

Expectation smelled of wet, rusted metal. It was heavy, and oppressive, and it stopped her from living.

With stiff fingers, Ruby reached into her pocket and stroked, barely sensing, the glossy image on the card. She was under obligation. But still, the wind pushed her. Tempted her. Begged to carry her away. If she stayed, she was very likely to lose her mind.

"Damn it, there is nothing for it." She argued all the time within herself, but the smells and the wind and the heavy snow were muting her protests. "Damn it all to hell," she snapped at the wind. "I'd be a terrible mother anyhow."

Ruby took large, reaching steps away from the jail and crossed the road. She walked along the sidewalk, lifting her feet high in an effort to navigate the rising snow till she was at the corner with that plush green curtain and golden lettering on the window: Royal Canadian Post. Ruby opened the door with its faint tinkle.

"The door now, quick!"

Slipping inside, she shut it tightly behind her.

The cast iron stove reminded Ruby of the burning furnace in Engine Two that would roar with heat as Andy, Matthew's coal man, would slave away keeping it piping hot. Once she'd been too close when he'd knocked aside the grating to fling another shovel-full, and the heat had pushed her backwards, baking her skin and singeing her brows. Burnt hair smells worse than indigestion.

The black pot-belly stove of the post office was no real comparison, but with its aura of heat and window of flames, it was a good point of remembrance on a blistering winter's day.

"Thought I'd see you blow-in, what with Jesiah occupied."

Ruby knelt down before the stove and held out her red raw fingers, watching as flames enveloped the log behind the glass.

"News travels quickly, eh?" she replied.

"Doesn't it just?" Hot cinnamon hearts. The Postmaster's wife smelled like hostility and spices, clove and cinnamon warmed together. And her arms would be crossed, too.

Mrs. Brennan was an import from the old country. "A true Irish lass," the men would call her as she walked by with her Saturday market shopping and little Patrick by the ear. "A proud one," they'd all mumble. The old postmaster had married her on the spot the day she rolled into town. Back then she'd been young and pretty. More cinnamon than fire. At least, that's what she had told Ruby, 'I was just a girl back then, years off from a woman.' Now she was taller and more present, four children under her belt, with three of them raised and gone. Times had hardened Matilda Brennan. She was not a person to waste her smiles.

So when this Indian girl walked into her store and asked, perfectly politely, 'May I please buy a stamp and card?' and wrote, in perfect hand, a letter to her mother; not a spelling error, not a hesitant scribble, not even a drop of uncertainty, except for the way she glanced around and scrunched her nose. (It was a terrible habit for a woman, to scrunch her nose like that, as though she were a badger.) When she passed back the postcard and said she was Jesiah's new girl, well, she hadn't said it like that, had she? This young blow-in had said: "My name is Ruby Claire Pierre. Jesiah and I have stopped into town." As though she didn't know a 'stop in' was to stop and not continue.

But all that was half a year ago, and here she was now with child, running like mad through the snow. It was no wonder they called her a witch. And the alcohol those two were brewing, that was a scandal in itself. But when Ruby had walked up to Matilda's post office counter and passed her the postcard, and Matilda had seen that she used proper English with proper cursive script, and must have had a good education ... well, a surprise like that could warm you to anyone, couldn't it? Or at least a wee bit, enough to allow Matilda's careful mind to imagine why a woman like Ruby shouldn't be caged in a town like this. And so she had understood when Ruby approached her with the cookie tin.

Hot cinnamon hearts, indeed; Matilda Brennan scrubbed every day with soap.

Ruby glanced away from the fire and looked at the postmaster's wife. Arms crossed, like she'd figured.

"We did well last night."

"I don't want to hear about your sinning."

"We did well."

Ruby stood up from the fire, toes still numb, and pulled out a bag of coins to show Mrs. Brennan.

"Should be enough here to skim." And she shook out its contents, pennies, nickels, and even a few dimes rolled across the table. Jesiah never counted the money. He'd take his share in drink instead, that was till Ruby lectured him silly and made him feel his shame. But he never counted the money, and each night she stole away some and stashed it in the cookie tin for her Something Claire.

Deceit smelled like sweating bodies, locked in a room and turning to stink.

She reached down into her basket and pulled out a postcard. This card wasn't to the mothers. Instead it showed illustrated kittens playing with bright pink spools of yarn, and had "Happy Birthday to a darling girl" printed in large, looping letters.

"Stamp, please?"

Matilda gently touched the postcard. Taking one penny from the coins, she licked a stamp of King George V and glued it to the back, then stamped it properly over the top with the date: January 24th, 1928. The back of the postcard was crammed full of Ruby's birthday messages for when her daughter turned three.

"Three years old?" replied Matilda, "Ruby, she won't be able to read."

Ruby stared at the postcard. "Jesiah can read it to her," she mumbled.

Ruby watched as Matilda studied her message and nodded quietly. They had their arrangement, not that the postmaster's wife had anything to gain, but she was a kind woman at heart; she would guard the postcards.

The outside storm was roaring through the street, thrashing against the window with its pressure and filling the streets with opaque whiteness.

"You're a fool of a girl, anyhow. But don't go out in that weather. Stop for a while," said Matilda.

Ruby shook her head. Reaching into her cold pocket, she pulled out the letter from the mothers. "And here, put this in the tin, too."

Victoria Falls, Victoria slid across the counter.

"How many more months then?" asked Mrs. Brennan.

"Five or so," replied Ruby. "And then that will be that."

And then she will be free. Free and gone, like the wind. Jesiah will have his supporters, and the baby. It was his baby too, after all. And the town wouldn't leave him on his own.

"Stay for a cup of tea."

"Not today," replied Ruby. The storm was calling, ripping through the streets with the force of a near hurricane. "Got to make Jesiah dinner, and then dig up the still, you know." Ruby slid the bag of money across to the red-head. "Put it in the cookie tin, okay? I'll tell Jesiah the money was misplaced in the storm."

Matilda put her hand on the small pile on the table: the postcards, the money. She stood ram-rod straight and nodded her head.

"All right then."

"All right," replied Ruby Claire Brown.

Stepping away from the counter, with one hand across her growing middle and the other tucked through the basket handle, Ruby opened the post office door with a quick tinkling of the bell. Snow flailed in around her like reaching fingers.

"The door!" called the postmaster's wife.

Breathing in the coldness of the storm with its scent of fresh nothingness—the most wonderful, exhilarating scent of them all—Ruby stepped out into the whipping blizzard. And she disappeared, as was her nature, into the total whiteness.

The Miss Pierres, 1905

Edmonton, Alberta

Matthew stepped onto the salted platform of Edmonton, Alberta and raised a whistle to his lips, screaming out a high pitched shriek. "All aboard!" he boomed. Wrapping his Canadian Pacific royal blue trench more closely around his body, he began waving on the flocks of passengers. "Trans-Canadian Pacific to Toronto, Ottawa, Montreal, and Quebec City is now ready for boarding. Ladies and gentlemen, please board the train."

Porters in maroon jumpsuits and caps hurried across the platform lifting trunks, helping women, pointing out cabins. Matthew strolled beside the train and nodded to his passengers. He glanced down to check the wheels, the link-and-pins, the brakes. Ice could be a problem in February and he didn't want problems on his maiden voyage.

"All aboard!"

Matthew did a time check: 12.10 in the afternoon and everything was running to schedule. As it should, and as it would, so long as Matthew Barnes was in charge. One minute and counting till departure.

Holding out his pocket watch, Matthew tapped the case with satisfaction.

"All aboard!" he called again.

Last-minute riders wrapped in furs and shawls and Hudson Bay colours were slowly but surely packing themselves onto the train as the biting February winds pushed at their backs to hurry them along.

Ice was forming upon Matthew's moustache, which he twitched back and forth.

"Hurry up now!"

The last of the passengers were climbing abroad — except for one: a sorry-state of a girl dragging a huge trunk behind her with one hand, and clutching her stomach with the other.

Matthew knew his job. He whistled at a porter and waved the boy along, then marched across to the passenger-in-need.

"All alone, ma'am?"

She couldn't have been more than fourteen-year-old, blonde as corn silk too, from what hair he could see from beneath her kerchief.

"Yes," she replied, glancing quickly between the approaching men. "All alone." The words evaporated into frozen steam, rising in small clouds from her lips as she spoke. She was like the ice queen, or maybe an ice princess, cast off and fragile.

"Are you unwell," he asked.

"I'll be fine in a moment. I'm with child."

It was a hidden fact within Matthew's family that his mother, Matilda Barnes née Craiova, had had him by a man who wasn't his father. The secret had never gone beyond the family circle. "A bad choice and too much liquor," was all his mother would say when the subject arose. Then, after some thought, she would add, "But you never know from where miracles derive." And then she'd wink at her Matthew and cluck her tongue with satisfaction.

Therefore, when Matthew, as a newly appointed conductor, spoke with this wide-eyed, lone girl struggling across the platform with a trunk that looked ready to quit, something in his mind flickered back to his dear mother and how she might have looked after her 'first husband' had quite suddenly 'passed away', and she herself had set off to Winnipeg in search of another life.

Edward Pike came running along, straightening his uniform and rubbing his red-raw fingers, nearly slipping on a patch of ice, before skidding to a halt and relieving the girl of her trunk.

"Your ticket, ma'am?" asked Eddy.

She passed the porter her flimsy yellow slip—third class passage—

and glanced between them to the train, to her trunk, to the ground. Edward passed back the ticket, "Quebec City then," and turned away, dragging the trunk behind him.

Matthew blew his whistle again, lips nearly freezing to the metal. "Put her in the Ruby berth, Edward."

"The Ruby, sir?"

"The Ruby," Matthew replied, then turned to the girl. "You're welcome to our deluxe carriage."

It was a long way to go for a girl in that condition. He imagined her on the wooden bench sleeping with a rolled-up scarf beneath her tiny head. There wasn't even central heating in the third-class carriages, just a wood stove blasting uneven waves of heat fuelled by whatever could be scavenged from the stops.

The Ruby was a reserve cabin for last-minute guests of a certain prestige. Damn daft idea, in Matthew's opinion, having a place reserved for the Queen should she ever decide to show up and grace the Canadian Pacific. But occasionally it came in handy, as Matthew's predecessor, former Conductor Hanes, had discovered, when a first-class couple had had a row and insisted on separate berths, or a rider had had too much drink and needed to recover composure.

Hanes had said just last week, on his final run across the country, that the Mayor of Edmonton's daughter had taken the berth when all other berths were full and insisted on a separate room from her father, who snored so loudly that Hanes provided complimentary cotton buds to all first-class passengers.

So really it was no bother to upgrade this sorry state of a woman before him, who shivered and shook and kept staring down at her boots.

"A little warm wine's what you need, ma'am," said Matthew, gesturing her to follow Edward. No ring on her finger, he noticed, and they'd turned a fine shade of blue. "A girl in your state needs her rest, we must think of the baby. Edward," Matthew turned to his deputy porter, "see that she's settled in."

And he straightened his long blue jacket with the swipe of a gloved hand, raising the whistle to his lips once more as he walked away down the platform.

"All aboard!" he called to the emptying station.

Glancing back, Edward was nearly having to drag the girl into the front carriage. She stood resolutely on the spot, glancing back at Matthew and at the third class cabins far along the train.

"Come along, then!" he called in his best conductor voice, though when the air turned this cold, it nearly strangled the lungs. When she *still* didn't budge, he turned away from the final inspections and headed back to where she stood rooted.

"Your name, Ma'am? Or is it Miss?"

"Sir, it's Miss," she softly replied.

"Your name Miss. Or is Miss your name?"

"My name's Mary, Mary Claire Pierre." Her voice wasn't as he'd expected. It was clear, without a back country accent. In fact, there might have been traces of French in her phrasing, which was strange for the prairies.

"Right, Miss Pierre, you have been promoted to a first-class sleeper, unless you'd prefer the wooden benches and crowds of third class?"

She finally shook her head. "Thank you. I'll take the bed."

Matthew nodded to Edward, who once again began dragging the trunk, this time followed by the girl.

And he marched away, giving one last whistle for good measure as the seer-offs stood back from the tracks and the people on the train pressed their faces against the glass, waving goodbye and rubbing away the frost.

Matthew, walking briskly back toward the engine, pulled out a yellow flag, and gave a satisfied wave to the engineer, Fred, who blew the horn with a resounding "Hoot" of steam and power. As the wheels began to turn and the great snake of steel started moving, Matthew hopped onto the middle carriage and watched the slowly disappearing platform with its reducing crowd of relatives and well-wishers puffing out their own small clouds of smoke as their mouths formed words of goodbye and farewell, all lost over the chugging engine of the Number Two.

Chugga, chugga, chugga. Fred, the engineer, blew the horn once more, "Whoo, whoo!" called the train.

And off they went, marking the maiden voyage of Matthew Daniel Barnes, conductor of Transcontinental Canadian Pacific Engine Two. It was a cold but promising start to what he hoped would be a very, very long journey.

***

Travel across the country took, if running to schedule with no unforeseen delays, twelve full days, including rest stops—two of which had already passed under Hanes's final guidance before they arrived at Edmonton, the remainder for Matthew alone to manage. He had ten days to reach Quebec City safely. There would be no tardiness, as per company regulation. "They set their clocks by us, Matthew," Hanes used to announce with each passing village. The now retired conductor had been working that line since its ribbon-cutting day. He knew where children threw the most snowballs, where the cows were always on the tracks, where the grizzlies tended to run beside the passing cars. Every vibration, every tick, every whirring of the train had a meaning for Hanes—Conductor Hanes didn't just ride the railway, he *was* the railway.

The old conductor had discovered Matthew some twenty-five years ago while Matthew had been sitting by a grain silo with his pencil in hand and writing. He was always in the same spot with every pass of the train, writing furiously as the engine whirred and the horn sounded. This would have been all the conductor would have ever known of the scribbling boy in the working-class wear had not an escaped herd of cows massed upon the tracks way back in 1880, halting the charging train in its tracks and allowed Hanes, normally bound by schedule and purpose, to step away from his rail line and ask the farm boy what he was writing on "that there pad of paper?"

"The train, sir," Matthew had answered. "I'm writing the train."

And indeed he had been. Wonderful phrases of wind-wrapping power, snaking hisses of steam, the quaking of earth and the bursting of speed. This, the conductor realized, was true appreciation of trains. In that moment, he offered the boy a porter position. Matthew never looked back; he'd found his place in life alongside the conductor. But when Hanes announced his retirement from the rails and then appointed Matthew his successor, well, that was the best damn thing to happen on the saddest day in his entire life.

"They set their clocks by us, you know," Matthew told the young girl in the Ruby berth as she sipped her mulled wine and laid her head against the cabin wall. One of the boys should have brought the girl her drink, but there was something so familiar, as if she were his own daughter somehow, that suggested he should bring the drink himself.

"People must love your train," she replied. Again she tasted the steaming drink. Matthew had added two extra cloves for a stronger smell, plus two extra sugar cubes for good measure.

"It's my first run as a conductor; I have high standards to meet, of course."

She smiled gently and let her head fall more heavily against the cabin wall. Her nose was still red-raw from the cold.

"Though I'm not sure why I'm telling you that. You just remind me so much of my mother. She was also pregnant on her own, for a time." He also wasn't sure why he was telling her that bit either. No one ever spoke about it, not even his own mother. Matthew had found out about her widow-pregnancy from his father after a night of too much drink from Farmer Burton's still.

"Everyone tells me everything," she said. Yawning, sinking even further into the berth's plush lined wall, she added, "I don't know why. *Maman* says its magic. She hates magic. *Seulement le diable a besoin de la magic.*"

The girl was dream-talking now. Off in another land. But still, Matthew kept going: "I'll ask Edward to bring you some blankets and make the bed." He turned up the radiator for the sleeping girl. "Just warming the room," he whispered. "Turn it down if the heat becomes too much."

The wine rested beside her on the red velvet berth. Matthew carefully picked it up and placed it on the window-side table, then lifted the girl's flimsy jacket, draping it across her small, pregnant body. Somehow he felt as though he'd known her from before, from somewhere or sometime he couldn't remember.

"Right," said Matthew to himself. Stepping from the cabin, he brushed off the last drops of melted snow from his shoulders. "Time to work."

Cornstalk, Manitoba

Rule one of the Canadian Pacific Trans-Canada Passenger Line: no free rides. The train hoppers loved to catch a ride between the cracks and crevices of the standard everyday trains. They hid on the roofs, they hid between cars, they hid in the freights, they hid in the washrooms, they jammed themselves in everywhere. Except on the Matthew's train—no sir, thank you very much. The Canadian Pacific was a glamorous lady to be treated with reverence. She needed constant vigilance against those train hoppers: every porter (Edward, László and Philip), every mechanic (Marcus, who was also an engineer along with Fred), every coal monkey (young Bertalan and young Sámson) and every conductor was on guard. Matthew felt on guard in his blue suit and cap, with a pad of tickets in his pocket and a handlebar moustache right down to his chin, which he'd grown for his inauguration after Hanes advised him he looked 'too fresh faced' for the new position.

The Canadian Pacific was a great big shining example of all things good and wonderful. No hopper was going to soil her reputation. Hanes had placed the responsibility in Matthew's hands when passing along the ticket book. "Chase 'em off, man. Chase 'em away."

And those free-riding hoppers knew it too—she was *the* train to ride if they could steal the chance. Matthew had a secret pride in the quality of hoppers that his lady train attracted. They were of a better class. From making high-quality ticket forgeries, to wearing disguises (dressing as women, as if a porter wouldn't notice a man eating an orange from his corset after several hours of not affording the lunch cart), to creative hiding places. Heck, Matthew had even found one once hiding under a dining table, legs between Lady

Balmont's ankles. The poor old woman had thought it was her dog, Chester, licking her feet. That had been a rider to remember. It was said, though not by Matthew, that if a rider made the journey coast to coast without detection, he'd be entitled to a free seat for life. But Matthew had checked the rule book over and over and not found a single reference to hoppers except one that read: "Unauthorized riders must be expelled from the train as the nearest platform approaches" (i.e., throw 'em off!).

Which is why Matthew was in a bit of a state when exiting the first-class berths into the second-class rows. With that girl in the front, he'd neglected his inspections, and that meant extra vigilance was required. After all, he was maintaining a reputation, wasn't he? "Constant vigilance," Hanes had prescribed. "Throw 'em off," the book demanded.

"Tickets please," Matthew requested as the second-class rides sat row after row, wrapped to their chins in winter jackets and scarves. He turned back to the door and fiddled with the thermometer, raising it two degrees. "Tickets." Passengers began to jostle in their seats, snapping open suitcases, unbuttoning purses.

Matthew moved along the carriages, collecting and checking tickets, nodding and smiling and answering questions from his guests. And it was in carriage four that he found his very first hopper of his inaugural journey. An easy pick, granted, but Hanes would have been pleased at how Matthew had spotted the fellow in the crowd. Slouched against the frozen window pane, face right up against the frost (it'd freeze there if the fellow wasn't careful), with his hat pulled low, and his moose pelt collar lifted up high, gloves still on both hands and dark, heavy boots. He reminded Matthew of that invisible man story he'd been reading, all bundled up without a patch of skin to show. The fellow was sleeping.

"Ticket please, sir?"

Nothing.

"Sir, ticket please?"

Nothing. The lady in the row before slightly turned her attention toward them, so did the couple in the row behind. Well this wasn't new for Matthew; while he'd never been the senior conductor of the

CP before, he'd certainly sussed out hoppers.

"Sir, your ticket?"

The sleeping man shuffled slightly in his sleep, as though disturbed by a fly, and sunk lower against the window.

Matthew leaned forward and lifted the man's hat. Ah, he knew it, one of those wild fellows dressed up to look presentable. Long tattered hair, unwashed and unkempt, fell from the hat.

"Sir. That's enough. Wake up."

"Oh!"

And with a few snorts and wide-blinking eyes, the man was 'roused' from sleep.

Matthew straightened himself. "Ticket, sir?"

All he got from the man was a sheepish grin, and "Ticket, no?" It was little wonder the fellow was trying to pull such an amateurish trick; he'd probably only been in the country for a week or two.

Edward, good boy that he was, had just walked into the cabin. Matthew had better things to do, and Edward could handle a straightforward case like this: get the payment or kick the hopper off at the next stop.

"Edward," Matthew waved over the young assistant as he was lifting a suitcase into the upper shelf for a lady.

"Sir!"

"Deal with this, won't you?"

"Yes sir!"

"Edward," Matthew leaned in close to the boy.

"Yes, sir?"

"I'm not your drill sergeant, boy. Relax."

And Edward relaxed noticeably. Even smiling. He had one of those playful half smiles that made you feel in on a joke.

"Right," mumbled Matthew to himself, ripping out a page from his ticket book for Edward—as if a hopper would be paying—and moving along the car.

"Tickets, please? Tickets?"

After sorting through the second-class riders and heading over to the darker, smoky recess of third-class berths, Matthew was called away by László, his middle porter, in a panic. Mr. Recess of cubby 12A, first class, had allowed his gloves to smolder in an attempt to warm them over the heater. While the small fire was contained (with the opening of a window, and throwing away the burnt gloves), the panic in the entire car had herded all the passengers down into the dining car, which was now person-to-person thick with bodies, and not a soul could move, let alone order a bite to eat.

And so Matthew's hunt for hoppers was cut short for the day, which was just as well since he had pages of paperwork to review and a menu to approve and orders to be set and telegrams to dispatch. By the time the panic settled and everyone returned to their cabins (or was seated for dinner), it was half-past eight in the evening. Too late, most certainly, for disturbing the passengers by checking tickets.

Edgelake, Ontario

The morning of the 23rd of February, 1905, Matthew woke chilled to the bone. Staff sleeping cars were located between the first and second-class dining cars, car seven to be exact, and had central heating tapped in from the second-class cars. Shivering in his berth, he sat up, cap sliding off his head, and pulled back the heavy curtains to stare at the frosted darkness. A few farm lights whipped past, but otherwise nothing but fields of night, stars and ice as the train pulled closer to Thunder Bay. He raised a hand to the small vent beside his desk and shook his head. Cold air issued from the vent. The whole damn train must have been freezing.

Matthew turned on his small electric light and checked the time: 4.25 am. Maybe, just maybe, if he fixed the problem now, if the grace of God were with him, he could avoid the shivering complaints of passengers as they woke from their frozen sleep.

Sliding down from his bunk, Matthew slipped two stocking-covered feet into his conductor boots, swapped his nightcap for his conductor hat, and pulled on his large dark blue jacket with the CPR emblem embroidered onto the chest. Turning off his small light, he grabbed a lamp with stiff fingers (they were more and more stiff in the mornings lately) and lit the wick as he stepped out into the corridor.

There was the rocking, the constant *clack-clacking, thump-thumping,* but nothing else, except the cold.

He moved through the dining cart where the yellow light of his lamp shone on empty tables, empty chairs, empty counters, and then he continued onward to the second-class berths—six people to a room, three bunks stacked on top of each other for each side, curtains of each cubby drawn together. Here, Matthew stopped and felt the radiator: it was warm. He put a hand against the vent: it was cold.

Continuing on, he came across the rows of seated sleepers, passengers stretched out on the reclining seats (innovation of the CPR) and buried beneath blanket upon blanket, fur upon fur. It was warmer here, with all these bodies sleeping together.

Again Matthew checked the radiators: warm. He checked the vents: cold. Holding his lamp up to the thermometer, he turned the gauge a few degrees higher, then carried on down the line of cart after cart, checking the radiators, checking the vents. Eventually he arrived at the final second-class car, leading onto third (third class had a cast-iron stove, not central heating), mostly empty of passengers since the train was not *always* so full between prairie towns.

He pushed open the carriage door as an ice-cold wind slapped him across the face.

"Mother Mary!" he cursed.

Dropping the lamp with a sudden rocking of the train, flame flickering in the gusting wind, Matthew's eyes struggled to adjust to the pale silver glow of the moonlight. All the windows were open, even the door to third class was open! And there in the midst of the whirlwind the girl was standing against an open window. Her loose hair was rising wildly in the breeze and her eyes were closed against the moonlight. With a blanket thrown loosely around her shoulders, arms stretched outward through the window, the wind poured in around her.

"Miss Pierre?"

Last he'd seen of the pregnant girl, she was taking her meal in the dining cart and leaning, nearly hiding, into the pages of her menu. But here she was now: winter reincarnate, more pale than the moon, more wild than the wind, half out the window and likely to catch her death.

"Miss Pierre?" he asked again.

She did a double-take when he spoke.

"And what if it is?" she replied.

"Think of the child, Miss Pierre! You'll catch your death leaning out the window like that!"

She drew her arms back into the car and sat down on the seat. Matthew picked up his lamp and re-lit it, renewing the yellow cast of light across the cabin seats. How had she managed to open the third-class door? Following CPR regulations that door was always locked at night. She must have picked it. '*She's crazy*,' thought Matthew, '*I've taken on a mad woman*.'

"Help me close these windows," he said, but she just sat there, staring upward toward the moon, running her hands along her pale, exposed arms.

"It is a little cold," she replied. "But I was stifled with the smoke. And we were all coughing and shifting in our sleep. Can't do any harm to open a few windows, can it? You know, it's incredibly warm back there, nearly choking."

Matthew glanced at the girl as she stood up from the seat and headed back toward the third-class entrance. Sleepwalking! She must be sleepwalking. She'd gotten up in her sleep and returned to third class. Though he couldn't blame her with those characters up front, Mr. Recess with his kid gloves, and so on. Now here she was like the ghost of winter. She must have still been dreaming.

"Miss Pierre," he beckoned, shutting one window after another, "come with me now, you are sleeping."

"I'm sleeping?"

"Yes, you are sleepwalking."

"I can promise you, I am very much awake."

"Impossible, child. Impossible." He did his best to sooth her.

Matthew was not an unlearnt man; he knew full well the trauma a person would suffer if woken from a state of sleepwalking hypnosis. "*Shh*, now."

"Are you the conductor?" she asked.

"Yes."

"In your nightgown?"

Matthew looked down at his open jacket and bare legs, striped nightgown hanging just below his knees.

"Yes, dear. In my nightgown."

"Well," she replied, "maybe I *am* sleeping."

He took her frozen hand. "Come on, I'll guide you to your cabin. *Shh*, quiet goes it, don't wake the other passengers—or yourself."

"*Shh*," she replied. "Let's not wake anyone."

"And no more sleeping in third class, promise me."

"If you insist, I suppose," she replied, letting him lead her along. "After all, this is only a dream."

And so he lead the ghost girl, the pregnant girl, the third-class girl behind him toward her assigned cabin at the front of the train. She was a strange contradiction—pleasant, mild and timid, then suddenly ferocious, wild and reckless. Certainly, as his own mother would have said, a girl of two faces.

Ottawa, Ontario

After the sleepwalking incident Matthew decided to keep a closer eye on Miss Pierre. After all, she could have caught her death the previous night, which would have been all kinds of terrible, not to mention a stain on his reputation as a reliable and steady conductor.

He decided that, having taken Miss Pierre under his care, he had, in a sense, adopted Miss Pierre. After all, as a confirmed bachelor he had little to no chance of having children, though Matthew figured he'd be a good fatherly type of man if given the chance. And so he decided that at least for the length of the train ride, he'd be a guardian to the girl.

But sometimes, maybe because she was so young and unsettled, or maybe because she was with child, sometimes the girl was a complete contradiction. One minute she'd be tucked up warm in the library of first class, nearly hugging the radiator for that bit of extra heat, and then ten minutes later he'd spot her with her head out the window, screaming and laughing to the children of Sickton, or Hamlet, or some other small town as the train slowed down and they threw snowballs. "You can't hit the side of a barn!" she'd be calling with laughter and waving.

Matthew, of course, always pulled her back inside.

"You'll catch your death, young lady."

"I'll never catch my death," she'd reply whenever he'd scold her. "I hardly feel the cold."

Which in itself was confusing, because only that previous evening she'd been head down into a pile of postcards all spread out on the dining cart table, and when Mr. Smithson cracked open his window following an after-meal cigar (Mrs. Smithson hated the dirty habit, she announced to the entire car of diners, and wished for a little fresh air), Miss Pierre had looked up with those large grey eyes of hers toward the window, and shivered—*shivered!* as she asked, quietly, for Edward (he was playing server that evening, the CPR being temporarily short staffed) to bring her a pot of hot tea. Matthew had been sitting just behind Miss Pierre when Mr. Smithson opened the window and she had shivered, and he was so perplexed he couldn't finish his rhubarb preserve and toast.

And that was why he'd invited her along to scout for hoppers. "Ticket taking," he'd told her, "with a little bit of extra fun." And she'd been too polite to decline, though she was clearly attached to her radiator and reading. It was getting to the point where Matthew was so confused, so nervous about the girl, that he wasn't comfortable having her out of sight for more than half an hour.

"You'll see how a train really runs," he promised.

And she smiled her gentle smile, and tucked away her postcards into a large tin, picking up a knitted shawl and following him into the corridor.

Today Matthew was determined to search third class. He'd been so overwhelmed by the new tasks of conducting that he'd so far avoided the two most difficult cars. As he picked his way through first class and over to second, Miss Pierre followed behind like a shadow. "You see these widows?" he gestured to her at the frost-covered windows. "These windows are doubled, you see?" And he tapped the glass as they left car number four. "That means they keep the cold out."

"Like an extra blanket?"

He stopped as he opened the door between cars four and five. "Well, you are clever, aren't you?"

Miss Pierre smiled and blushed. "My mother often said I was too clever for my own good. She thought the both of us were a couple of demons."

"Who are the both of you?"

"My sister and I."

Matthew stopped between the two cars where the train most rocked and roared. To the right and left were long, glass windows, and the left-side tracks were whipping past as fast as could be. "What are you going to do when you get to Quebec city?" he shouted. The train tracks answered: *clunk, clack, clunk, clack,* and the wind whistled through the cracks. "Now that you're all alone?"

"I won't be alone," she shouted back over the roar. Her hands wrapped around the bump on her body.

"That baby won't be much help, Miss Pierre."

"She'll be the best thing in my life, Mr. Barnes."

Matthew had been spending quite a deal of time with the girl, and while he knew it was inappropriate to ask, the words just fell from his mouth.

"Where's the father?"

She did a double take—then pushed down her eyes with a furrowed brow. "He's been sent to prison. My father had him taken away."

Matthew's hand was on the door to the fifth cabin, but he still didn't open it. Suddenly she looked like the wild ice queen once again, hair tied back in braids, but blonde pieces flying loose—eyes fixed out of the window, watching the passing scenery as if her life depended on the fields of the Ottawa Valley.

"Denis was Métis, Mr. Barnes. A kind, smart young man. So what do they expect? They take these children and train them to act like us, and after a while some can't even remember their homes. And there I was, and there he was, and Mother and Father were leading the school, and I loved him. Can't two people just love one another? Why does there need to be rules?"

She looked at Matthew with such a piercing glare; her little chin raised up in defiance.

Matthew didn't reply. He didn't know what to say. A crazy girl with an Indian boyfriend knocked up and five months gone with child, an Indian child, and *still* there was something about her. There was something he couldn't let go that said to him, '*It doesn't matter now, Matthew Barnes. You decided to take care of her so long as she's on this train, eh, and now she's yours to carry.*'

But Miss Pierre was already brimming with tears as the rumble and the wind and the cold wrapped round them in the corridor between carriages.

"Excuse me," she uttered, suddenly reverting into her quietness. Matthew barely heard her over the noise. "I'm not well," she added.

And off she went as he stood there, red faced and feeling his own shame at probing too far.

"Damn it," muttered Matthew. "What's wrong with me?"

Opening the door to the fifth car, he stepped into the heated space and looked at the rows of passengers. Sighing, he took off his spectacles and cleaned them on his handkerchief. Then, replacing the glasses, he filled up his voice with resignation: "Tickets? Tickets, please?" And carried on along the train alone.

Matthew had a successful day. In second class he'd ousted one hopper tucked into the toilet area who kept calling (with a poor impression of an elderly woman's voice) that she was, "in a tight spot at the moment," and "wouldn't he be a dear and order her a pot of tea to help the process?"

Then moving on, stepping between cars five and six, he'd come across an older hopper smoking a pipe and leaning against the window. Matthew had asked the man for his ticket, to which the man replied (tapping his ashes down through the grate), "No ticket, sir. Just here till the train slows." He was a gentleman hopper, it seemed, who knew how the game worked. Next village that passed the old fellow had emptied his pipe out the doorway, tucked it into his jacket, and jumped from the train into a snow bank.

Opening the door to the filled third-class car, Matthew was hit with a blast of heat and voices singing *Oh, You Beautiful Doll.* They always did this, the third class riders. They had two cars to spread out across, but always, *always* they clustered into one and sang the journey across Canada.

The air pulsed with heat from the wood stove and crammed bodies, despite the several open windows. Third class was where winter came to die and sweat poured from the bodies of many tired, humming, travelling people.

It was a slice of madness.

And yet...

And yet, his feet were tapping. There was a melody of voices swirling round the stench of sweat, and the open windows dazzled with the light of the mid-day sun. The passengers' laughter and conversation mixed into the music and noise of the train. Matthew hoped it wasn't the fiddler in the corner who was there without a ticket; it'd be a shame to throw off the talented fellow.

Just as he raised the whistle to his lip and blew on it—loud and high and clear—to bring the room to a halt and for a moment gain their attention ... just as he filled his lungs once more to shout out the well-trained words: *Tickets, please!* Just as he was about to finish his daily checks, she came back and stole the show.

"Who do you think you are?" she demanded to know.

Matthew turned around. Miss Pierre stood behind him, blanket wrapped tight around her shoulders and face red, pregnant bump stuck out high on her body as though it were pointing distinctly in his direction.

"Who do you think you are, sir? Asking about the father and such? You don't think that's upsetting? A smart man like you can't realize when he's acting a fool? If you weren't so kind, I'd wring your neck."

She had flipped her coin, the crazy girl.

Matthew considered for a moment whether she was sleepwalking again. But no, not this time. There was no ghost-like expression. There was fire and fury; it radiated from her like the hot stove in the corner.

He was not an uneducated man and had heard about these passions in which women could throw themselves. In his favourite magazine, *The Gentleman*, Matthew had read an article quoting Dr. Freud, who warned against this very condition in women; describing it as the Electra Complex, deriving from an inherent longing and jealousy over their very own fathers. Miss Pierre clearly had man troubles, and was expelling her frustration on him. Not to mention that Matthew *had* asked a few too many questions between cars four and five.

"Miss Pierre," he replied.

"Don't you Miss Pierre me."

Everyone was watching. Matthew took off his glasses and rubbed them with his handkerchief. Then, turned to the cabin. "Tickets, please!"

No one moved.

"Got your tickets? Good! Carry on with yourselves," he said without glancing at a single ticket and walked through the cabin toward the final passenger cart of the train, hearing through the continuing silence (above the rumbling tracks and stifled laughs). Miss Pierre's feet stomped along behind him.

As Matthew knew it would be, the last passenger car was nearly empty except for one fellow spread out on the wooden bench along the wall. A second cast iron stove was pumping here as well; Toronto had been a good place for scrap wood scavenging what with all its construction. The temperature in the cabin was well above thirty degrees. Matthew took off his hat.

"Ticket, please?" he asked gently. The young man in the corner held up a ball of yellow paper, scrunched up and illegible, and then tucked it back into his pocket. It looked like a third class ticket.

"What do you have to say for yourself?" asked Miss Pierre.

Matthew went over to the sleeping man.

"Sir, may I see that ticket?"

The man held out the ball of paper and then tucked it back into his pocket.

"Don't ignore me, Mr. Barnes." Miss Pierre was right up behind him, still stomping her feet, still red in the face.

"Sir," Matthew bent down face level to the resting man. "I need to read that ticket." And he slipped his fingers gently into the fellow's pocket. It was as Matthew had suspected. The ticket was for Thunder Bay to Mississauga. The man had long ridden past his stop. "You cheeky devil."

The boy sat up.

"Non, mais, il faut que j'aille a mon marriage. Ma blonde va me tuer si je ne suis pas là. Si tu me fais debarquer je vais manquer mon marriage."

"Sir, I do not understand you, but this ticket has expired. You have to leave the train at the next village. It's coming up shortly, in fact; please, proceed to the doorway."

"But he's got a wedding to go to. He's getting married," said Miss Pierre, now leaning over Matthew's shoulder.

"You speak French?"

"Of course I speak French."

"And he's getting married?"

"That's what he says."

"When?"

"Quel jour est le marriage?" asked Miss Pierre.

"Dans deux jours. Le père de ma fiancée va me tuer si je le manque. C'est vrai il va me tuer."

"He's getting married in two days. And his future father-in-law has threatened his life if he misses the ceremony."

Matthew stood up and rubbed the expired ticket between his finger tips. Everyone always had a reason for hopping the train. Conductor

Hanes had never minded their excuses: it was produce a ticket or get off. He'd even once kicked off a fellow travelling to Edmonton to see his new-born baby boy; Matthew had thrown the young man into the nearest hay stack and the whole thing had been a bit heart-breaking.

"Fine," replied Matthew. "We need someone to shovel coal in the engine room. Bertalan is sick in bed and Edward's not made for coal tossing. Can you translate that? He can stay if he can shovel."

Miss Pierre explained. The man wasn't enthusiastic, but reluctantly agreed. He must have been serious when he said he was afraid of his father-in-law.

"Tell him to go up to the engine and explain to Marcus; he speaks French. I'll come along in thirty minutes to see that he's up there shovelling."

Miss Pierre translated. Nodding, the young fellow stood up and left the cabin. Miss Pierre then stomped her feet, though this time not as heavily.

"Are you still ignoring me, Mr Barnes?"

"Conductor Barnes, Miss Pierre."

Her fire seemed to have cooled. She went to a window and threw it wide open, leaning over the frame and out into the blinding daylight and whiteness.

"I don't engage with young ladies in a passion. Never have, never will."

"I'm in a passion?" she asked, glancing back from the window.

"Yes, you are. You're excited and jealous of your father and I can't help you. Though I do apologize for my questions. They were excessive."

"Can't say I'm jealous of anyone, Conductor Barnes, least of all my father. He's a repressed man, and he's got no joy in his life."

The bold statement was surprising, considering she'd just reprimanded him for asking too many questions. But she kept talking.

"Can't even see people in love, you know? He flies into his own sort of passion. Talks about purification and sanctity." She spat out the window. "Heard enough of that talk from his sermons, eh, didn't need to hear it every other second too. And then he takes an innocent, stupid, mistake and uses it as an excuse to beat his daughter black and blue. Black and blue all across the arms and legs and side—not the face mind you, 'cause he's too clever for that. What choice was there but to leave? He would have killed the baby too, if he could have. I've never seen a man so angry. And our mother, well, she just went outside and stood by the fence the entire time, staring down at the road from what I could see. It's what she does every time he loses his temper on us or the school children. What causes a woman to become so weak? Where did all her *passion* go?

"So when you ask those questions, you don't know it, but that's a large can of worms. A huge can of worms. Even the bruises look fresh, and it was weeks back, that beating."

Matthew sat on the wooden bench where the hopper had slept. He took off his spectacles and gave them a thorough cleaning with his handkerchief.

"I'm sorry to have upset you," he said. Suddenly he felt exhausted.

"I'm sorry to have embarrassed you," she replied. "But I do get into 'passions' once in a while, though it's got little to do with anyone's 'brilliant' theories on women."

"I just couldn't help myself from asking. It's like I feel responsible for you." He didn't want to admit it, because he certainly didn't want to give her the wrong impression. She was so young, after all, and he really had no use for silly young ladies, but there was something about her that reminded him of his mother. "And no one deserves a beating, not like that either."

She came away from the window and sat beside him. "How long till we reach Quebec City?" she asked.

"Tomorrow morning," replied Matthew.

Miss Pierre nodded.

"I've sure loved this train, Conductor Barnes. The way it rocks when you want to sleep, and how it jostles when it's time to wake. I love that *clackity-clackity-clackity* it keeps singing to me, and the fields with their different smells. Did you know that the provinces smell different? Even in winter, they all smell different. And the movement, I love the movement. All I wanted to do was escape, and on this train we're escaping every moment. It's a beautiful feeling."

Matthew agreed: it was a beautiful feeling.

"And what will you do once in Quebec City?" asked Matthew.

She shook her head slowly, her large eyes scanning far into nothingness, past the cooker, past the cabin, past the windows, past the fields of snow and sky.

"Damned if I know, Conductor. But something will work out. I feel it right inside me. Everything will be fine, eventually."

And they sat there side-by-side staring far-off into nothing.

Quebec City, Quebec

In the winter, Quebec City became a grand ice palace with the Chateau Frontenac bravely facing the river's wind and the train station hiding comfortably at the base near Vieux Quebec.

The city was the landing place for many immigrants. In some ways it was an enticing omen: the cobbled streets, narrow alleys and leaning buildings were said to be much like Europe. In other ways it was a frozen slap across the face: ice on the road, ice on the trees, ice in your hair, ice in your lungs. On a brilliant winter day with blue skies that dazzled and fresh snowfall across the ground, a person could get lost in the intensity of the light. It was at once beautiful and painful. Attractive and repulsive.

And then there were the celebrations. The *Bonhomme,* a living snowman with a blood-red sash, wandered the festival-filled streets. Wafts of burning sugar filled the air as the maple sellers boiled their syrup. Fiddlers stood red nosed, frozen fingered and hopping, numb foot to numb foot as they inflicted impassioned damage upon their age-old instruments, thanking the occasional passer-by for the few coins. Ships arrived with foreign goods, barrels rolled along the ice-covered tracks, food was sold in the midwinter market including steaming pots of boiling soup, dead livestock hung and dried, and jars of preserve to offer a taste of lost summer sweetness.

Quebec City was the end of the line and the start of the world. Matthew couldn't help thinking that it would swallow Miss Pierre whole—baby and all.

***

At 10 a.m. the Canadian Pacific pulled into Quebec City station and began to unload its goods. Wheat from the prairies, lumber galore, coal for the East Coast, furs for Europe, mail from all over. Matthew had to oversee the distribution of goods, then they'd reload, restock, and return: items from Europe, people from Europe, fish from the coast, more lumber, but shaved and smoothed, more and more. There was always more to load, more to move, more to do. And so when he had said goodbye to Miss Pierre that morning over the breakfast porridge—she'd had her head so far into that bowl he'd thought she'd nearly drown, though she said she was just enjoying the warmth—it had been rushed and, in his mind, entirely unfinished.

But what could he do? She wasn't his daughter. She wasn't his anything. With a temper like hers she'd settle fine. He kept thinking of their conversation the day before, the way she had described the train. It was just like him, just like the young Matthew of the fields. That love for the rails was inside of her, and yet, it wasn't his place to ask her to stay. A young woman with child? What would Conductor Hanes have said?

And still, as he directed the train crew to load the Hudson Bay order from England, he kept thinking over and over: it'll swallow her whole.

But no matter, now. Once off the train, once on her way, she stopped being his responsibility.

Stopped being his responsibility.

He scanned the list and ticked the boxes, then pulled out his pocket watch and checked the time: 13:42.

Passengers would be loading, Edward and László would have finished preparing the cabins; it was time to reappear at the front of the train. Matthew pulled out his whistle, newly polished, and gave a long, high-pitched blow. "Loading up, men. Loading up. Let's get this show on the road." That was a touch of Hanes, of course. He always 'got the show on the road', and in perfect time too; Matthew was running late. Not to protocol.

As snowflakes began to drop heavily from the sky, he hurried toward the front of the waiting train, where passengers were steadily loading onto the cars. "All aboard," he called, and his eyes darted to the entrance, just in case...

"All aboard!"

Edward was welcoming the first-class passengers and writing down their names. Matthew walked up behind the boy. "Eddy?"

"Yes, sir?"

"Did the girl get off all right?"

Edward gave a shrug. "She set off first thing. Everything seemed in order."

"Did you help her with the trunk?"

Edward tipped his maroon hat forward and scratched the base of his head. "Can't say that I did, sir. She must have had help from another passenger."

Matthew nodded. "Fine, that's fine." And then, "All aboard!" as the last few passengers ran to catch the train. Marcus in the engine room was waiting for the yellow flag. Matthew looked amongst the well-wishers and lingering salted-fish sellers.

"Last call!"

With the flourish of Hanes passed down through years of training, Matthew pulled out the yellow flag from his jacket and waved it for Marcus. Immediately the train screamed, shooting a column of steam high into the air.

"Next stop, Montreal!" called Matthew, stepping on to the moving staircase, as the train chugged, chugged, chugged away from the station.

"Tickets, please?"

Matthew walked down the aisle as women and men rifled through their pockets and bags, holding up the pink slips of second-class tickets. Matthew punched the slips one at a time.

"Tickets?" he asked again.

A rosy-cheeked man carrying a wicker basket was sitting propped up against the corner seat at the end of car four, absorbed in his paper, *Le Bulletin.*

"Ticket, sir?" asked Matthew with a sigh.

The man was scratching his head, clutching the basket against him, bringing the article right up to his eyes.

"Ticket, sir?" Then again, more loudly ... much more loudly: "Monsieur, ticket!"

"*Augh!*" The man started and lost control of his basket as his paper dropped to the ground and the basket tumbled after. Eggs—fresh, large and fragile, dropped across the cabin floor, splattering in yolk bombs.

Matthew took off his glasses and cleaned them with his handkerchief. Everyone turned to stare.

"*Je suis désolé monsieur, j'étais absorbé avec cet article de La Presse. Je m'excuse du dégât, tient prend mon billet.*" And he held out his pink second-class ticket for Matthew to examine.

Glancing round for a porter, but there was not an Edward, or a László, or a Sámson in sight, Matthew sighed to himself with resignation. He took the ticket and punched it, then headed to the back cubby near the exit to find a bucket and, hopefully, if the pipes hadn't frozen, some water.

As he swung back the cupboard door, Matthew gave a yelp, "Mother Mary!" and jumped from the doorway.

Inside, hunched down in her school dress, jacket and blanket splayed across the cleaning fluids was Miss Pierre, looking green with asphyxiation.

"Conductor Barnes, oh, thank God, I was choking with those chemicals."

He pulled her from the cubby.

"Girl, are you truly out of your mind? What are you doing there?"

"I'm sorry, Conductor, I know you hate the hoppers. But we're all out of money, and that city is more cold than the Alberta plain on a freezing winter night. We can't stay there. We have no shelter."

She kept saying "*We* can't stay, *we're* so sorry, *we're* biding our time." Matthew reckoned she must have been delirious from the fumes. He took off his glasses.

"Clearly you're delirious."

"I am?"

"The fumes have gone to your head."

"They did?"

"Absolutely."

And then *he* nearly fainted. Out of the closet under the jacket and blanket rose a *second* Miss Pierre.

"She might be delirious, but I'm perfectly sane. It was one damned dumb idea to hide in this closet," said the second Miss Pierre.

The first Miss Pierre turned to the newest Miss Pierre. "I told you he'd find us, Lizzy."

The second Miss Pierre, Lizzy, pulled off her jacket and blanket as she stepped into the car, then pushed down the corridor window. The first Miss Pierre, Mary, shivered.

"Doesn't matter," Lizzy replied. "We've gone over half the line under one ticket, and you know what that means?"

"No," replied Mary.

Matthew was too stunned to speak. He was looking at the same girl twice over. Again he cleaned his glasses, but it didn't help. Here they were with the same big grey eyes, same corn-silk hair, same small nose, same furrowed brow. They were same, same, same, right to the last detail. Maybe he was the one who was delirious.

"It means that together we've hopped the length of the *whole* track. And on the CPR that means one thing and one thing only: we're allowed to stay on the train, no charge."

"No charge?" Matthew snapped out of his trance. "No charge, young lady?"

"No charge," replied Lizzy.

Mary slouched against the wall, hands holding her middle. Lizzy was immediately by her side: "Just take deep breaths Mary, it's just the spins from getting up too quick. Deep breaths." The girls breathed together.

"You're both pregnant?" asked Matthew.

Lizzy pushed at her pregnant belly, shifting it right to left, until an old feather pillow fell out from the bottom of her dress. "You've got to let us stay."

"It's against regulations."

"Now come on, Matthew," replied Lizzy. "We know the rules. If you count the both of us as one, and most people do 'cause we're twins, we've hopped the entire length of the line between us."

Matthew pulled out his official CPR regulation booklet and began to flip through the pages. "Only thing it says here about hoppers is to throw 'em off."

Mary gave him the look: that same look she'd given him back on the platform in Saskatchewan. "You're going to throw us off? Really?"

What was there to do? After all, the city would swallow them whole, the winter would freeze poor Mary, and besides, he liked having her—*them,* around. Matthew sighed and cleaned his glasses once more. "I still can't believe there's two of you."

Hanes wouldn't have been pleased that these two ladies were claiming a hopping right to the train; he would have instructed Matthew to throw them off at the next town. "It was an awful trick you pulled." Edward was always fumbling with the tea service. Matthew had been thinking of hiring another hand once they arrived back in Victoria, though a fellow, of course, given that women and trains don't always mix well with the small quarters and surplus of men. Though these two had each other. And yet it had been such a blatant lie.

But then there was the baby. Matthew had never thought it possible to have a child. He knew he would never marry, let alone have children. And yet, he worried. The baby and the girls, they'd be swallowed whole if they weren't more careful.

Matthew was a soft-hearted man, after all. He wasn't some kind of *monster.* By now his glasses were crystal clean, yet he kept on rubbing them in silence. Finally daring to look up into their faces, Matthew chewed upon his decision.

The Miss Pierres waited. The train rocked back and forth, *click-clacking, click-clacking*, and the February wind blasted through the semi-open window. They looked like ice nymphs in the wind, flying across the country on a magical train that would take them everywhere they'd ever dreamed of going, and Matthew would see that they went safely.

Finally he relented. "You can stay."

Screams and laughter erupted in the small hall as the girls launched themselves against him; Matthew dropped the regulation booklet and managed to catch his falling spectacles. The twins each kissed him on the cheek.

"You'll never regret it, Matthew," said Lizzy.

"Not for a single moment," said Mary, smiling like he'd never seen her smile.

You'll never regret it, they promised. Matthew allowed himself to laugh. He knew there'd be no regrets.

Bending over into the cubby, he pulled out a mop and bucket. Handing them to the girls, he said with a widening grin, "And isn't this lucky, I've got a job for you already."

Anna Claire Pierre, 1890

Anna Claire Pierre, née Angyal, pushed aside her thick maroon curtains as the tractor pulled up to the broken, snow-buried garden fence. Through the frost-covered window she watched her mother thank the young Jenson boy for the ride and climb down the massive wheel of the tractor onto the snow-packed road. She'd given the boy a feather, Anna noticed, a red feather.

"Jesus save me, here she comes," whispered Anna. Her mama stepped through the crack in the gate.

The rosary beads quivered on the nail, hanging by the doorway to ward off evils. The crucifix stood more erect and spread, bearing up for the challenge. And in her hand, rubbed between forefinger and thumb, was the small gold cross Richard had given her for their wedding, a great comfort to her whenever he was away. On the sitting room table, next to the jar of preserves, loaf of bread, and butter from the dairy was a postcard date-marked March 3rd, 1890 . The picture was of a Wild West girl sitting with her gun, smiling at the camera. On the other side was her mother's scribbling in large and looping cursive.

As a child, Anna used to watch with fixation as her mother wrote postcards for Anna's grandmother with an inky quill that dripped onto the table, the black splatters wiped away by her mother's moving sleeve. Her mother would often have Anna write her own name in the remaining corner of the card. Anna would grasp the quill in her small fist, and slowly write out in large, imperfect letters, 'A-N-N-A,' and then 'XOXO', so that it was ANNAXOXO. There was an "xoxo" on the end of the Wild West post card as well; it read: "Coming to visit, be there Thursday after next. Haven't had your jam in ages. Would love salted butter too. Your Mama, *xoxo*." Anna had received the postcard this morning, on the very Thursday her mother was due to arrive.

Anna's mother, Aliza Claire Angyal—back held straight, wearing a long dark riding jacket and wolf-fur wrap—walked cautiously toward the house, carpet bag in one hand, bottle of wine in the other, minding the patches of slippery ice.

The farm was none too impressive in the winter. The garden was buried in mounds of dirty snow, it hadn't dropped a flake in weeks to cover the yellow and dirt and grit from the road. And the yard wasn't much to see either. Out by the water well, Richard had flooded an area for some skating. He was obsessed with his ice hockey, but this time of night it was nearly impossible to see, and the repainted barn was near invisible in the darkness. They had painted it black, Richard saying it would give natural heating in the winter and Anna agreeing that it certainly *might* get warm, though it never actually did. That was where the school children were to sleep once they arrived tomorrow morning. Tomorrow. Soon.

But here was her mother instead, heading up the path.

"Anna, quit staring and come help a tired woman with her bag," called her mama, glancing toward the window.

Anna jumped back from the glass and pulled a hair clip from her apron pocket, securing her bun with an extra fastener. The Holy Mary looked over from the fireplace mantel with approval and, Anna sensed, compassion.

Picking up her own brown knitted shawl, throwing it over her shoulders, Anna walked into the entrance hall, pushed back the heavy foyer drapes and opened the large front door.

In blew the March wind, wet and freezing.

Out stepped Anna into the night, nervous and six-months pregnant.

"Mother, this is a surprise."

"Surprise? I sent you a card two weeks ago."

"Mail arrived today, Mother."

Anna took the carpet bag from her Mama as they walked into the house.

"You disappear, elope with that French preacher, and this is where you end up? Middle of nowhere from what I can tell."

"Manitoba is an up-and-coming place, Mother."

"What's this 'Mother' business? Call me Mama or Aliza, now you're a married woman."

Anna closed the door behind them, shooing her mother in further and shutting the hall curtain to block the cold. The fire in the sitting room was roaring with two blocks of wood, biting back the hard March weather, not to mention the kitchen stove piping away with a pot of tea and that evening's dinner stewing in the pot. Anna had had a mad-dash afternoon trying to sort everything before her mother arrived. If it hadn't been for the six Hail Marys and seven Our Fathers over the snowy rabbit that afternoon as she skinned and prepped the dinner, Anna might have gone faint for lack of breath and too much panic. How could a woman in her condition be expected to *run* so much in one day and *not* feel like dying?

Thank Jesus the Jenson boy had called round with the root vegetables and milk that morning. Otherwise her mother would have been walking from the station; Anna was in no state to take the horses.

"Oh." Aliza turned her back to the fire, hand still gripping the bottle. "You do look big. Last I saw you were a tiny, skinny thing."

"I'm six months."

"Six months? Doesn't feel more than a week since I last saw you, Anna, but here you are."

Anna straightened herself proper, bump protruding from her waist, and pulled her shawl around more tightly. "Here I am," said Anna.

Aliza nodded, pulling off her red gloves.

"Well, the spirit's always been on your side, hasn't she, Anna?"

"God's a man, Mama."

"God is a god, Anna. Now, is this all for me?"

Sitting down in Richard's overstuffed chair, she helped herself to the bread with butter and jam.

"Did you give young Jenson a feather?"

"I may have."

"Mother!"

"Mama."

"Mama, you can't go giving these people feathers and the like. They're God's people; I don't need them thinking my own mother's a witch."

Aliza had peeled away her wrap and overcoat, revealing an off-the-shoulder bright yellow dress trimmed with pink floral edges. It was satin. She'd travelled in satin.

"Who's a witch?" asked Anna's mother, shrugging her exposed shoulders. "Not me, that's for certain. I just happened to find this lovely red feather last week in a snow bank, and took it for a lucky omen. And that Jenson child is such a sweet little boy, I told him if he took that feather and gave it to his best girl, she'd fall straight in love with him. Not 'cause it's magic, but 'cause it's a sweet thing for a boy to do. And you know that works. Didn't your Mr. Pierre do the very same thing?"

Anna sat down opposite her mother and the garish dress. In her opinion, women shouldn't expose their shoulders, particularly not at her mama's age.

"He gave me no feather."

"No, he gave you a tiny gold cross, and everything you'd ever dreamed suddenly came true."

The fire sparked.

"Nonsense," replied Anna. She helped herself to bread and jam.

"Where is he anyhow?" asked Aliza. "Couldn't even meet me at the station? I remember that man coming into town all fire and brimstone. Talk about passion. Though I might have called it raving madness, hollering from that soap box like a man possessed, fist pumping up and down, shaking off the dust and spiders."

"He's a great speaker, Mama."

"So where's he off to now? Can't I be formally introduced to my new son-in-law?"

Anna glanced at the Holy Mother on the mantel, taking a moment of solace in the virgin's kind expression.

"He's collecting some children, though he should be back soon. Not sure when, maybe tomorrow. We're starting a school."

Aliza licked the butter off her fingers. "What kind of school then? Natural sciences?" She smiled, showing her golden tooth, and leaned back in the chair. "I could come and show 'em how to read the stars. What do you think of that?"

"Mama, you've already got a job."

"And you don't want your crazy mama too close to your flock. You can say it, go on."

Anna sighed and glanced at the wine bottle on the table. All she needed to do was pick it up, swing it hard, and they'd both have a good night sleep.

"That's fine, you know," continued Aliza. "It's in the blood, that's all. I knew from the day you were born you'd go off far, far away. Can't fight the blood."

"You're ridiculous."

The rosary beads shook upon the nail as wisps of wind pushed through the curtains. Slips of cold air melted into the heated room, mixing into the aroma of damp wool, smoke and rabbit stew.

"I *am* ridiculous; it's part of my charm." Anna's mother winked. "Anyhow. I knew the day you were born that you weren't meant for the circus. You came out with a look on your face so serious, so deadly serious. I said to Géza, 'This girl's of neither you nor me, she must be some other family's child.' But he said that his family was full of serious faces, and his was just the exception. So I guess that's from your father's side. But running away, well, that's the Claire blood thick and true. We're not happy without the wind on our backs."

"I got married."

"Doesn't matter, same difference. I congratulate you on your new life. And the children too."

"We'll be getting maybe five or six little Indians, and maybe some half bloods too. And that's just for starters. Richard says we'll teach the Indian right out of them—kill the Indian, save the child. They'll be good little Christians before next Christmas."

Anna pictured a large pine tree decorated with acorns and popcorn strings and maybe even tinsel, if the province came through with more money. And all around her, little dark-faced students would sit and sing *Silent Night*, voices pure and clear, like angels from heaven above.

What felt to be a long time ago, a Reverend's wife had given young Anna a tiny yellow bible. She'd only been about ten-years-old, and was told that miracles and love were in those pages, along with power and constraint. Constraint: it rung like a bell in her small child ears. Constraint. Something her mother's magic never mastered. Anna had learned to love God, and love Jesus, and love Mary too. She had learned to calm her wildness through proper prayer and to raise her soul where it belonged with full loving devotion to God. Her God. The one God. It had been an incredible feeling, and an island of peace as she'd tolerated moving town-to-town and being part of the circus. Anna had benefited, and soon the Indian children would benefit as well. Wildness never helped anyone. They had to learn. Didn't they? They did. They had to. Their souls could be saved, even if her own mother was a goner.

Richard was certain about this plan.

She picked up a piece of bread and nibbled on the crust. "We're civilizing in a civilized manner." Anna softly replied between her bites. "Doing them a favour."

"I don't mean those poor Indian children. Though I could give you some words about that, separating a child from its parents just ain't right, Anna. I would have killed anyone who tried to steal you from my arms."

Anna turned three shades of red. Her mother leaned forward, putting a hand onto her arm before Anna could summon the energy to storm from the room.

"I meant the children in your belly," said Aliza. Anna's mother appeared very old as the firelight streamed across her face, filling in the crevices and lines. So much a mother, too, with the soothing drop of her voice. "Congratulations on a fine set of girls. I wonder which will come out first?"

Anna dropped her piece of bread and jam, wrapping her arm

across her pregnant belly and leaning back from the table. "Now don't you go doing any of that voodoo stuff with my baby."

"Babies, Anna. Why do you think you're so damn big?"

"Watch your language, Mama."

Aliza laughed softly and reached into her purse. She pulled out a small, pink, threadbare drawstring bag faded into patches of colour and shiny bits of string, placing it onto the table. Once, long ago before either woman was a speck on the horizon, it'd been embroidered with roses and humming birds. It was a lady's purse.

"I don't want to disturb your new life, Anna, but you left without the postcards."

Aliza picked up the postcard that Anna had left on the shallow table. She smiled, flipping it over and examining the Wild West photograph: "Gotta love this girl's gumption, eh? Shooting gophers in the field for dinner. She's a survivor, just like us." She untied the drawstring, opening the bag, and dropped the postcard in with the others.

"Richard doesn't want my corresponding—"

"Richard doesn't need to know. He's not here, is he?"

Anna didn't touch the bag. "How are Géza and Jozsó, anyhow?" she asked.

"They're fine and they say hello." Jozsó was her brother and a tightrope walker. Their father, Géza, was a well-known daredevil. Anna, unlike her brother or her parents, had never liked the big top. It was too dirty, too noisy, too out of control. With every year she grew, Anna's eyes had focused more upon the makeup than the beauty, the toothless lion over the showy handlers, the drunken clowns instead of their happy parade. Her own mama was the biggest liar of them all. She was Queen Aliza of the Night, fortune teller supreme, and tucked away in a corner tent filled with smoke and candles as she read innocent palms, looking into their futures while asking for another dollar, and then another as the reading become more interesting. All to tell people what they mostly already knew. It was shameful.

"We'll be travelling near your town next month when it's a bit warmer, just a day's ride away, I think. You could come for a visit, or I could drop by again when we pass?" suggested her mother. Aliza picked up her piece of bread and studied it in the firelight.

Anna shrugged her very young, very covered shoulders. "School will be up and running."

Aliza nodded in return and gave her daughter a gentle smile. "Well, you'll have your hands full, then."

"Let me go and check on dinner," replied Anna. "Would you like a cup of tea?"

"You always were such a lady, Anna, for such a little girl. Here." Aliza passed Anna the bottle of wine. "Uncork this for me."

They were, in a sense, mirror images, same loose posture that could flick over into stubborn rigidness, same short nose, same long neck, same round face, and the same blue eyes with the same dark circles underneath. Except for the hair. Aliza dyed away her light brown with a dark maroon colour. Anna had gotten her corn-silk blonde from Géza. The line was drawn by hair and age.

But they were both women now.

Anna took the bottle of wine and walked towards the kitchen, crossing into the unlit corridor and lingering in the darkness.

She was remembering running as a girl through fields of yellow cornstalks, picking up the dropped ears and throwing them high into the air. The circus always set up in the fields, paying off some farmer to lend them his land. She liked the farms. Sometimes the women at the farm houses would welcome her onto their verandas, charmed by the wild circus girl, and would offer her tea and cookies—true country sophistication. She loved those verandas: the quiet, the stillness, the dignity. That was until her mama appeared in her gypsy dress, hair untamed and barefooted, calling Anna, in the Hungarian tongue of Géza's language, for the evening meal. The ladies on their porches would recoil, or worse, invite her witch of a mother up for tea and ask for a reading.

Anna hated to be near her mother when she gave a reading. It was like a vibration in the bones. It was an earth-bound magic that her mother tapped into and the power resonated through Anna, a feeling of connection to everything around: the sky, the air, the fields, the people, the world. It was raw and unrefined, basely physical and very tempting. Anna despised temptation.

The hallway in her home had no photographs on the walls. Richard wouldn't allow that sort of thing, but as she again began to move toward the kitchen, she glanced above the doorway; there hung Jesus Christ on the crucifix. He had suffered for his love. Anna had suffered too, and she was strong enough to persevere. She would reform. She would be better.

Sometimes absentmindedly she picked up stones, lucky stones, and thoughtlessly dropped them into her pocket. Richard had found some the other day in her petticoat. She'd lied, said they were a present from little Marie who'd collected them on the lane. But Anna was a terrible liar and as a preacher, Richard had studied witching. He threw the rocks at her as she knelt in the corner. Magic wasn't allowed.

But the bible stories *were* a sort of magic, a beautiful and guiding magic. Jesus, up there on his cross dying an agonizing death was filled by God with a very potent power. He'd paid a high price, hadn't he?

"You need help in there?" called Aliza from the sitting room.

"No," replied Anna.

Anna stepped into the dim kitchen and went to the corner cupboard, taking out a large black cookie tin. She tipped the contents onto her table to find a corkscrew. Lifting the bottle of unlabelled red wine she uncorked it with a gentle 'pop'.

Two girls? Twin girls?

Richard was set on a boy. Anna didn't want news about a girl, let alone *two*.

She pulled back the heavy window curtain and glanced into the yard. Through the silvered darkness her eyes drifted from the barn to the makeshift school room; they had built it onto the stables to save a wall. She worried the children might steal away the horses, though Richard said they were only children and they would be brought to heel. They'd behave, and it would be all right, Richard promised. They'd have a working farm, teaching practical trades and doing God's will in the process. Anna was to be a school teacher. She'd teach them about the Bible, help them read stories of Jesus and lead them in their daily prayers. Bright and eager children would sit around her in a circle, and she'd read to them in the field. They could have tea in the afternoon after the chores were all done. Richard said it would be perfect.

The rabbit skin was hanging up to dry on a string near the stove. Inside the pot the meat had begun to melt into the potatoes and the carrots were turning mushy. She'd chosen a large pot to leave room for tomorrow's leftovers. The children could fill their stomachs before heading to the barn if they arrived by tomorrow. Richard wasn't sure how long the collection would take.

Her mind flicked back and forth between lighting a fire in the old furnace to heat up the barn or not, but if they didn't arrive till next Wednesday it'd be a waste of wood. She stroked the rabbit fur as she gazed into the empty darkness.

Her mother would want the fur. She'd use it to cast a spell for some desperate, last-pennies vagabond hoping to raise his luck. But Anna needed it for the baby. She was going to line the crib in rabbit skins. Half of her thought of writing a prayer into the hide to protect and bless her child. The other, more reasonable half rejected the idea. She'd hang up a rosary instead.

The tea boiled. Thick cloth in hand, she transferred the kettle from the stove to the table, placing a mat underneath the cast iron and sweeping away the mess from the cookie tin. The scent of mint drifted from the water. At noon she'd added a clove for sharpness, along with a few dried orange slices and nearly swirled it with her long-hanging braid, whispering words of health and happiness, then she'd stopped herself and thrown her hair high into a bun.

The steam rose from the kettle in twisting whirls, catching the oil lamp's light and disappearing into the warmth of the kitchen air. Richard would have said she was cooking the entire house. He'd pinch her cheek and say, "Now don't go using all the logs," and she'd shut the flue to save the embers. But over in the barn there was a strong draft through the boards, and the air was filled with coldness.

His black-paint idea wasn't helping, and the straw beds would only be so good in the slow-to-fade winter weather. Spring was around the corner, but cold was cold. Maybe she would get up early and light a fire, just in case the children arrived, and then see that her mama caught the first train too, since Richard couldn't stand the sight of Aliza.

Then Anna heard them.

Bells.

Jingling jangling with hoof beats too. They were coming. He was home.

"Jesus, Mary, Joseph."

She dropped the kettle back onto the stove and turned up the oil lamp to full glow. "Great Lord above," muttered Anna, "he's gonna lose his head."

Looking at the uncorked bottle of wine and the table covered with scattered bits, Anna grabbed the large black cookie tin. She'd received it from Mrs. Murry on the first day Richard had carried her over the threshold. Her neighbour had dropped by with a tin of Florida oranges (half of which Anna had promptly dried), and ever since then she'd kept all sorts of odds and ends in the tin. Now she held it under her arm and hurried along the corridor toward the sitting room.

Aliza was up and looking through the front window.

"That Ree-chard just arrived?" she asked, drawing out the name with a gross French accent.

"Now you behave yourself, Mama, unless you want to never see your granddaughters. Richard doesn't know you're even here, and the last time..." No, there was no use in remembering the last time. "Just behave yourself, Mama."

Anna put the cookie tin on the table and opened the lid, scooping up the tattered drawstring bag and dropping it in with a thud. "And don't mention these, he *hates* our side of the family, as you well know."

"Nice to see you're both alike."

"As you well know, Mama."

"He seems to like you just fine."

"I'm a Pierre now. Reborn and everything. He doesn't know that I wrote you last autumn, and you aren't going to tell him either." Anna hustled back to the corridor, slowed by the incredible weight of her body, eyes glancing up at poor Jesus on the cross, sacrificing himself for the greater cause. She nodded, giving a quick prayer: "*Dear Lord, this isn't so large as sitting on a cross and dying like you did, and I'd never try to pretend it was, but do let them get along, Lord. For me. For us. Let us all get along.*"

Into the kitchen she dimmed the lamp to a mere whisper of light. Through the kitchen wall came the high cries of children and Richard's deep call of her name: "Anna? Anna, you hear me?"

Scooping up the collection of bits, she poured the mess over the bag of postcards and covered it all with the orange grove lid. Richard never dealt with odds and ends, he'd never look in the cookie tin, not while Anna was there to fish him out some string, or the cork, or whatever needed searching. Opening the corner cupboard, she shoved it in as far back as she could reach.

"Anna, now," he shouted from outside, "come help with the children."

Aliza was in the kitchen doorway, wolf fur wrapped again round her shoulders, hair falling free in heaps of loose curls and glowing in the orange light. She looked older, composed, not scared, and more beautiful than Anna, too. More everything than Anna.

"You want me to go out and give him a hand? I may know some of their languages. It might bring the little ones comfort."

Anna pictured her mother leading the group in a chant with her 'hoo'ing and her 'haa'ing as the bewildered, long-haired and dirty children wrapped in their blankets and dressed in their furs followed suit. Richard would explode.

"No," replied Anna. "None of that allowed—we're civilizing them, Mama, not adding to the mess." Pushing past her mama, she ran back to the sitting room, no easy feat for a woman of six months and carrying twins, and threw on her brown knit shawl, hurrying again toward the kitchen back door, stepping out of her slippers and into her working boots. "Stay here, eat more jam. Wine's on the table, and please," Anna opened the door and held out the oil lamp before her face, squinting into the darkness before looking back at her mother, "please Mama, just please, act like a good *Christian* woman. For the love of God, just be good." And out she stepped into the snow, slamming the door behind her and leaving her mama—her crazy, godless, witch of a mama, alone to wait in the dark steaming kitchen.

***

It was a mess. The whole cursed thing was a mess. Anna had stepped out into the ice-cold night to meet the angry cries of children being pushed as a group further toward the barn by her husband who kept shouting over his shoulder: "Come and give a hand, Anna."

"Richard," she called, hurrying to catch up with the corralled mob moving further away from the house. "Richard, what about their uniforms? I've got it all in the attic. We were told to change 'em right away." After the Archer house had had its auction and all the old children's school outfits were up for sale, she and Richard had managed to secure the lot. It was regulation for boarding schools to change and bathe the children first thing. Change 'em, wash 'em, and burn the old rags.

It was then she really saw them under the glow of her lamp's weak light. Children, yes, wild children with long, straight black hair. They were little people, covered in furs, and beads, and feathers and glistening in the lamplight, with shining eyes of tears, and leaking noses of frozen snot.

They saw her. They saw a pregnant child who was not much older than the oldest of them, and they began to hiss and cuss. Richard didn't understand a word. Anna understood a few. Her mother would have grasped it all, and, Anna was sure, felt the hot drippings of shame for what they were doing to these children.

Jesus Mary Joseph, good God Almighty, this is horrible, thought Anna. There were six of them in all, tied together with rope around their waists and shackled at the wrists. Richard had gotten the farm dog from his post; Blackie was barking and snapping like a spirit possessed. She'd never seen the dog act so fiercely.

"We ain't changing nothing tonight," said Richard, pulling the rope and dragging them further.

But she could smell the urine. The little ones had wet themselves.

"Richard, I'll just go and get—"

"Anna Pierre, you will listen when I've spoken. We ain't changing nothing tonight. Not after the fight they gave me."

He stopped before the barn, handing her the rope and shotgun, keeping Blackie barking and snapping by his side, and walked over to the barn door to unlatch the lock. "During a stop in Bridgeside the damned little things started running in all directions, I lost half of them at the cross roads, and the rest are here with me now. Had to tie 'em up."

The barn door swung open revealing pitch blackness. Anna thought about the furnace, and the fire, and the rabbit stew.

"I've got enough dinner for all of 'em." She passed the rope back to Richard, trying not to pull them any further. "And it won't take a minute to light the furnace."

"Furnace!" called Richard in his deep preacher's voice. "Lord knows these children aren't deserving of any heat tonight."

And with the force of a full grown man against the protests of a small group of children, he dragged them all further—Blackie snapping and barking all the while—into the darkness of the barn, and re-emerged, free of the load and dog by his side. Nodding to his wife before turning round and re-latching the barn door.

"But they'll freeze!" cried Anna.

"They'll learn," replied Richard.

Sliding the bar through the latch he turned from the barn and released Blackie from his leash. The dog yelped and wagged its tail for his master before running off to pester the horses.

"Never seen Blackie act so violent," whispered Anna. "He's going to bite one of them next."

"Animals can sense things, Anna. They know where the devil lurks." He took the lamp from her shaking hand. "Give it time and we'll make things right. They'll be happy here, you'll see."

And off he walked, light in hand, toward the farm house, leaving Anna alone in the dark, with the barn, with the cries and pounding on the secured barn door. For a long moment, Anna imagined throwing off the bar and setting the children free, or at least lighting the furnace. The urge resonated through her, vibrating the tips of her frozen fingers, stirring her to step forward, lift the bolt.

Bang!

A rifle shot called from the farm house.

"Mama!" cried Anna, wrapping tight her shawls and doing her best to hurry across the yard. "Don't you shoot her, Richard!" shouted Anna. "Don't you shoot my mama."

And as she rushed though the moonlit night toward the house, as she panicked about her mother and husband, some little voice, some nagging shaking deep-rooted voice, called her back toward the barn, losing power with her every step forward, called her back toward the children, to the latch, to their fear. But Richard was shouting, and her mother, *Thank you Lord, thank you Jesus*, was shouting back. She pushed away the feeling and hurried along the snow-packed yard. Hurrying with twins in her belly. Hurrying under the moon, that powerful moon. Back toward her house, back toward her kin, and back, she could smell it now as she opened the screen and reached for the door, back to the stew; that damned rabbit stew, turning charcoal on the stove.

***

Down in the sitting room the fire smoldered with the fading embers of last Christmas's pine tree, now burnt down from the sappy log into small, blackened pieces of glowing coals. And through the dark, barely lit room, upon the mantel and hidden amongst the shadows stood the Virgin Mary with a look of compassion. Her painted ceramic eyes stared across at the empty sofa, the empty chair, the low table with bread and butter. She watched, mouth upturned at the edges, holding one hand across her heart, and the other reached outward.

The room was cold with midnight air flowing in through the broken window, stealing away the fire's heat. It had been shattered by the rifle bullet. Wine was spilt and seeping into the rag carpet. Jam was splattered across the dusty floorboards.

And in the kitchen etched by the reaching shadows cast out from the nearly emptied oil lamp, wrapped in the heat of the cast iron stove, were the wife, the husband and the witch.

They scraped at their near-empty bowls of stew, and chewed upon the burnt pieces of meat

The gun was against the back door. Richard's rosary was on the table. The postcards were hidden from sight.

Before, in the chaos, Anna had grabbed the beads from the nail on the wall and shoved them onto her husband's chest. "For the Lord's sake, Richard, put down the gun!" she'd begged.

She had managed to get them down to dinner. Food, at least, brought silence, and Anna savoured the silence.

Anna had already read the Bible twice over before meeting Richard. She didn't need any convincing about how beautiful Eden sounded and the birth of baby Jesus. Psalms would play inside her head as she followed along in her woman-child humming. It was a lovely feeling.

She knew all along about the backwardness of the circus. She felt the sinfulness deep inside her. It shook, it vibrated.

And then she'd met Richard.

The circus had arrived in Colville and was parading through the town. She trailed at the end of the group while herding along some of the younger circus children, walking beside with her brother and some of the younger tumblers. And there had been Richard, up on a soap crate preaching about the final days of redemption, casting out his fire and brimstone across the enraptured crowd, with his brow sweating and his brown hair shaking free from its carefully combed parting, dark eyes boring down into his watchers, bare arms pumping with conviction ... Anna felt a different kind of stirring in the pit of her stomach. It wasn't power, it didn't vibrate—it swelled, rushed, and spilt. It was helplessness. Pure and total helplessness.

Bliss at the shaking of his ever pointing, ever demanding finger.

And Richard had promised her, he'd promised her on the day that he proposed an elopement, that she could be reborn. She could be recreated. She would be free.

***

"Would anyone else like more?" whispered Anna, rising from the table and taking her own bowl to the cauldron set beside the oven.

Anna glanced over at her mother who was slipping the frills of her satin gown up onto her shoulder and watching Anna scrape the sides of the pot. There was now a change in her mother. Aliza looked so exhausted, unlike before when she'd arrived with the postcards and wine. Though it wasn't Richard who had wearied Aliza. Anna's mother had been all set to fight and scratch with her fingers dipped into the hot paprika bag, kept in case of emergency, in her dress pocket. She would have scratched him in the eyes and set them on fire with the spice. She would rip out his hair and bite off his ear. She'd do it all with pleasure, Anna knew, if not for her, if not for Anna. Aliza would often say that Anna showed more promise, more power, more magic than any Claire before her. And in that room, the now abandoned sitting room at the front of the dark house, Aliza had been ram-rod straight and ready to battle Richard, but then Anna had thrown herself between them, pleading (Aliza had muttered this when Richard left to quiet Blackie in the yard) "Like a slave to its master."

Aliza spoke softly as Anna scooped another serving-spoon portion into her bowl. "Make sure you eat plenty of peppers, and drink plenty of milk, Annuco, for the last trimester. And suck out the bones for their marrow. Here," she put the rabbit bone onto the table, "start with this. The marrow is good for babies."

Richard's hand slowly reached out and collected the bone, moving it beside his beads. "Bones are for the pigs," he replied, staring down into his stew. "We don't eat slop."

"Bones are full of the animal's strength, and that will keep her strong."

Richard looked up, spoon hovering above his bowl. "We don't eat slop." He reached to the rosary and rubbed a bead between his forefinger and thumb, staring at Aliza.

Aliza stared back.

Anna stood at the stove and watched them. She longed to grab that bone from the table and suck it dry—pulling out the strength of the snow rabbit, revelling in its freedom as it had leapt, flew, soared across the winter fields.

The serving spoon slipped from her fingers and clanged as it hit the ground. Her husband and mother broke their stare. Sliding down against the counter, she picked the spoon up and dropped it into the cleaning bucket.

"Sorry."

Richard shook his head and pushed himself away from the table. "I'm going to bed. I've had enough of this day." And scooping up the rosary he stood up from his seat and moved the chair back against the table.

"Aliza." He nodded to Anna's mother, once more matching her glare, before bending down. "Sweetheart," he said and kissed Anna on the forehead.

Anna stared down into her steaming bowl of burnt rabbit stew.

"Richard," replied her mother. "Sleep well. Don't have bad dreams."

Anna glanced up at her husband to see his head tilt back, as though avoiding a rock thrown his way (or a curse rather, for what would the witch do to him in his sleep?) and step back, crossing himself.

"Don't be here in the morning," he uttered, taking the oil lamp that hung beside the door and side-stepping out of the kitchen.

"Don't worry, I won't be," replied Aliza, staring no longer at Richard, who had left, but at Anna.

Anna sat back at the table and dipped into the mash, chewing upon a burnt piece of meat. When she was younger she, her brother, Jozsó, and her mother (Géza was always off, flirting with some random rich woman or locked away drinking with the ring master.

Her mother said he was a wonderful father but a terrible husband, and that was simply life), would sit around midnight campfires with the half-painted clowns, the lion tamer's assistant, the seamstress and the fat lady, and roasting groundhogs on the spit, burning the bellies, fingers and toes till they were crispy, brown and delicious. Burnt had never been a problem back then, not when it was out in the field. Here in the kitchen it branded her an inattentive housewife. A failure in culinary skills. But regardless, Anna swallowed the stew.

She scooped up another spoonful, this time full of breaking potato and barely solid carrots, and slid it into her mouth. Eventually, Anna's young, tired blue eyes looked across the table toward the wrinkled and wearied eyes that watched her eating.

With her mother there were always shadows to move through, power to choose.

With Richard there was no debate. It was relieving.

"Why did you come here?" asked Anna. She sucked on the small tin spoon, holding its warmth against her tongue.

"To see how you were doing."

"I'm fine," replied Anna. She reached out her free hand and stroked her mother's arm.

"Yes," Aliza said, turning up her palm and touching Anna's arm in return. "I'm afraid you are."

Anna sighed. She leaned back in her chair, pulling her fingers away. "I knew you wouldn't understand."

"I understand. You're like the dog outside. You're devoted."

"I'm at ease," hissed Anna, leaning forward again. The bun on her head had all but fallen apart, with blonde strands loose in all directions, circling her head in the light like a gentle halo. "It's better this way."

"His way."

"His way, Mother."

"I heard those children tonight. They were crying. You know children like that, you grew up playing with a few of them. And here you are, letting them cry in the darkness."

Anna pushed away her stew.

"It's just for one night."

"How are you going to replace their mothers and fathers? How are you going to soothe away their terrors. You can't do it, Anna. You can't do that. You and Richard, are their terror. My own daughter..."

"I've got nothing but goodness and charity in my heart. I'm going to bring to those children what saved me: love, guidance, and God."

Aliza spat onto the floor. "*I* gave you guidance, love, and all the wonder you needed."

"You don't understand, Mother."

"Mama."

"Mother."

"No," replied Aliza, "I don't understand."

The two women sat in silence for several minutes, sweating from the heat of the stove and watching one another.

"Anna darling, I can't stay, you know. I can't see you like this."

Anna said nothing.

"Anna, we'll be passing through Helmwick. You can always write us, you know that, just send it general mail to the post office. If you need me I'll come on the first train. If you need me—"

"Mother, please." Anna waved away the concern. She wasn't a little girl any longer. She was about to be a mother herself.

Aliza stood up from the table and picked up her bag, pulling out her riding jacket and fur, draping them over her shoulders.

"You're leaving now? At this hour? You'll freeze."

"If it's warm enough for those children, it's warm enough for me. I'll catch the first train to Bridgend and transfer over to Godshill."

"Mother."

"Anna, please, no more of this 'mother'."

"Aliza, please, stay till morning."

Anna stood from the table, taking her own brown shawl and wrapping it around her slender shoulders.

Both women had tears in their eyes.

Both women hesitated.

***

Once upon a time Anna and her mother had hung their feet off the beaver dam, staring across at the flooded back-field pond below. Anna, with her hair in long yellow braids, had been tossing pebbles as Aliza pointed to the ripples. “You see, Anna, how these ripples make circle after circle, and it all comes from the same pebble. The circles get bigger and further apart, but they all have the exact same centre. You see that?”

And young Anna had nodded.

“No matter how far they stretch,” Aliza continued, “those ripples are connected. They have the same heart, the same point of creation. And nothing can change that, not even distance or separation or time.”

Anna again nodded, tossing a small pink pebble. She watched how the circles formed one after another, and moved further and further and further away, eventually lapping up to the pond bank where Jozsó sat fishing for guppies.

“That’s like us, Anna,” said Aliza, stroking the back of her daughter’s small head. “You and I are like the ripples. No matter what happens, no matter how far away we go, we will always be connected—always of the same pebble and the same heart.

And Anna had thrown all her pebbles, watching them splash and radiate with layer after layer of ripples, then she laid her head against her mother’s shoulders.

“Are Jozsó and Papa ripples too?” she’d asked.

“They’re more like trees, Anna. They put down roots and grow outward, keeping their names and passing on their legacy. But you and I—we’re women, and so we’re a little different; we grow up and marry, have children to whom we’re devoted, and in doing so we’ll always spread away. Away, and away and away. But our hearts stay connected, our hearts form our chain. We’re like the ripples. Isn’t that nice?”

Anna picked up her braid and sucked on the end for a few moments, then said “It’s very nice, Mama, but also sad.”

Aliza had nodded and stroked her young daughter's blond hair. "You're a clever girl, Anna. A very clever girl."

There in the heat of the farmhouse, Aliza, looking older and more exhausted than ever before, turned from the kitchen and felt her way along the dark hall toward the front door and sitting room entrance. Anna followed with the oil lamp in hand, crying now, just softly, as her mother pulled back the winter curtain and opened the front door.

The sharp March breeze flew into the corridor, freezing their tears. Anna shivered and wrapped her shawl tighter.

"Do you—" began Aliza.

"What?" Anna stepped up closer and dropped the curtain behind her.

Aliza was standing upon the threshold, facing the moon-touched frozen garden and looking back over her shoulder. "Do you promise to keep the postcards. Don't let him find them. And the name, will you pass on the name, Anna?"

Anna's tears sprang hot and salty, cooling in the circling winter wind. "I promise," she said.

"Do you really promise, Anna?"

"I promise, Mama."

"If you insist on nothing else—"

"I will insist on that."

"My good girl." Aliza leaned forward and kissed her daughter on the forehead.

Anna leaned forward too, stomach pressing against Aliza's furs, and wrapped her arms around her mother, kissing her on the cheek.

"Good bye, Aliza."

"Good bye, Anna."

Breaking apart, Anna stepped back and Aliza turned away. Aliza, with steady creaking steps and back held ram-rod straight, dark hair swirling in a mass around her wrapped shoulders—the witch, the woman, the untamed mother—made her way toward the broken garden gate.

Standing in the doorway, watching as her mama left, oil lamp in hand and hair having given up the battle and completely fallen from its bun, stomach bulging and fingers shaking, Anna gave a final wave. "I love you, Mama," she called once more.

Aliza blew a kiss from the road, then began to walk away.

Anna stepped back from the doorway, and shut the heavy oak door. She turned the key, locking it, then pulled the curtain across to seal out the cold. For better or worse she had made her decision. It filled her with strength and weakness all at once. But that was what a woman had to do, she had to choose. That was it. She had chosen. It was done.

Taking a pin from her pocket, Anna gathered her fine hair and twisted it once again into a bun atop her head. She turned down her lamp to a tiny glow. She wiped away her tears. Her back straightened and her sniffling stopped.

Richard would be waiting, his toes would be cold and he'd need her to warm them. He'd be waiting for the sound of her footsteps upon the stairs.

"I'm coming now, Richard," she called into the darkness of the corridor and staircase.

Anna headed up the stairs toward her husband, one step at a time, holding her stomach and clutching the railing as the steps creaked beneath her weight.

"I'm coming right up," she assured the darkness. "Everything will look better in the morning," she promised aloud. "I'm certain of it," she said once more. "I'm certain of it. Everything will be okay."

She had made her choice. It was done.

And everything would be okay.

Aliza Claire Angyal, 1874

Here's our girl, fresh off the donkey and protruding with an unborn baby-to-be. Only three days ago she ran away from her small trading-post town of De Mer on the edge of Thunder Bay, taking nothing more than a carpet bag, her two-year-old son and her gentle stead, 'Donkey'. (And believe me, she's not ignorant of the image—a pregnant woman of seven months, riding on a donkey because of her husband. It was a significant picture, but less impressive in reality, as her bum developed sores, her son never stopped squirming and the donkey took to wandering from the path to examine every newly melted patch of grass.)

Five days of riding and she's finally arrived. Standing there in her blue housedress and layers of black knitted shawls, sucking on the tip of her long braided hair as it hangs from her kerchief. Aliza is thinking; she's trying to consider what comes next. Except you can never really be sure what comes next, not even when writing your own story. So instead she plays with her hair, strains her eyes, and watches as smoke begins to escape through the Big Top entrance.

Aliza Claire Angyal peeked around the tent flap and gazed into the heart of *Barnes and Son World's Greatest Traveling Circus*. White-faced clowns with red bulb noses were running from the tent and shouting in French to one another, passing without noticing her as they hurried to the elephant watering trough and back toward the centre ring. By the bucketfull they tossed the water onto the burning cannon. Catching the spray was a man rolling across the ground and cursing the circus, cape burnt next to nothing and body covered with soot. By the side of this mess was the infamous

Buster Barnes, ring master extraordinaire; Aliza had heard about him and recognized the fellow in a moment with his handlebar moustache that curled at the tips and his enormous belly that rose and fell with every exclamation like a ball bouncing on the waves. "Oh, Mother! Mother! Mother!" the ring master shouted from his giant performer's mouth. He stomped at the licks of flame that were creeping across the hay-strewn ground. Aliza waved at the escaping smoke and turned away from the choking air.

"You've got something on your skirt, dear," said a sequin-covered, feathered-headpiece-wearing woman passing into the circus tent. She looked over Aliza, easy-like, then glided onward into the smoke.

Aliza straightened up, pulling her shawl tighter. The circus woman swivelled past the stands toward the commotion of the centre ring. Aliza glared after her as she became lost in the thickening haze of smoke.

"That's my son," she whispered to herself and dropped her hand to Jozsó, who clung at her dress and was sucking his thumb.

Then, as natural as breath, or sleep, or watching the stars, a little voice spoke aloud in her head,

'Star of moon and eye of bat,

Cause that woman to grow fat.'

And the breeze stirred round her gently, and pushed the smoke away from Aliza's eyes.

Carefully bending down, it was getting harder now since she'd grown so big, she lifted her son from the ground. Jozsó was two-years-old, and she was seven months pregnant; lifting him had become an adventure. As her little boy climbed into her arms and she struggled to stand, her giant body disagreed with the intended direction. Instead of standing upward, Aliza slowly teetered sideways and fell into a pile of straw.

"Dear Lord, not again."

She looked up into the face of Donkey, who looked down with long-lashed, sleepy eyes. Reaching into her pocket, she pulled out a carrot top (saved from yesterday's meal of vegetable ends and chicken bone soup) and passed it to the animal. Jozsó kicked his legs into the hay and pointed at the passing clowns, touching his nose as if it too had a large red bulb.

Laying on the ground, still feeling the world spin, Aliza listened to a deep, bellowing shout from inside the tent: "The flaps!" it demanded. "Open the flaps." A large group of clowns rushed back out of the tent, several tripping over each other's giant footwear, then bouncing back up to rush ahead. Not one noticed Aliza on the ground, trying to push herself up. (*It is a well known fact that clowns are highly focused, so much so, that they don't even notice when another pulls out a pie and shoves it into their face. They just keep on juggling.*) Within mere moments the clowns returned as a group carrying several ladders. Jozsó watched, open mouthed and absorbed as the floppy-footed, red-haired, white-faced parade headed back into the smoke, calling, "Hup, Hup" as they passed. They never saw things like this in De Mer, that was for sure.

Jozsó clapped his chubby hands.

Aliza grunted as she rolled onto her side, "Just hold Mommy's back, Darling."

She grabbed Donkey's rein to help rise from the straw.

"Thank you," she said and she curtsied slightly to Donkey. She walked away from the tent not worrying about the donkey running off, because donkeys never run anywhere.

Piece of cloth and string to merge,

give me faith,

give me courage.

Scanning the mess of bright caravans and busy performers, her eyes caught the passing breeze full of milkweed seeds, and followed them till it settled upon the largest, most golden and glitz-covered carriage of the entire lot. *Well*, she considered, *what happens next will never be known until it happens, so time to make it happen.* She hadn't travelled five days by Donkey just to stand on the sidelines. She straightened her back, holding both son and bag, and stomped across the grounds, stepping around a small herd of pigs being yapped at by tutu-wearing dogs, and narrowly avoiding collision with a man on his giant unicycle. The elephants waved at her with their trunks, but

Aliza didn't notice.

No one was going to dictate her life. Not one person. If Aliza wanted to join the circus, then that was exactly what she was going to do.

Marching up to the decorative caravan, she took a seat upon the wooden step that led to the canary-yellow door. Jozsó scrambled down to the bottom step. Aliza reached into her carpet bag and pulled out a small velvet purse. Opening the purse she took out a card of paper and began to draw the circus tent with a loose piece of charcoal.

She waited, nose bright red in the early spring cold, Jozsó laughing and pointing at the passing performers, thumb stuck inside his mouth still, and with the unborn baby shifting inside her body. It always fidgeted when she felt nervous. Lately it wouldn't stop.

She had managed to draw a sketch of the scene and write half a letter to her mother before the ring master exited the circus tent. He was smoking a cigar and waving his top hat in front of his red, sweating face. He shouted after a crowd of young boys and jumped out of range as Donkey tried to kick him in the side. In spite of being such a sweaty, ugly man, Aliza could see that he was attractive. There was something magnetic about him. It might have been his largeness, his girth, or the way his voice would vibrate in your bones long after he'd finished speaking. Her heart began to pound with nerves while the baby inside pressed against her stomach, almost banging to get out. The ringmaster turned toward the carriage and narrowed his eyes upon the woman and child sitting on his steps.

His black boots stomped across the grounds, splashing through the puddles.

"A young lady? On my doorstep?" he bellowed, stopping in front of Aliza and rolling the tip of his handlebar moustache, cigar hanging from his giant lips.

Aliza tucked her charcoal and cards back into the purse, scooping up her little boy and raising him onto her hip. She tried to stand, projecting upward with intention, but was struck by the spins again. Tipping forward on the horizontal, she dived into the air and headed toward the ground.

"Sir!" she called, falling.

If you'd like a dramatic illustration of Aliza's fall from the caravan steps, consider a hundred and fifty foot oak deep in the forest: as the axe strikes its final blow, the oak freezes briefly in time, perhaps remembering the highlights of its long-lived and quiet life, then crashes downward in a graceful, trunk-curving death fall. Or imagine a seven-month pregnant woman dizzy with child and exhausted from days of riding on a stubborn donkey, who, as she tumbles to the ground, realizes that indignation and anger are not enough to feed a body that's eating for two, and this journey to the muddy, cold ground was inevitable for a person in her position.

Ringmaster Barnes watched as Aliza tipped forward with child, bag and belly attached. Buster Barnes was many things: a showman, a gambler, a star, a business man, and most certainly a cheat; but he was not, to be sure, a brute. His enormous hands scooped up the falling woman and her little boy together, bouncing them against his stomach and catching them as they changed direction.

"Mother!" he shouted in his announcer's boom. The trick dogs sniffing near the trailer began to yelp; the elephants rose their trunks and sprayed water into the air (they suspected another fire); the jugglers dropped their knives to the detriment of two separate toes on two separate feet; and the clowns looked up from their cream pie baking, thus not seeing Andrew, the farmer's son, who stole a lime custard pie from Daisy Dots' cooling table.

Aliza was lifted from her feet in the ringmaster's arms. The yellow caravan door swung open, and through the darkened entrance an old, bent woman with a cane hobbled into the doorway.

"What's this?" she bellowed.

"We've got a fainter," replied the ringmaster, climbing up the steps and trying to enter the caravan backwards (it was quite a squeeze with his and Aliza's bodies combined and Jozsó still clinging to his mother's side).

"Boots!" shouted his mother, striking her son's leg with her cane. The ringmaster did a little dance as he juggled Aliza and child while kicking off his mud-caked footwear.

Aliza watched as the bent-over woman nimbly worked on her

boots as well. "I haven't passed out," asserted Aliza. But the old mother kept working at her laces, finally slipping off the boots and revealing Aliza's over-darned socks.

Neither son nor mother took notice of Aliza's consciousness and requests to, "Please put me down."

As the ringmaster's mother guided Buster and Aliza (still in his arms, with Jozsó climbing onto the large man's shoulders) sideways into their home, a gathering crowd of performers watched the commotion. Apparently an exploding cannon gave no cause for concern (except, of course, for the clowns, who considered it their duty to extinguish everything that flamed, particularly considering it was usually *them* who most often started the fires), but to see Buster Barnes with a woman in his arms, well, *that* was quite the event.

"Put the kettle on Buster," ordered his old mother. "The girl's in need of steeped ginger tea!"

And with that Mrs. Barnes made sure the door was closed tight, shutting them off from the circus outside.

***

Cup of tea and food to savour,
let fortunes fall in my favour.
Dark as night and musty too,
let these people feel my due.
Forward backward sideways going
let them know without them knowing.

Inside the caravan steam rose from Aliza's mug of tea, which was heavy with the scent of ginger root and citrus. Taking another sip of the powerful drink, she rested the mug upon her belly and managed a mouthful of cabbage stew before carefully placing her dish onto the small table beside the narrow hay-stuffed mattress on which she now sat. This was quite an accomplishment considering the table was covered with trinkets. The entire caravan was full of them: photographs on boardwalks, taffy in bowls, whistles from capitals, banners for sports teams, vials of maple syrup, and postcards, Aliza noted, from all around the world.

Jozsó sat happily on the rag carpet, pillaging a large straw basket full of brightly coloured yarn. One by one he picked out the balls, squeezing them between his hands and throwing them over at the ring master, laughing in delight. The ring master sat opposite Aliza with his own steaming cup of tea and plate of sour cabbage. He'd spent the past quarter of an hour pacing silently in his stocking feet—mud-covered boots on the mat by the door—as his mother brewed the tea and heated stewed cabbage. Aliza had attempted to start the conversation, only to be repeatedly hushed as the ringmaster massaged the temples of his head. Now, with a look of determination, he was ignoring the flying balls of yarn. Beside him on a low, cluttered shelf was his ringmaster top hat. Hanging on the door was his red jacket with long coat tails and black, shiny buttons.

Buster Barnes pivoted forward over his giant belly and gave Aliza the squint eye. Humming to himself, the man rolled the tip of his black moustache in and out of its curl. Aliza glanced between him and his mother, who was bent over the stove and ignoring them both.

"Did you see the cannon fire?" began the ringmaster.

"I saw the cannon," replied Aliza.

"Oh, mother. What a mess." He pointed to the poster on the wall behind Aliza. "Géza the Great, world-renowned flying trapeze artist and dare devil extraordinaire, and we can't even get a working cannon to shoot him through the air!"

"That cannon cost a pretty penny, Buster," added his mother. Carefully, she poured her own cup of tea and produced a stool from behind the closet curtain. Hobbling over to the young people, Mother Barnes placed herself down beside her son. With her cane, she poked at the scattered balls of yarn.

"Of course it did. Where do you think we get cannons from? Not this wild country. That's a specially-designed, custom-made, highly-innovative man-shooting cannon from *Italia*. The *Gialliano* brothers sent it direct from their *Napoli* workshop. It cost a fortune! Took three months to arrive. Crossed oceans and continents. Was handled by only the best, to be used by only the best! I don't pay a fortune for faulty cannons. You know what I think? I think it was those Bailey Brothers. They've got their circus spies all over this continent."

"Sabotage," said his mother.

"Sabotage," answered Buster.

"Sabotage?" asked Aliza.

"Sabotage!" Buster declared, shaking his hand into the air and throwing a forkful of cabbage across the room.

His mother glared at the mess.

"I can't imagine anyone is sabotaging your circus," replied Aliza. "Chances are, Géza simply has no idea what he's doing."

"You, my dear, have no idea what you're saying," said Mother Barnes. She put down her tea and re-tied the red kerchief around her head, winking at Aliza as she fixed the knot beneath her chin.

Aliza was slightly startled. She wondered whether she ought to wink in reply.

"This is nothing but a small countryside girl, Mother. She wouldn't know about our Géza, world-renowned, crowd-awing, knighted, sanctified, and ingenious angel of the sky. Ordered *him* straight from *Italia* as well, that man. Cost me a fortune."

Aliza was becoming steadily more confused.

"Géza is from Italy?" she asked.

"Of course," replied the ringmaster.

"I always thought he was Hungarian."

"Hungarian!"

Mother Barnes quieted her son with a tap on his leg. "Dear girl, have you heard rumours?"

"No."

The ringmaster's face was turning red. "He's from *Italia*."

"Well, I suppose you may know best." Aliza had been instructed by her mother, Marianne Claire Rivers, to insist, when engaged in polite conversation, that the other person *may* know best. Even if they were a total fool, it was simply polite. However, Aliza had trouble stopping at 'simply polite'.

"Though I thought," she continued, rubbing the curly hair on

Jozsó's head as he threw another ball of yarn, "that for certain he was a Hun."

"And why is that?" The ring master and his mother leaned forward.

Aliza pulled her shawls tighter. "Because he's my husband, of course," she replied.

"Husband!" bellowed Buster Barnes.

Mother Barnes coughed into her cup.

The ringmaster was wide-eyed. "He is your—"

"Husband. Married May 1872, and just going on two years now."

Buster Barnes blinked slowly. If this homely little thing was Géza's wife, it would be ruinous. Géza the Great wore golden capes and had god-like looks, he shined in the air as he leapt bar to bar: glittering and smiling and waving to the ladies. He *was* the show, apart from the animals. Not even the horse riders and their tricks could compete. And while the clowns kept the pace, Géza, that glorious specimen of a man, was the thrill of the circus. A star; he was Buster's star. The only people who knew Géza wasn't actually from *Italia* were Géza, Buster and Mother Barnes. If this shawl-wrapped, braided-haired, plain-faced, child-carrying, hugely pregnant woman whom he'd planned to politely escort to the nearest train station and abandon with a pat on the shoulder was really Géza's wife, they had a problem. There was nothing worse than a *wife* when it came to guarding secrets.

This wasn't going to do. He'd paid a contract and committed to cannons, to the trapeze, to a *safety net* for goodness' sake, all in the name of Géza the Flying God who startled men, owned the sky, and possessed women. (Rich widows, mostly, who paid highly in the forms of bonds, jewellery and gold for some company with Buster's Star.)

"Mother?"

The old woman was loudly tapping the side of her mug. "What?"

"Get Géza in here. Now."

"You get Géza, dear. I'm finishing my tea."

"That's entirely unnecessary," Aliza tried to stand, but slipped forward from the hay-stuffed mattress onto the floor, tipping onto her knees. She would never have purposely begged. In fact, she had intended to rise straight away and, on her feet, demand compliance, yet here she was kneeling on the carpet; her stance didn't match her darkening tone as she pointed toward the ringmaster with her small, charcoal-stained finger.

"Now you listen to me," she said. Jozsó looked up from the yarn; he knew that tone of voice. "Géza hasn't told anyone about me for a reason, and I'm not here to change things."

"What do you want?" he asked. Buster Barnes pushed aside his plate of cabbage. His large face was beginning to look pointed as he narrowed his eyes and pursed his fat lips.

Aliza scooped up her Jozsó, who had turned back to the mess of yarn and was about to throw another ball at the ring master's knees. She straightened her back and lifted her chin.

"I'm here to join the circus, plain and simple."

Which is when her little darling, separated from his fun, began to cry.

It is a well known fact that there's nothing more grating than the sound of a young child's cry. As a species, we have been conditioned to react to the ear-piercing wail. If you've never had a baby (and therefore never developed a tolerance), then try to outlast the crescendo of screams ripping at your sanity one lungful after another. Please, try it. You'll never win.

Aliza stared at the ringmaster.

Jozsó screamed.

Mother Barnes sipped her tea.

And Buster Barnes stood from his chair and boomed over the child: "I've got a cannon to fix!"

Grabbing his plate and spoon, he scooped the last soppy bits of cabbage into his mouth. Then, reaching for his black top hat and slipping his boots over his knitted socks, he puffed up in the chest like a blow fish. Turning toward Aliza and her child as he exited the caravan, he gave them a final, angry glance.

"Mother, give her a tent. This woman is our now our witch. Twenty cents a fortune and split 2 to 18 in our favour, for the favour."

"But that's not—"

"No arguments!"

And he stepped outside, slamming the door behind him.

"And your husband's from Italy, dear," said Mother Barnes, tapping her cane. "It makes him appear far more romantic. And do try to keep quiet about the marriage, it's not good for his image."

"Fine."

"Fine." Mother Barnes picked up a ball of yarn and handed it to Jozsó, who immediately stopped crying. "Now let's get you a tent, and you can find Géza later."

***

Aliza hadn't travelled three days on Donkey without giving the matter some thought. She was here, Jozsó was here, and Géza was with them now, despite living under a different identity, an *unmarried* identity. But this was going to be a good idea, once the details sorted themselves out. Everything was going to work out well.

Except for the hair. Aliza wasn't sure about that.

As the afternoon passed and Mother Barnes ordered an unused tent to be pulled from the stables, and Aliza was introduced to Patricia Bailey. Patricia was a rouged, puffed, corseted and red-haired eruption, who carried a cushion of pins upon her wrist and a purse full of string spools. The London-born costume designer took one look at country-grown Aliza wore, clapped her hands with excitement, and then shot off across the grounds, lifting her many lacy, rainbow-coloured petticoats away from the mud, revealing bright yellow boots that splashed into the dirt. When she returned it was with her trunk, carried by Ernest the Strong Man, Patricia's sweetheart, so that she could have her maximum amount of fun upon this blank canvas of a woman.

The tent was placed beside the freak show, just outside the Caravan of Horrors. As the tent rose around them, Patricia discarded Aliza's cotton dress, saying it'd make excellent rags, exchanging it for the ex-Fat-Lady's now unused satin gown the colour of sweet cherry juice. (It was the only dress they could find to fit Aliza, who was too pregnant for a normal waistline. Patricia said the Fat Lady had been secretly losing weight, and when Ringmaster Barnes had discovered that, he threw her out of the circus saying she could either put on forty pounds, or find herself another job; so she found herself another job.) The dress looked ridiculous in Aliza's eyes, but Patricia insisted it was striking.

Patricia examined her model, biting her bright-red bottom lip. "I'm thinking black."

"Black?"

"Mother Barnes said you're a witch. No witch has mousy brown hair."

"I'm not a witch."

"But you will be."

"I'll be a fortune teller."

"Same thing."

"It's not."

Patricia waved her gloved hand. "The hair will be better black, it'll make you seem mysterious. Now, just one moment." Patricia left Aliza sitting on a small wooden chair in the newly erected pin-striped tent (once upon a time, Aliza imagined, it must have been a changing room upon the beach). She held her body as the baby inside her kicked at her ribs. Patricia returned with a large bottle of dye.

"Henna ink," she said, smiling widely. "Now Rapunzel, Rapunzel, let down your hair. And we're getting rid of the kerchief and braid."

Aliza gave up arguing. She let down her hair.

"Just wait till you see what I'm doing with your eyes. The hair, the face, the clothes: you'll be magnificent."

"Magical?"

"Powerful."

Aliza nodded. "Powerful is good."

***

When Aliza was a girl, which was before her younger sisters (twins, Augusta and Alice) had married two local brothers in Thunder Bay, Marcel and Marc; or her mother took to selling raspberry liquor to the passing hunters and tradesmen; or her father retired from his custom officer position; or Géza asked her for her hand in marriage (with the shotgun pointed at his head after her father had tracked down Géza and tied him up, dragging the boy on the back of a dog sled, to marry his daughter who was five months pregnant); before all of those things had happened, back when Aliza was a young girl living in Thunder Bay along the coast, she would walk down the path to her grandmother's cottage, and listen as her grandmother read tea leaves and talked about life in England.

Aliza's grandma knew the difference between witches and fortune tellers, which was that generally witches cursed and tellers flattered. Both, of course, had the same potential, but her grandmother insisted that perspective was essential. She cautioned Aliza, her Claire namesake and favourite grandchild, to never forget that. "You've got power in you," she would declare to the young Aliza, who even then wore her hair in one long braid and sucked at its end. "But many are scared of power. They were scared of me!"

They would take out the tea cups and put the water to boil, and her grandma would rub her wrinkled hands over the cast-iron as she dropped cloves into the boiling water, mumbling words beneath her breath. (Aliza's grandfather, at this point, would be out on the ice, fishing. One thing was always for certain, if he wasn't in the house asleep in the kitchen, he was out on the bay, fishing for trout.)

The water would boil. The cups would be filled. The leaves would float to the top and slowly emit their aroma. Cinnamon, cardamom, anise, and black tea—the rich, familiar scent filled their small room and wrapped itself around both the woman and the girl.

And they would drink the tea, concentrating on their fortunes.

Then, holding up the cup, Aliza's grandmother would read both their leaves.

"Oh, I see adventure in your future. A marriage, maybe?"

Aliza would giggle. Her grandmother always saw marriage.

"Now me." Her grandmother would squint into the cup and study it intently. "For me, I see a giant, smiling trout." And sure enough her husband would have caught the biggest fish he'd ever seen, and she would clean and cook it for their dinner.

Aliza could remember those cups of tea with her grandmother, who always foresaw adventure and fish. Aliza, meanwhile, had happily waited for her big adventure. Then one day it arrived, wide-shouldered and blond-haired with eyes more blue than the bay. Back then, before Buster Barnes had found him, Géza was a tumbler in a small traveling group, which was passing through Thunder Bay to the prairies, then the wild unclaimed lands of the west. He'd winked at Aliza as she watched him in the pub, transfixed while he juggled six mugs behind his back.

It wasn't until weeks later when his group had moved on without her (though she begged to join them, maybe juggle plates or dance with ribbons) that she realized she was with child. Her father had jumped onto his sled and driven off after the performance troop, gun loaded and ready to fire.

She remembered walking over to her grandmother's cottage through the blinding white snow. She remembered boiling the water, filling the cups with leaves and breathing as the room spun gently with heavy scents of spice. Her grandma sat and rocked by the fire.

They drank their tea in silence, until all the liquid had drained. Aliza passed her cup to her grandmother, and the old woman looked at the leaves and squinted hard at their pattern.

"What do you see, Gran?"

"What I always, see, Dear."

"Marriage?" asked Aliza.

"No, tea leaves." The woman pushed away the cup. "I only ever see the tea leaves."

After she and Géza married, they set up outside Thunder Bay in the small town of De Mer. And then, of course, he left again; there was no shotgun at his head to keep him home. He returned only every so often, when the circus passed by not too far away.

Aliza couldn't go back to Thunder Bay; she wouldn't admit her failure. Besides Géza was still charming, when he was around. But when she'd gotten pregnant again, that was when her frustration began to boil over.

Suddenly, she wanted her adventure and she couldn't wait another moment.

No one needed to be a witch, and no one needed to be all-knowing. They needed only to pretend; she'd learnt that from her grandmother's admission, and Aliza could pretend with the best of them. Aliza the 'Fortune Teller' was going to be a success. She'd damn well be a huge success.

Finally being given a mirror after Patricia finished with the dye and make up, Aliza was startled at the girl who glared back at her. Her dark hair was loose and wild around her face with its shocking red lips and charcoal-smudged eyes. The rest of her features seemed to cower behind the overwhelming changes. She sat up straight, she turned her head left and right. She squinted. She stared. She pulled her black shawls tighter.

Aliza turned to Patricia, who was nearly green with asphyxiation from waiting for the verdict. "It's perfect."

Patricia squealed with delight and spun in a circle. "I'll be right back!" she called as she danced a jig and gathered her tools.

"Where are you going?"

"To put the kettle on and find some tea. It's time for us to have a fortune!"

Patricia returned carrying a pot of steaming water and a tin of leaves. She glanced down at Jozsó who was whimpering at his mother's side. "What happened?" she asked.

"He's a little confused," replied Amelia. "Jozsó woke from his nap to see his mother, who was also not his mother. Didn't you, darling?"

Jozsó nodded as Amelia stroked his head.

"Knock, knock." Mother Barnes pushed back the tent flaps with her cane. The old woman clucked at Jozsó as he looked up toward her.

"There now, no more tears, you." Reaching into her pocket, she threw him a small ball of yellow yarn. Jozsó caught it and ducked beneath the table where Aliza was sitting.

"Fortune, anyone?" asked Mother Barnes, smiling and with a thousand lines that rippled from her grin. She leaned on her cane and appraised Aliza. Patricia set down the kettle and tea leaves, then pulled out two tin mugs from her petticoat pockets.

"That's a fine job, dear," added the ringmaster's mother. "Why don't you go and see to the feather headbands? The girls are getting awful sore for the lack of attention. And Monica says her seam has split."

Patricia curtsied, then shrugged toward Aliza. She left the tent.

Mother Barnes settled into the chair opposite Aliza. She untied her faded red kerchief, revealing grey hair pulled back tightly, and reached into her pockets. Her deeply wrinkled hand produced a small souvenir, a thin wooden whistle that read, 'Montreal' on one side, and a thimble with a picture of a lighthouse.

"Now let's see your tokens," she said.

Aliza shook her head. "Pardon?"

"Come on girl, let's see your tokens."

This definitely felt like a test.

Glancing around her Aliza wondered, what tokens? In the corner of her minuscule tent were bags of seed for the circus chickens (which would act as her bed for the night). Between her and Mother Barnes was a small round table. There was the carpet bag by her feet. Patricia's pocket mirror hung on a support beam.

"I don't have any tokens," she replied.

"Course you do, I sensed them the moment you fell through my door."

Aliza shook her head again.

Mother Barnes gave an exasperated sigh, and reached with the hook of her cane under Aliza's skirt, making Aliza yelp, and pulled over Aliza's carpet bag. Undoing the buckle, the old woman retrieved the lady's purse.

"Here now. These."

Mother Barnes shook out the postcards and letters, tsking at their blackened edges and examining each card one after the other on the table between her and Aliza. She stopped at Aliza's sketch of the circus grounds.

"How do you feel when you draw these things?"

Several of the postcards had been drawn, at least the more recent ones, in Aliza's charcoal-smeared hand. She had a light touch in capturing the business of her home—swirls of skins and hunters lining up outside the customs house; fish that swam in the waters of the bay; buggies driving down the single busy street in De Mer; Maypoles standing on yards at Easter topped with letters from suitors to their sweethearts; a log cabin, her grandmother's, tucked back into the bay's lining forest flooded over with a carpet of wildflowers; her own mother's patient face as she had had her portrait drawn.

"I don't feel anything when I draw them," said Aliza.

"Come now, try and remember."

Aliza's brow bunched and she carefully took the drawings from the old woman, flipping them over to read their messages: "Marcus Johanson built the pole so high, Augusta had to knock it down with an axe to claim the note." "Things are quiet at home. Papa has spent much time at the office, and mother has perfected the brine." "Tea on Tuesday will be fine."

Whenever Géza wrote home, sending some sparkle-covered postcard from this or that city, she would keep them separate from her stash of letters between her mother and sisters. Somehow they didn't feel the same. "I guess I feel light when I draw. I feel separated. Like I can see the picture, but it's not really *me* doing the drawing. Someone else is in there taking over my hand."

Mother Barnes tapped her thimble on the table. "Exactly. And that's all there is to witching."

"I don't understand."

"Take me and my tokens. You think it's just a lot of junk, do you? An old woman and her habits? Not a chance!" She blew hard on the Montreal souvenir whistle and struck her cane against the table, making the cups jump.

As the whistle faded from their ears, Mother Barnes' face sagged, becoming suddenly empty, and her shoulders sank inward from their proud, pushed-back position. But before Aliza could exclaim, "Oh my!" and call for help, the old woman came back to life. Blinking her eyes, pulling up and smiling with a look of extreme satisfaction.

Aliza, uncertain what was happening, put down her postcards and opened the tea tin, shaking the aromatic black leaves into the cups. She poured on the boiling water. This was an odd sort of test, and she had little energy for it. (Five days on a donkey and anyone's temper will be short. Five days on a donkey when seven months pregnant and with a two-year-old child to mind, nothing but chicken bones and scraps of meat for a meal because she'd eaten all provisions on the third day following an extreme craving for roast, and it's a miracle she hadn't already fallen into a cloud of deep, penetrating exhaustion.)

"Um?" asked Aliza.

"Um!" replied Mother Barnes.

"Sorry?"

Mother Barnes picked up her whistle and thimble. "These little tokens are my moments of clarity. I just pick one up, use it somehow, and *whoosh* I'm back in time right when I first discovered the trinket. Just like that I've travelled through time. And just like that I can know what happens next. Not the me of then, mind you, but the me of now. With a twist of the wind I'm back in time, and can remember forward. So I say to whoever is listening something extremely clever, something like: 'Beware of stepping on a mouse!', and then come flying back to the present. Edward Greer stepped on a mouse around the time I stopped in Toronto and picked up this whistle. The poor mouse had it, and Edward would have too, you know, he was standing on the top stair when the mouse met his foot. But the fellow didn't fall. And he told me then, which I can see why now, that he didn't panic because he'd been expecting it all along. And it was my warning that saved his life!"

Aliza took a sip from her cup. It wasn't the first time she'd seen signs of dementia.

"Would you like your tea?" Aliza passed her a cup.

"Oh yes. Thank you, dear."

Aliza wondered whether now was a good time to ask after Géza. Patricia had relayed gossip that Aliza's secret husband was in a hot pot of trouble. All the ladies in camp were throwing tantrums. Somehow, through the miracle of eavesdropping ears and loose lips, it'd gotten out that he had a wife. Many hearts were broken.

"But more than that!" Mother Barnes stomped her cane on the ground again. "I can see what's going on all around me too, and that's far more valuable than a little time travelling. You, girl, have the gift. I can see it in your hesitation. Come now, tell me something that you know."

Aliza had to pass this test, her husband needed to be watched and that would only happen if she stayed with the circus. The tea was scalding hot and the leaves were still oozing swirls of brown flavour; it would be a while before she'd have to read their fortunes. Aliza considered predicting a fish in Mother Barnes' future, or a marriage.

"Come on girl."

"I know my sister will have a daughter in the summer."

"How do you know?"

"I just know."

"Would this be Augusta?"

"How do you know that?"

"It's on the card, Dear." Mother Barnes took a sip of the burning tea. "And you 'just know' it will be a girl."

Aliza slowly nodded.

"What about yourself?"

Aliza frowned and looked at her large bump. "I can't see anything. Whoever she or he is, they're not showing themselves to me."

"And how do you know that?"

"I just know."

"Why won't they show themselves?"

"Well, it's certainly not their fault."

"What isn't?"

"Oh, everything. Jozsó was meant to be a girl, but he turned out a boy. That's fine with me, of course, I gave him Claire as a middle name regardless, only spelt C-L-A-I-R without the 'e' since it feels more masculine. But my mother and grandmother wouldn't accept it. And now I'm pregnant again. Géza didn't want a second child, but he never argues with a bottle of good liquor and my mother, she distills and brews the very best you'll ever taste. This time I did things proper, married and man on top, and we should be having a girl—before my sister has hers; it's only proper. Except..."

"Except?"

"Except nothing has felt proper for a damn long time. Which is why I'm here. And none of this is the baby's fault, but at the same time, he or she's not made it any easier either. Stubborn little thing."

"So, you are in an argument with this baby?"

Aliza laughed very loudly and gulped her tea. "Argument! No one can have an argument with an unborn child."

"And yet, you hold a grudge." The old woman drained her cup; she slid it across the table and patted Aliza's hand. "That's another matter for later. All you need to do right now is read my fortune. Tell me, what do you see?"

"Tea leaves."

"What else do you see?"

Aliza had asked to join the circus. Granted, she imagined they'd have her taking tickets or popping popcorn or minding the children. But she'd asked to join the circus. Besides, she had fortune telling in her blood—real or not, it was there. She lifted Mother Barnes' mug and looked at the scattered, soaked brown tea leaves. She imagined the woman before her with the trinkets, travelling through time. If she were to sketch it, she'd create a swirl on the paper and the world would be full of laughing, disbelieving faces.

Charcoal to hold and sketches to draw

How can I see all that she saw?

From the hanging flaps entered a breeze, gently swirling along the room and pushing lightly against her face. She could smell wet grass and mud and that burnt, sweet scent of cotton candy, folding and rippling across one another. If she were to sketch it, Aliza would draw a face with a thousand lines and long, dark hair floating in the water and smiling at the sky. She'd draw a hand, a man's hand, reaching down to claim the woman from the water.

"You feel free inside the water, free of all the pain and the pressures, like you can let go of your body and float up into heaven. And there's someone who wants to keep you safe, to pull you away from that feeling and back to life, back to your lives."

Mother Barnes nodded slightly.

"He is your father?"

The old woman sighed. "Let's not worry about who or what he is. He could be life in general, obligations, love, or he *could* be my father. Papa never wanted me to run off to the circus. But can you see that this is more about the feeling? You've a sense that there's a part of me, or a part of us—'cause don't you mistake this girl, there's always a part of yourself in every reading—that longs to be free of all these things." Mother Barnes gave a vague wave with her hand. "I ran away from home in the end, much like you, and somehow ended up here. And yes, life is getting slower, more draining every day. I'm a very old woman, and sometimes it seems easier to just let go. Though my son could never manage properly without me. Now read your leaves, girl, and see what you see."

Aliza finished off the cooled drink and looked down into the cup. She tried to imagine herself in the tent, surrounded by an entertaining sort of madness and looking like a giant flesh wound in her deep red dress with her baby waiting to arrive. Her little unborn baby, tangled up in the mess of Aliza's life, of her doubts, aching to be free, and not yet ready to leave. Aliza didn't understand any of it.

"I see tea leaves."

Mother Barnes tsked. "Oh well, Dear. When you're ready you can try again. I expect Géza will be along soon."

Aliza nodded. She felt as though she'd failed and she hated the feeling. It had a way of sticking in her stomach and turning her restlessness into a small, burning fury. But then, she could always turn to her little—

"Jozsó?" Her son wasn't on the ground anymore, he wasn't even in the tent. "Where's Jozsó?" asked Aliza.

Mother Barnes tapped around the floor with her cane, not finding the child. "Damned if I know," she replied.

"He must have crawled out. I've got to find him. What if an elephant *steps* on him?" Aliza stood up from the table, teetering slightly in the new boots that Patricia had assigned her, and feeling dizzy, as usual, with sudden movement.

"Here." Mother Barnes passed over the cane. "I can do without it."

"Thank you." Aliza grabbed the cane, and wrapping her shoulders with her self-knit shawl she hurried out of the tent. Panic and lights began to spin around her head. "Jozsó!" she called, walking out into the circus grounds. The sun had just set, and lamps were aglow across the field. From within the massive Big Top light was pouring upward into the sky and organs were playing in horrible unison as, toward the road side, people were pouring through the gates with their tickets, heading down for the circus and ready for a show.

"Jozsó!" called Aliza again. "Darling!"

Dizziness faded as adrenaline filled her. Aliza dove into the sea of carnival and performance, searching for her lost son.

She searched, but couldn't find him. She tried to focus on her little boy, but she couldn't get a fix.

Night so black and lights that shine

Help me find my son divine

No wind stirred. No breeze crept across her neck and tickled her hairs. No sign arrived to show her the way. Nothing. Even with the clowns and Patricia and the strong man, Ernest, scouring the circus grounds for her son, no one was finding her little boy. What if he'd been carried away? What if he'd been trampled underfoot. She pushed her way through the mass of performers who were rushing like mad in last-minute preparations for the show and yelled for her son. "Jozsó! Jozsó, honey!" But when that didn't work, Aliza changed her tact. "Géza! Géza you stupid goose! Where are you?"

All day long her own husband had ignored her, and now when their son was missing he *still* didn't materialize? That wasn't acceptable. This was exactly the sort of thing that made Aliza very, very angry. She was running on the fear, the fear that her son was lost and would be hurt. How could she have been so stupid not to notice him leaving?

How could I be so stupid?

"Géza!" she screamed.

"He's over there, honey," said one of the horse girls, fixing her headband in a small mirror and leading a horse toward the performer's entrance; she nodded to the far right side of the camp at the large carriage lit up from within. "He's been locked in his carriage all day—no visitors allowed. But you look determined enough."

And the young girl swung herself up onto the horse, fixed a bright smile on her face, and rode into the Big Top as the clowns came running out in the other direction, still smoking from their flaming daisy gag.

Aliza ran through the clowns and headed for the caravan. Locked in all day? Locked in while she was out here, losing herself and her son in this circus?

"Géza!" she called as she stormed the carriage and slammed the cane against the door. "Géza Béla Angyal, you open this door right now or I'll break every one of your windows!" Again, she pounded the door with her cane. "Open up!"

And just as she was leaning over from the ladder, about to smash her first window, there came a beam of light from the caravan door as it opened slightly. Aliza pushed open the door. She was struck with the smell of cigars as she stepped through into the yellow light of the room and shut the door behind her.

Géza was crouched in a ball against the far corner. With singed hair and still in his burnt golden cape, he looked an absolute wreck.

"Géza?" Aliza stepped in further, forgetting to wipe her boots. "Géza, what's wrong with you?"

"It's over, Liza. It's all over."

"What's over?"

"My career!"

Géza tore his eyes away from the mirrored wall and glanced at his wife, then stopped, and looked again.

"What happened to *you?*"

"I've joined the circus."

Géza blinked. He uncurled from his ball. "You've joined the circus? What as?"

"A fortune teller."

"Your eyes are so black."

"So are yours."

Géza's normally sharp blue eyes were surrounded by two rings of puffy dark purple.

"Did Mr. Barnes do this to you?" asked Aliza.

"Buster? Of course not. He'd never."

"Did the women finally get you?"

"Those girls who've been knocking on my door all day calling, 'Géza, oh Géza darling?' Not a chance."

Aliza carefully lowered herself down beside her husband. This was the real Géza, not the star on the posters or the one who'd in a blur of De Mer liquor gotten her pregnant. This was the crumbling, careful and deeply-complicated man that she'd fallen in love with after having been married. The lust had worn off, but a certain kind of dedicated love had remained.

"Géza," whispered Aliza. "Why are you hiding in your caravan? Didn't you know I was here?"

"Oh, Buster mentioned it when he came knocking, though I didn't believe him."

"And?"

"And my career is absolutely over! Liza, I can't fly out of that cannon for the life of me. I've tried and tried, and every time it ends in flames. Buster said I could have anything in the world, and I was fool enough to ask for a cannon."

Again he curled himself into a ball.

"Géza, we have to find Jozsó. I've lost him. I can't find him anywhere."

Géza looked up from his ball. "You brought Jozsó?"

"Well, I couldn't well leave him at home."

"You could have left him with your mother."

"Géza Angyal, I never leave the ones I love most."

If Géza had a selfish streak that stretched from coast to coast, Aliza had a self-righteous one to match.

Géza shook his head. "It's all too much, Liza. It's all too much for me today. I am an artist, not a clown."

"Yes, you are what you are." She stood up from her husband and grabbed him by the ear. "And we're going to find Jozsó, right now."

Opening the caravan door, Aliza clung to Géza's ear as he finally consented to be pulled from his nest and taken across the circus yard to the sideshow and Aliza's tent.

***

Aliza had been in labour for ten hours when Jozsó had arrived to the world. Géza hadn't been there; he was down south in Niagara Falls for an early summer show. Buster Barnes had just taken him on as a daredevil on the high wire and he was making his first tour. Her mother had managed the delivery with direction from Aliza's grandma, her mom's arms pulling the child from her daughter's loins. Slick, wet and mucus-covered, the baby arrived in the world and shocked them, utterly shocked them as they took a look and saw—gasp and horror—that it was a boy.

But Jozsó was a good little baby. He hardly cried when the generations of women began wailing all around him. The grandmother cried out in shock. The mother burst into tears of mixed emotions. The sisters cried at the pain they'd witnessed. Only Aliza and Jozsó were calm in the circle of women. Only they knew the very simple truth: little Jozsó, to be christened Jozsó Clair Angyal, was the very best thing to have happened ever in the entire world. And Aliza lifted him onto her stomach and smiled at his squashed, blind, baby's expression. And she whispered him a little poem.

Little Jozsó don't you know
All the ways you'd like to go?
Little Jozsó can't you see
All the things you're meant to be?
Sky of blue and winds that blow,
May you always know you know.
Dreams that sail and hopes that fly,
May you live until you die.
Perfection comes, perfection goes,
Yet you have the most darling nose.
Ten fingers here, ten toes as well,
You've put me under a lovely spell.

She had written it on a postcard a day before his birth (having had a strong feeling, but telling no one, that she'd be having a baby boy). He'd been overdue and she was becoming desperate. In fear, she had written her baby the poem and drawn a picture of her love in smeared, swirling charcoal, and she had promised, quietly within herself, to give this postcard should it be able to arrive very soon. Otherwise the poem might be sent off to Niagara Falls, or across the world to another little baby who had been good and arrived on time.

Everything had turned out all right. So long as he was with her, so long as she could see him, everything seemed to be just fine. But then she'd gotten pregnant for a second time, and she couldn't *see* this new baby. Why couldn't she see it?

And why couldn't she find Jozsó?

Throwing back her fortunetelling tent flaps, with Mother Barnes having disappeared, Aliza sat down at her small table and picked up the lady's purse, emptying it out onto the table and sorting through the postcards. Géza rubbed his ear and watched his wife at work.

Pushing aside the letters and postcards, Aliza found the picture she'd drawn earlier that day.

"Yes!" she cried, and picked up the card. She studied the picture, holding it to the candlelight, and squinted through her charcoal-smudged eyes. "There! Oh, Géza, do you see him? Right there in the picture!"

"What is that?"

"It's the picture I drew while waiting for the conductor. But I must have know somehow. Mrs Barnes says these are my tokens. I must have known without knowing. He's got to be there!"

And rising from the table, she dropped the postcard and began to run once more across the grounds. This time there were no dizzy spells. This time she could feel the breeze pulling her along. Around the caravans, over the poodles, past the elephants. Géza followed behind her, burnt cape flapping, and nearing the cannon by the entrance that was to be wheeled into centre stage—readying for the shot. Aliza ran up to her Donkey, still waiting patiently by the performers' entrance to the show, and looked down beneath its feet.

There, curled up in a small ball with the yellow yarn between his arms, was Jozsó fast asleep.

"Oh Donkey," Aliza said, kissing the animal's nose before bending down carefully and scooping up her son.

"Hello, Donkey," said Géza to the beast. "Didn't expect to see you."

And Aliza lifted her son and held him tightly, closely within her arms. She kissed his sleeping face, she kissed his ball of yarn, she kissed his light curly hair.

"I found him, Géza," she said, turning to her husband.

"Hello Jozsó," he replied. Géza kissed his son's head.

The ringmaster in the centre ring waved his arms as he spotted Géza through the performers' entrance and announced in bellowing tones: "Géza the Great has arrived! And for his first spectacle, he will *fly* across the tent—shoot by the cannon of death, and live to soar another day!"

And with that Géza was suddenly transformed from the snivelling, broken man into a golden-clad god. Chest puffed and muscles flexed he waved at the waiting ringmaster, pushed back his singed blond hair, and nodded to the clowns who began pushing the cannon into the ring. Through a smile so wide and tight it was ready to snap, he turned to Aliza.

"Pray for me Liza, and don't let Jozsó forget his father."

He then turned to the crowd and ran into the rings, arms held above his head as the crowd cheered for their hero. Aliza watched as her husband glanced back, just once, and nodded toward her and Jozsó.

She sighed, then whispered to herself, "Let's see what happens next."

Géza was vain and he was disinterested, and yet he was so very real with her. And Jozsó wouldn't like to grow up without a father; after all, why else had she come to the circus? Simply put, she had done it for her family. Because everything needed to be set right, even when they felt so mixed up and confused. She still didn't recognize the baby within her, but she knew the child in her arms. And time would tell, time would sort out the details.

Watching Géza as he climbed into the cannon, Aliza felt the breeze stir as she directed the wind toward him and uttered a little charm beneath her breath:

Nights of light and darkness day

Let everything turn out okay.

The fuse was lit. The cannon boomed. Géza flew: golden, soaring, with his cape flapping in the air.

Marianne Claire Rivers, 1851

Beyond the old cottage, seagulls circle above the crashing waves—waves that charge the eroding cliff face, above which, high up and far back, the Rivers Family's ancient Patriarchal home is situated. From the long green grass of the cliff top, with criss-crossing lines of flapping blue sheets, grey socks, and white petty coats, with the Atlantic ocean rising and falling all the way to the horizon, the Rivers' small claim to the Cape Breton coast was a sight to take away the breath. And further along the dirt road that slopes from the cottage toward the tidal streams, down the hill and just beyond the foot bridge, a little shack—one room with thatched roofing—has been built just beside the jetty's mouth.

Marianne Claire Rivers glanced over toward her small shack as the familiar breeze of salt and decay rushed up across the dunes and rose to the cliff-top cottage, testing the age-old clothing pins, and pulling at the loose strands of her dark braid.

Down at the shack, Marshall was standing on their front porch. He was dressed in his fisherman's garb, and waving at his wife while beaming with appreciation. Even from the top of the hill, Marshall's hair looked a huge mess of curls. She smiled at her husband and blew him a kiss. Some things, she reckoned, only a woman could manage.

Marianne stood straight (as straight as was possible, her back was aching right through her middle) and knocked on the door of her mother-in-law's cottage. Earlier that day she'd gone for a swim in the cold May water, but had left the luxury of the weightless ocean and wrapped herself in her maternity petticoat, long black skirt, loose cotton top, and layer upon layer of blue knitted shawls, secured in place with her whale-bone pin. Hair braided back, still damp with salt water, and having squeezed her swollen legs into her moccasin boots that reached above the knees, she'd stepped out of the shack and into the wheelbarrow, allowing her husband to push her up the hill, to his mother's home, where he quickly deposited her and ran back down the hill *before* she was allowed to knock, just as fast as his feet could manage.

Basket in arm, full up with vegetables and a smoked joint of ham, Marianne peered through the window of the Rivers' cottage to the darkened room beyond.

She knocked again.

"Bonnie Rivers, you're keeping a pregnant woman on her feet!"

While Marianne was all things gentle and kind, she knew how to handle those who were not of the same disposition.

She knocked again, this time more loudly.

"Bonnie, this is Marianne. You know I won't go away."

"Leave me be, Marianne Rivers," came a shout through the door. For a woman of later years, Mrs. Rivers could shout loud and clear.

Marianne tried the door. It was locked.

"Is Boyd there?"

"He might be."

"Boyd, you in there?"

There was no response. Marianne knew full well that Boyd was going out with Marshall to check the lobster traps around the bay, but Bonnie wasn't meant to know that. She'd given strict instructions that no Rivers along the Cape was to help Marshall with his fishing until he changed his mind about leaving home. But Boyd was soft as cotton, and would never say no to his son.

"Fine, Bonnie," said Marianne. "Either you let me in, or I'll make my own way through this door."

"Be off with you. I'm in no mood."

"*I'm in no mood!*" called Marianne, pointing a threatening finger at the closed door. The entire Rivers family lived upon the coastal edge of town. Neighbours were spaced generously apart, but with all this yelling of Marianne and Bonnie's, they were sure to come along the lane and listen to the fighting. Down the road, Fiona Campbell was already walking to her gate with a flock of children behind, making as though she were checking for David Kerr with the mail. Marianne hadn't yet heard the ring of the mailman's donkey bells, and knew Fiona hadn't either. Fiona Campbell with her upturned nose was doing nothing more than satisfying curiosity.

Marianne waved to her neighbour. Fiona waved back.

"Nice day, Fiona!"

"Gracious good!" replied Fiona.

And Fiona looked left and right along the lane, but David Kerr was nowhere as of yet.

"Well then," called Fiona. And wiping her hands on her apron, she turned round and headed back into the house, a line of red-headed children behind her.

Marianne turned round to the door. "Bonnie, I'm going to pick up this here piece of decorative drift wood in your garden and smash it through your window. You want me to do that? I swear to Mary and Joseph, I'll do it if you don't open this door. And *then* imagine what Fiona Campbell will be saying across town. Hmm?"

Marianne waited. The last thing she wanted was to bend over and pick up that log. She might not be able to get back up.

"You're a stubborn goat, Marianne La Fleur," called Marshall's mother.

Bonnie always use maiden names whenever she was fed up with daughter-in-laws.

"As are you Bonnie Sinclair."

Marianne did the same for mother-in-laws.

The door clicked and was opened a crack. Mrs. Rivers walked back toward the dim kitchen as Marianne pushed through the entrance and stepped into Marshall's childhood home. It wasn't a very large place, just a few good-sized rooms grouped together and supported with wooden beams from inland. The outside was salt encrusted with a lifetime along the ocean, and the inside was cluttered with family memories and traces of their trade: netting in the corners waiting to be repaired, driftwood piled by the hearth for burning, shells along every flat surface you could imagine.

Marianne put down her basket and eventually managed to step out of her boots, trading them for some black knitted slippers she pulled from her pocket. Taking the basket, she slowly hobbled her way along the corridor to the kitchen.

Bonnie was on the cot in the kitchen. The room was stuffy and hot, the curtains were drawn. Marshall's mother looked pale as cotton and more deflated than a jelly fish on the beach.

"By the way you were fighting me, I almost thought you'd eaten a horse and more this past week. But Marshall tells me you haven't touched a thing."

"I'm not hungry."

"Fine," replied Marianne. "But I'm starving and our stove is plugged. You mind if I make myself some dinner here?"

"Don't play your games, girl. I know your stove ain't plugged."

"No games here, Bonnie. A family of sparrows just laid eggs and I don't want to move the nest till the young ones have hatched and flown away."

"Couldn't have moved it before the babies arrived?"

"And where would they go otherwise? The seagulls would get them."

"Marianne, all that sweetness will rot your teeth."

Marianne put her basket on the kitchen table and walked over to the large windows, pulling back the drapes and letting in the light. Bonnie turned on her cot by the stove and faced the wall. The woman began mumbling to herself.

"What's that?" asked Marianne. Going to the cupboard, she pulled out a large pot and left it on the counter.

"I said, 'just like a child to fly away,' even birds are ungrateful to their mothers."

"Birds have no concept of gratitude; they just do what's natural." Marianne opened a drawer and pulled out a small knife. Then, sitting down before the basket at the table and pulling over the large cutting board, she grabbed a handful of carrots.

"You rinse those carrots?" asked Bonnie, peeking over her shoulder.

"Of course I did," replied Marianne. Marshall's mother's white hair was hanging loose across the cot. That was a bad sign. Normally the woman kept it high and tight in a bun.

Marianne peeled her carrot, then another, and then another. Moving aside the peels, she began to slice the carrots with a small paring knife. Soon the board was a mountain of carrot slices. Pushing back her chair, she moaned at the weight of the baby and stood up, getting the big pot and carrying it over to the stove. She lowered herself slowly down to the cupboard beside the stove, taking up the oil jar and pouring several 'glugs' into the pot. Putting away the oil, Marianne turned to the cutting board and brought it to the oven. "In we go," she whispered as the carrots splashed into the heating oil.

"I won't eat a thing," barked Mrs. Bonnie Rivers.

"The carrots are in the pot," replied Marianne. Picking a wooden spoon from the drawer, she pushed them around to cover the base. Then, taking a small log from the wood pile near the door, she opened the oven and added it to the burning embers.

"Don't you know better?" asked Bonnie, still facing the wall and not moving. "You cook the onions first. Gets rid of their sting and makes everything sweeter."

"I sure do know better," replied Marianne. "Carrots first brings out the yellow, and everyone likes a soup with strong colour."

Marshall's mother snorted. "Young girls think theys always knows best."

"All I know is that carrots go first."

"Onions first!" Mrs. Rivers turned away from the wall to stare down Marianne. "I've been cooking soup all my life, girl, and I knows about order."

"This recipe has been handed down generations," replied Marianne. She pushed at the carrots and looked out the window. "That essentially makes it historic."

Another snort from Bonnie. "Historic, my backside."

"That too, of course."

"Cheek!" But Mrs. Rivers suffered a momentary grin on the right side of her face (the left side, as always, being more stubborn), and propped herself up further on the cot. Her long white hair was pushed behind her shoulders, and her sharp blue eyes—sunken after a week of fasting—moved between her daughter-in-law and the table of food. Marianne kept her eyes on the pot.

"Smells good, no?" Marianne put down the spoon and returned to the cutting board, picking up two onions and cutting off their tops and bottoms, slicing them down their sides and pulling away their outer layer. Tears began to slip down her face. "Good Lord these onions."

"I've told you a hundred times, girl, you gots to whistle as you chop those onions."

"I can't whistle one note, and you know it." Marianne put down the knife and leaned back from the table. Her eyes stung sharp.

Without a word, Marshall's mother tentatively turned back the blankets and lifted herself from the cot. Gripping the back of a nearby wooden chair, she pushed it over to Marianne's side. Marianne had to stifle a gasp. Bonnie was still in her nightgown. It draped down from her square shoulders, contours of hanging breasts and large stomach appearing through the loose cotton as she pulled the chair up to the table. Her bent bare toes peered out from beneath the gown hem as Bonnie sat down upon the chair, wrapping her covered arms around her waist.

Marianne, for the two years she knew Marshall's mother (or Marshall for that matter) had never seen Bonnie in anything except the woman's practical grey dress and petticoat, kept together with an unseen but tightly tied girdle, and layer upon layer of aprons tied around her waist for the fish gutting. (Except during weddings and christenings, when Bonnie wore her 'special occasions' dress, a yellow gown with a bustle on its back, and opal buttons running from her chest to her neck, bringing the eye to her sturdy face that had the slightest suggestion of rouge from very well-pinched cheeks.) But here she was with her body shaking and long hair loose: weak, and yet determined as she kept her expression steady, leaning toward the onions. A whistle filled the kitchen, long and pure, then broke into the tune of *Row, Row, Row Your Boat* as Marshall's mother blew away the sting of the onions.

Blinking back tears, Marianne leaned forward and began to chop again to the tune. Soon she too was trying to whistle.

"You've gots to make it like you're blowing out a candle. Imagine a candle." Bonnie leaned forward and rested her elbows on the table, head slumping down upon her palms. Marianne pushed back her chair, lifted the cutting board, and hobbled over to the pot. Into the oil the chopped onions fell—*sizzle, pop*—and steamed. She basked in the sensations.

"Like this?" Marianne, eyes closed, tried to blow out an imaginary candle.

"You're just blowing."

"This?"

"You're just blowing harder, you gots to go gentle with whistling. And make your mouth more narrow than an 'O'—make it like an 'O' that's been sat on." Bonnie whistled again. "See?"

Marianne came back to the table. She tried once more. "Like that?"

"Sounds like the wind creeping through your lips."

"It's almost a whistle."

"Almost. I can't believe your mother never taught you how to whistle."

"She tried, actually. But it didn't take. My father can whistle though, and when he whistles, the entire forest stops to look around; raccoons fall out of trees and deer stop their running. No one whistles louder than my father."

"Hmm."

Mrs. Rivers went to push back from the table, but Marianne pushed back first. "Now you just hold on there because I brought along some juice. And if you won't eat, the least you can do is drink."

Reaching across to her basket, Marianne fished out her bottle of raspberry juice, which she had brewed and bottled last summer. Marianne was proud of her raspberry juice. There was nothing better than its sharp sweet flavour, and Mrs. Bonnie Rivers had never been able to resist another glass whenever offered.

"Don't want no drink," replied Bonnie.

"It's not eating, Bonnie. And you know well as anyone that if you don't drink, then no way you'll last a day, and then who will protest Marshall's leaving?" Marianne took two cups from the shelf and poured them both to the brim.

"This some joke to you, girl? Because I'm not playing." Mrs. Rivers looked up from her hands with those cold blue eyes and stared at Marianne for a moment. Marianne, on her side, took no notice of the angry glare and instead sipped the red juice, licking her lips as she set the cup back down.

"No joke, Bonnie," she said, gently smiling. "But you know I'm right."

"I don't know you're anything."

"You know I make one fine bottle of juice."

"That you do."

And Bonnie drank the juice in a careful sip. "You best be getting some water in that pot before it burns."

"Oh!"

Marianne reached forward again to the basket and pulled out a wrapped package, peeling back the paper to reveal the ham hock. One of Marshall's brothers, Ian, had smoked it just a week earlier when the pigs had been slaughtered, and Marianne had taken all the hocks before any of the other wives could notice they were gone.

Standing up again (all this sitting and standing was making her exhausted. If this baby didn't come soon she was going to lose her mind. How was it that women got the role of baby carrier when men were so much larger and stronger?) she dropped the hock into the pot, pulled it off the burner, and then, moaning as she bent down, she picked up the bucket and opened the kitchen's back door to the garden. "I'll just be a moment at the well, Bonnie. Finish that drink if you're going to lay down again."

"Who says I need to lay down?" barked Bonnie.

"Do as you like," replied Marianne. And she pushed off her slippers and stepped quickly into Boyd's spare shoes, going out the back door and leaving it open behind her.

Marianne worked upon the pump's red handle, up and down, and up and down. The pipe groaned. Cold water poured in gushes from the spout.

As she pumped with one hand, her other reached into the filling bucket and formed a cup. Marianne bent over to quench her thirst. Raspberry juice was fine and well, but nothing, not a damn thing, trumped the taste of fresh water. Fresh water. Beautiful water. Water gushing as her arm pumped, splashing as her mouth sipped, spraying across her boots, and overflowing the wooden bucket. She closed her eyes and drank straight from the spout.

Lord, that was good. Sometimes she marvelled at how wonderfully good life could be.

Up on the cliff Marianne could see for miles. She'd been raised closer to town where the cape crossed over toward the main land and her father left for his portages, raised with the city on her heels—never too far off, always reachable with its hum of noise and excitement. But what was better than *this* view? Miles upon miles of uninterrupted openness. It had suited her immediately when she first moved to the village. Not the quietness, no, not that at all, but the openness. The horizon promised so much greatness. It caused a swelling right inside her middle, and maybe the baby felt it too? It was a yearning to find the horizon, to cross it, to hold it. It was a feeling that life was more than she could ever imagine.

It was no wonder Bonnie felt sick at the idea of losing her Marshall. Boyd had inherited the cottage, and Bonnie had lived in the village all her life. Marshall's parents were part of the waves, coloured by the salt air, submerged in the view that stretched toward an endless number of forevers, and Marshall was part of this land too. Losing her youngest son would be like losing the sky. Losing a vital piece of the world.

But Marshall wasn't like his parents: his dreams had wandered beyond the fish and sea, and Marianne could understand in a way that his parents couldn't, that when he looked around him, he wasn't looking at the horizon, he was looking far beyond it. Adventure and change was a pull he couldn't deny. Marianne understood.

She stopped her pumping and looked down into the dark wooden bucket. Drops fell from the tip of her chin and rippled across the bucket's surface.

Marshall had wanted to go beyond the horizon. It was one of the reasons she'd fallen so hard in love with him, his idealistic dreaming. That and the broadness of his shoulders.

"But lord knows why men don't carry the babies," she said aloud, bending her knees and reaching for the bucket. "Lord knows why us *women* need to carry such weight." And she stopped and looked up at a small passing cloud behind which she suspected God was hiding. "Didn't you consider how much stronger they are? Didn't you consider? And here I am, bigger than a beached whale and just days from delivery, lugging a bucket of water. If I was a man, strength would be no problem, but you couldn't have considered that, could you?"

She often had these one-sided conversations. She figured if God could read her thoughts, there was no point in containing her opinions.

Just as she had moved back round to the door and saw it was still wide open, the sounds of bells filled the air between the waves and the gulls.

"Bonnie, I do believe the mail has arrived!" called Marianne as she put down the bucket. "I'll run round to collect the news."

Run, in the case of Marianne, more of less meant a careful walk, but she got to the gate as old David Kerr was passing with his pony, Lou Anne the Third, with the clanging bell tied around her neck to declare that the news had arrived. General rule of thumb with David Kerr was that you'd better come running when you heard Lou Anne the Third's bell ringing. Otherwise, letters from friends and family would be left under a rock near the path, and there was a considerable chance the birds would fly off with the paper before you read about the latest news in Halifax, or back home, in the Old Country.

David had been servicing the area since he was a young man, and he'd worked with one Lou Anne or another his entire life, raising his girls right up from their calf days. Now he and Lou Anne the Third were simply a couple of old folks, strolling down the lane and handing out some letters. David himself had taken to carrying the mail in a large sack, which was slunk across his shoulders. Lou Anne the Third's back couldn't tolerate the weight any longer, but he said she still enjoyed the walk.

Catching her breath as she waved at David Kerr, Marianne opened the gate and stepped toward him.

"Oh Mrs. Rivers, I don't expect you should be rushing down the path like that."

"It's no trouble, Mr. Kerr," gasped Marianne, still choked for words from her efforts. She waved her hands toward his sack. "Any mail?"

"Nothing for Boyd or Bonnie this week." While David was on formal terms with Marianne, he'd known Boyd and Bonnie since they were children together. He'd even almost courted Bonnie for one week as a young man of thirteen. But she'd pinched his cheek too hard after he'd whispered to the other boys about her fancy eyes, and that kind of force in a woman wasn't much to David Kerr's taste. Instead he'd found his first Lou Anne upon being hired by the Royal Canadian Mail office, and a more gentle lady he'd never known. "But I do have a card for you, ma'am, from Halifax."

"Mama wrote?" Marianne's grin doubled and she clapped into the air. "Please let me have it, Mr. Kerr! She's gonna be coming round any day now, you know? My mama has midwifing in her blood and won't trust any doctor to oversee the labour."

"Not even those fancy doctors back in Halifax?"

"Hmm, Mr. Kerr?" Marianne suddenly had a vision of her mother spotting her all the way from Hilerton, seeing her daughter swimming in the ocean and toting buckets of water. It would be very bad, indeed, if she found out Marianne was running around. But Marianne had tried bed rest and it hadn't suited her one bit.

"Don't know," replied David Kerr. "But with you being from the city, I just figured you might have a city doctor." He passed her the postcard.

"No doctors at all," replied Marianne as she accepted the card from David's hand. "Just my mother. She's the best, anyhow." Marianne glanced at the picture her father had painted in watercolours upon the recipe card; it was of his old canoe from back in his portaging days, and at the head of the canoe was him and her mother, looking straight ahead out over the water. "Besides," she looked back up at David Kerr as he glanced down the lane toward Felicity's home, where Felicity was waiting at the gate with her gaggle of children. "Besides, she just plain insists on delivering. Be arriving any day I reckon. Which is why I've got to get Bonnie to cooperate."

"I heard Bonnie was giving some trouble," said David. "That don't surprise me. Always was stubborn over one thing or another."

"You said it, Mr. Kerr, not me," Marianne replied with a wink. "Thanks very much for the mail. Have a lovely day, Mr. Kerr and good bye, Lou Anne."

"Good bye, Mrs. Rivers. And wish Marshall good luck in case I don't see him before the two of you leave. Tell him it is an honour to join the Canadian Customs, and he's doing our nation proud."

Marianne tucked the card into her pocket. It seemed as though the entire village knew of their leaving, and of Bonnie's final protest.

"I will, Mr. Kerr. I will. Take care."

"Good day to you."

And moving from the fence, David Kerr and Lou Anne the Third meandered on their way, down the lane to their next conversation as they carried on with their day. *Heck of a job* considered Marianne, *going about all day visiting friends.* Although she remembered just a few months prior David Kerr and his pony trudging through a blizzard with his sack full of mail. The Canadian Post was a romantic vocation, much like Canadian Customs, reasoned Marianne. "Women," she figured aloud "romanticize their feelings, while men, well, they romanticize their work. They all want to be heroes." But secretly she felt they *were* all heroes in their own right. To imagine Marshall as a customs agent was a thrill; he would even receive a uniform when they transferred at Montreal for his Thunder Bay assignment. Her husband in a uniform ... well, if that wasn't the finest prospect, she couldn't imagine what was.

And it was in this dream-like state she had wandered back up the stone path and back around the house to the wide-open door. It was while thinking of the brass buttons and square shoulders that Marianne picked up the bucket of water—only to immediately drop it with a splash. Looking through the doorway, there sprawled across the ground face up and eyes closed, like a puppet with cut strings, was Bonnie.

"Good Lord, Bonnie!"

Carefully lowering herself to the ground beside the old woman, Marianne patted the side of Bonnie's face, then bent over and felt for breath upon her cheek. It was there, but only just so. Shuffling over toward her mother-in-law's bare feet, she lifted them one at a time and placed the legs upon Bonnie's chair.

This wasn't the first time Marianne had seen someone faint. Once she'd become a young woman, she'd been allowed to join her mother during the birthings. Marianne wasn't allowed in the bedroom, but she was in charge of tending to the men who paced outside the door and twisted their caps into balls. Many fainted. That was how she'd met Marshall's second oldest brother, and how she ultimately met Marshall. Abram's wife had a sister who'd moved to Halifax and had used Marianne's mother for her four children's births. So when Gabby, Abram's wife, had gotten pregnant, she'd gone off to the city and stayed with her sister till the baby came. Abram had passed out just as soon as Gabby had started with the shouting.

Marianne cupped water from the bucket and splashed a handful into Bonnie's face.

"Bonnie!" called Marianne. "Bonnie, you hear me? You wake up right now."

Leaning down to her mother-in-law's ear, Marianne whispered a few words of the Lord's prayer, hoping he wasn't too offended about her earlier attack on His judgement.

"Bonnie," she then said, patting the woman's face. "Bonnie, I'm making you the loveliest soup. Won't you wake up?"

Her face was grey and sunken.

"Don't you go being so selfish by dying on us!"

With a gasp, Bonnie turned her head just slightly, and her mouth fell open.

A snore began to fill the room.

Marianne nearly yelped at the enormous sound. It resonated

between the rooms, and continued on and on till Bonnie's mouth widened so large, and her nose scrunched so high, Marianne was nearly certain that Marshall's mother was about to turn herself inside out.

"Bonnie Sinclair, you wake up this very moment!"

Leaning back from the old woman, she continued to scold. "Here I am thinking you're dead, but you're just sleeping? Bonnie? Bonnie can you hear me?"

Bonnie swallowed the last of her loud, rhythmic snores and blinked up toward her daughter-in-law. "I didn't fall asleep. I tried to close that darn door and the whole room tilted sideways. Can't help it if I fall asleep after collapsing, can I?"

"The room didn't turn sideways, Bonnie. You just lost the blood in your head. And no wonder, over a week without food! And here I was always thinking that a Rivers woman never played the fool. But there you are on the floor, drooling and snoring just like the cat in its chair."

Bonnie tried to push herself up with shaking arms. "Like the cat," she replied. "That cat's so lazy, it wouldn't swipe a mouse if I dangled one in front of her."

Marianne grunted as she pushed against her mother-in-law and helped the woman rise to a sitting position on the floor.

"Now, Bonnie, I'm going to finish this soup, and you're going to drink the broth a few sips at a time, till you're able to handle eating food again."

"I'm not hungry."

"You are starving. And Lord knows I haven't the energy for all this," she added, gasping again from the effort of rising.

The baby was doing twists against Marianne's pelvis, and her back was radiating a deep, spreading ache. "But you've got to eat this soup because it's killing everyone around you to see you wither away. And maybe you'll win Bonnie, maybe Marshall will give in and not move to Thunder Bay. Maybe he'll never leave your side again, but you'll be killing his dream then, you see? Killing it dead, and you know he was never meant for fishing. Doesn't have it in his soul like

Ian, Murray, Jason, Abram, Tyler or even Boyd. You should have seen Marshall when he read that flyer. He said to me: 'Marianne, I'm going to become an agent—that's what I'm going to do. The Canadian Customs Authority will never have met an officer so honourable, so willing and able.' I've never heard him get as excited about a good pull of crab."

Marianne went over to the bucket of water and pushed it along the ground with her feet over to the cast iron stove. "But here you are, protesting his decision to leave the coast. And it's not that I don't feel for you Bonnie, because I know what it's like to leave your family; some of us know it well, no doubt. But with what you're doing, well you're giving us a horrible sort of choice. Either we kill you, or you kill him. Your own son too. Downright shameful, in my opinion."

Bonnie remained on the floor, gently shaking and silent. Marianne pulled the blanket from the cot and wrapped it around the old woman's tiny shoulders.

"This is going to be the best soup you've ever tasted, Bonnie," whispered Marianne. "I promise on my own mother's soul."

"Well then," muttered Bonnie.

Marianne poured the water into the pot, and sat back down at the kitchen table. Minutes passed, and the women stayed silent; Bonnie weak on the ground and Marianne reaching with her heavy arms around, trying to rub away the lower back pain. Steam began to rise from the pot; the soup began gurgling with a ferocious bubbling, shooting heat and humidity up to the ceiling and all through the air. Rising again, Marianne stoked the fire inside the stove and, hands wrapped with tea towels, moved the pot over to an area of lesser heat. Slowly the bubbling reduced to a simmer, and still the women waited together in silence, breathing in the thickening smell of carrots, onions, potatoes and ham melting into the cumin, paprika, pepper and salt that Marianne had only just remembered to add.

"Ssssss," steamed the soup.

"Rumm pshhh rummm pshhh" broke the waves.

"Squa! Squa!" cried a seagull.

"*Slllurp,*" went Bonnie, sipping her juice.

"*Ba, ba, ba,*" thought the baby, though no one could hear her.

Reaching into her apron pocket, Marianne fished out the postcard from her own parents, Amelia and Eric La Fleur. Her father was wonderful with a pencil; he could sketch nearly anything he saw. When she was a little girl and he'd be home between his journeys, he used to draw pictures of all the animals they encountered in the deep forest: wildcats, bears, owls, wolves, beavers, rabbits, you name it. He'd tell her stories of his trapping as he drew out the wilderness. Living in the city Marianne had never seen a wildcat or a wolf, not even after moving out to the cape with Marshall and his family—the most she'd ever seen were passing whales, huge and dominating, and then several times a year a massive dead shark strung up in the harbour.

Her mother had written the postcard. For all her father's skills, he was terrible with his composition.

> *Dearest Marianne,*
>
> *Sealing up the house for our visit to yours. I'm delivering babies night and day; there was the Simmons girl this past week. But I'm saving my best for you, darling. We're going to be ready. There will be no complications. I am certain because I am certain.*
>
> *Sincerely,*
>
> *your mama and papa*

Ever since learning of the pregnancy, her mother's postcards had always ended with 'There will be no complications. I am certain because I am certain.' And because her mother was positive, Marianne was not very worried. Maybe a little. Particularly as of late with the pains and the way her legs felt so big and her back was often aching. But everything would be fine. She was certain because her mother was certain.

Bonnie was kneeling up and raised herself onto the cot. Sitting there on the edge in her nightgown, with the blanket wrapped across her shoulders, she craned her neck in that ever familiar style that Marshall shared. It was the 'what are you doing?' neck crane.

"You don't get many letters, do you Bonnie?"

"I don't write many," quipped Bonnie, pulling back her neck and suddenly examining her cuticles with great interest.

"But you do write?"

"Right you are. I keep record of all the household expenses, and the Christmas gifts each year, and the profits from the season, and the cost of the boats and nets. I write all the time, just about."

Marianne passed the postcard over to her mother-in-law. "Would you write us if we left?"

"Oh, I don't go in for fancy stuff like letter writing."

"It's not too fancy, Bonnie."

"Looks it with all the loops your mother gives to her letters, and your father's little pictures."

This wasn't the first postcard Bonnie had read from Marianne's family. She often accepted all Rivers Family postage from David Kerr, and passed along the letters and notes once she'd had her fill of first-hand news.

"Well it doesn't have to be so very precious. We use recipe cards sometimes, when there are no blank ones in the study. You have plenty of those, I'm sure."

"Of course."

"And a pencil."

"No doubt."

"Well then, all you need is a stamp and address, and you'll be set."

Marianne glanced toward the stove top. The soup was releasing a thin column of uninterrupted steam. Near enough and it would be ready for eating. Marianne stood from her table and went over to the corner cupboard. Opening the door, she pushed through the shelves till she found the recipe box and a stub of a pencil. Returning to the table, she picked up the cutting board, and then shuffled over to the cot and put herself down beside the woman.

"Now here, you give it a try right now."

Bonnie gave her a squint-eyed look. Marianne put the cutting board on the woman's lap, and opened the recipe box, flipping through the cards to the back. "Here!" she pulled out a blank card and placed it on the board in front of Bonnie. "And a pencil for you."

"This pencil's too tiny for proper fancy writing."

"Just do your best, that's all. We can always burn it if it's too messy."

Bonnie Rivers was nearly sixty-five years old. She'd gotten married early, had four miscarriages and then four baby boys, one after the other. Her entire life she'd lived by the ocean and stared out every morning toward the horizon as the sun crept over the line between the earth and the sky. She washed her floors and tied the nets. She scrubbed the sheets and chased away the gulls. She'd learnt arithmetic to help with the money, and she'd travelled to Halifax on more than six different occasions, once being to enter her pie in the custard competition after word had spread that the previous year's winner had had burnt caramel as her topping, and Bonnie knew as well as anyone that caramel should never be burnt. She'd seen her boys grow older, and her husband stronger, and her family spread out like a tree with deep roots. Every evening she'd take in the laundry and kiss her husband on his forehead before serving the catch from the previous day. And every year she counted her blessings for what the lord had given. But she'd never needed to write a letter, not even once, because the Lord had given her so much in this small space they called their home, and everyone she'd ever loved, and everyone she'd ever known was right here, just a walk away.

Bonnie held the pencil stub between her fingers and looked down at the empty recipe card with its light blue lines and fading yellow complexion. They were getting old, her cards, and she was feeling much the same.

"You know," she said quietly, "women in my family have been known to live well into their nineties."

"I can believe that, you're all so stubborn."

Bonnie laughed gently. "Marshall likes to smile and laugh. It's no wonder he picked you to be his wife. Funny, he always said, was a far better thing than too much pretty."

"Well, lucky for him, he got both with me, eh?"

"That he did."

Marianne watched as her mother-in-law stared down at the paper on the board.

"You can write him a letter right now, if you want. I'll see that he gets it."

A tear slid down Bonnie Rivers' face and trailed off down her neck, below the ruffles of her gown.

"You start it, 'My dearest Marshall,' and then say whatever is most upon your heart."

Bonnie was making tiny circles with the pencil as more tears slid across her face.

"Then, to end it, you write, 'With love, your Ma.'"

Marianne watched in silence as the old woman sat and stared at the paper. Bonnie felt the edges of the card, she rubbed the tip of her pencil, and then, carefully and with tiny curving loops, she wrote.

'My dearest Marshall you always looked toward the shore and you never liked to swim. So take off with you if you must. Wash your face and visit again before I die. I'm letting you go, there will be no more fuss. With love, your Ma.'

Pausing a moment she scribbled one last line: *'And don't forget to write.'*

Bonnie put down the pencil and passed the card to Marianne. Marianne took the card, but before Bonnie released her grip, she whispered softly to her daughter-in-law, "One day you'll feel what this hurt is like."

Marianne swallowed the streak of pain that shot through her abdomen as the baby twisted upward against her stomach and pushed out with its little feet. She patted her mother-in-law on the arm, then brushed away some of the long white hair that was stuck against the old woman's cheek. "Would you like a bowl of soup, Bonnie?"

Bonnie let go of the letter. "Yes," she replied. Picking a pin from her sleeve, Bonnie began to pull back her hair into a high white bun. "Yes, I reckon it's about time for soup."

Marianne pushed herself up, tucking the letter into her apron pocket. Moving to the cupboard she took out two deep bowls and a long wooden spoon. Turning back toward the stove top, she scooped out two servings of the meat soup. Sitting back down beside her mother-in-law and passing the woman her lunch.

"Careful now, Bonnie, it's hot."

The women sat in the kitchen and looked out the window, watching the seagulls rise and fall in the distance, and their thoughts flew beside them, over the dunes and the waters, down to the shores and the docks, out to the boats where the men were pulling in their loads, and further toward the horizon where the sun was high in the sky.

"But I will miss this place," whispered Marianne.

Bonnie gave a quiet sigh. "It will miss you too."

Amelia Claire Stives, 1826

Amelia had never known the rock of a boat until she boarded the Royal Sovereign Cromarty that night of June 23rd 1826. Of course, that didn't make her an unworldly sort of girl, worldliness belonging as much to the heart as it does to the feet. She'd always looked toward the horizons, and wondered what was beyond. And yet, even as she ran away from the fields of Devon, she carried memories of home.

She could describe the feeling of dirt as it crumbled through her young fingers while she searched for millipedes; she could remember how the farmers' crops of cabbage and strawberries filled the entire landscape with row upon row of order; she knew well what a barn door looked like on a warm summer's day as the heat radiated off the peeling red paint; and she would never forget the long dark braid that twisted so thickly to hang down her mother's back and curled at the tip with a blue ribbon tied into a bow. Her mother used to tickle young Amelia's nose with that very rope of hair, tied neatly with its ribbon.

Amelia was good at remembering the things she loved most, and, for this reason, would forever carry those impressions in the memory of her heart. Whether that was her choice, her curse, or her magic, you would have to ask Amelia yourself. One thing is certain: when she jumped before the Captain Lyanburrner's carriage with blood smeared across her face and offered him a trade; as they arrived at the port past midnight and she stepped onto the massive barge; as the plank pulled up and the boat pushed away to separate her from England ... you couldn't have dragged her back for all the memories, cabbages, hair ribbons or millipedes in the entire world.

***

Amelia sucked her phlegm inward, amassing it at the back of her throat. She stopped to shyly smile at the group of ripe-smelling, close-standing men and wink at the curious wives behind them. She curled a tip of her loose red hair, then let it fall as she turned back toward the water. Snorting deeply, with mucus raising onto the back of her tongue, Amelia leaned her waist across the bar and pushed out her chest with an intake of air. In a snapping moment, she shot it all back and sent the wad of spit flying.

It flew—it glided—it wavered. It hit the smooth blue water.

"Oh ho! Beat that if you're able!" Amelia spun toward the watching crowd. She blew her opponent a kiss, and waved at the now disapproving cluster of women. "Amelia the great, at your service," she said, licking a trace of spit from her lips while eyeing some of the husbands and leaning a hip against the railing.

"Amelia the whore, more like it," whispered the man who stood beside her with the bag of coins in his hand. "Calm it down, girl."

Amelia smiled and ticked his pouch of money.

"Back home they called me a witch," she whispered into his ear. "Whore is an improvement, don't you think, Mr. Snider?"

Mr. Arnold Snider turned away from the woman and slapped a hand upon the shoulder of William McKay. "Now Willie, this is it. Let's not be shown up by the weaker sex."

Willie fixed his eyes in concentration. He too sucked back long and turned toward the crowd to rouse their support, flexing his muscles while doing a quick jig. Amelia actually liked the fellow very much. Willie was one of the few who would dance with her and not receive a wifely scolding. But of course, that didn't mean she could let him win.

"Air of passing go away, come again another day," she whispered beneath her breath.

Willie turned back to the railing and—like a lion about to roar—leaned back then threw himself forward, launching his wad of spit through the air.

It sank.

"Lord above!" cursed Willie, keenly aware he'd just lost one whole dollar.

"Who's the weaker sex?" asked Amelia, holding out her hand before Mr. Snider for her share as he doled out the takings to the few who had bet in her favour.

"Winner, my friends, goes to the capable lady," announced Mr. Snider.

Willie turned toward the pair of them as the men and wives began to leave. "Real women don't spit like that," said Willie. He looked over the railing in hopes that somehow his gob would reappear.

Amelia pushed herself off the railing and smiled at her opponent and occasional dance partner. She had a way of smiling that warmed her entire freckled face, made it glow in the cheeks and brightened her lips so that they matched her red hair quite nicely. Most men, when struck by Amelia's smile, thought of strawberries and sweet wine.

"There now, don't take it badly. I grew up with five brothers and no mother in sight," she said, cooing in her soothing voice.

"A woman is not meant to spit." William McKay stuffed his hands into his pockets and kicked at the deck. Amelia placed a hand upon his shoulder and swung in close against his side. Suddenly Willie found himself thinking of home. At this time of year, late May, the berries would be hanging from their stems, nearly dripping into his wife's basket as she plucked them for the market. His wife was a tiny thing with dark hair so frizzy it sprang out in all directions. She was going to follow, just as soon as he made his fortune.

Amelia picked a few pennies from Mr. Snider's counting hands and slipped them into Willie's pocket, winking at him as he woke from his reflection. "For being a good sport, and for having a good heart," she whispered. "Off you go."

William blinked and left.

"There now, I told you I'd win." Amelia slid over to Mr. Snider who was still frozen in shock from Amelia's sudden act of charity.

"There's three cent you gave away!" replied Mr. Snider, the boat's resident provider of entertainment so long as Captain Lyanburrner wasn't in the near area. "Three cents of my takings. If you want to be kind to someone, do it with your own money."

He was, in a sense, a ring master of activities; one moment organizing a card game in the bunks, next moment testing feats of strength, later challenging spectators to follow the ball, and then, when people had lost interest for the day, counting his earnings with a barely suppressed giddiness. Everyone knew Mr. Snider was a swindler, but after nearly two months on ship they were grateful for any distraction. Slowly but surely he was collecting all the spare half pennies, pennies and nickels on the boat. Soon enough it would be gold teeth and silver cutlery, if he could just twist a few arms before they were too close to land.

Amelia had cursed Mr. Snider with boils the second night aboard as she lost her dinner ration to a game of cards. He, in turn, red and blotched, had learnt of her secret talents.

"Just because you're a witch, dear young Amelia, doesn't mean you can give away my money."

"My dear Mr. Snider," Amelia leaned into the small man. She wasn't a large woman whatsoever, but then again, Mr. Snider wasn't a large man. They watched one another eye-to-eye. Amelia whispered into his ear. "I've got a beautiful shiny knife on my person just eager for some fun. So, if you call me that word once more, I'll direct it to your nether-parts, then slice your middle upwards."

Mr. Arnold Snider set his jaw, gripped his handful of change more tightly and looked over Amelia, moving between the witch's earnest wide smile, exposed bosom and dirty-nailed hand that rested so casually near the pocket upon the hip that wasn't pressed against him. He squinted at her.

"Men don't know the half of what a woman like you can manage."

"You better hope they don't," she replied.

Amelia stared down at the crafty Mr. Snider whose looks were essentially on par with a rat, and yet whose pockets hung heavy with coins and cash. Sliding herself even closer to the now trapped and bent-backward Mr. Arnold, Amelia pushed her massive chest just below his face, issuing a scent of summer berries on her breath.

(A remarkable feat of personal hygiene after nearly two months of salted beef and dried biscuits.)

"I bet all the girls on this ship are hoping for you," she said as she once again tickled the money pouch clasped firmly in Mr. Snider's fist.

"For me?"

"A man in your position, a man who can organize."

"I organize everything on this ship," Mr. Snider gulped.

"Are you aware, Mr. Snider, that a woman in my position must do her very best?" Amelia waved an arm away from the man, back toward the open water. "Nothing is waiting on the other side, nothing owed, nothing promised."

"Yet you are here."

"And yet I am here."

"Why is that?"

Amelia turned back to Mr. Snider and whispered again into his ear. "I like adventure."

Mr. Snider gulped.

"I have talent, you know, Arnold," continued Amelia as her small, dirty finger played with the scarf around his neck. "A girl doesn't grow in a house of men without learning a few things about needs."

"Oh," replied the man now relegated to 'Arnold'.

"And I am, after all, a business woman. Trading my goods and knowledge. Preparing for this next big adventure."

"Are you suggesting we work out a deal?"

"I'm suggesting far better things, Arnold, than simply a deal. A partnership seems more appropriate, with certain benefits. It would hardly cost you a thing."

Mr. Snider's hand tightened over his pouch. "Women are a luxury, but money, money is—"

Amelia sighed against his cheek and relaxed her head upon his shoulder, allowing her remarkably clean hair to fall across him. She traced her fingers along his arm. Arnold's eyes sunk low as he was filled with memories of the field and the smell of earth after a spring-time rain. He inhaled the sweetness that was country air and savoured it upon his tongue. It felt as though the skies might open once again and shower down upon him.

He shuttered and loosened his grip.

"How much?"

"A reasonable amount."

"You can't have all of it."

"I'd never ask. Only, perhaps half would be a fair value?"

Arnold tried to resist the witch, her breath upon his neck, her warmth against his body. Part of him wanted to toss her into the ocean, let her flail in the waves and disappear altogether. But that smell, the land, those feelings... After fifty-two days on the water, fifty-two days of staring toward the giant masts and willing them to move the boat more quickly... that touch of another seemed to have more value. This could be the best decision he ever made. And half his earnings from the journey? Reasonable enough!

Mr. Snider was thoroughly lost in Amelia, who continued to trace his fingers, his arm and his neck.

She didn't do this often, but she did it whenever necessary. After all, there were times when a woman had to employ her assets. The Captain had been enjoying certain assets for some time now, and in return she received free passage plus rations and the occasional scented bar of soap. Mr. Snider was going to help with the finances. It was business. This was all business.

"What do you say?" asked Amelia, moving her hand onto Mr. Snider's thigh.

"Oh yes, yes indeed."

Which is when the entire world began to tilt and the ship rocked violently sideways, throwing man, woman and child across the deck.

There was screaming, falling; Amelia tried to grab at something, but came up short with little more than the lapels of Mr. Snider's jacket.

Together they slid across the deck as the coins flew from their hands, people fell across them, barrels were flying and the opposite railing rushed up to slam into their bodies, soaking them with the ocean's thrashing waves.

"Witch!" he proclaimed, as the ship suddenly rocked back in the opposing direction, and again they slid across the deck, him pushing away from her, she grabbing him with furious hands, rolling over one another and crashing into the banister.

"Witch!" Snider called again. Amelia fell upon him as the boat shifted back to the other side.

"Witch!"

"Shut up, Mr. Snider," she sneered. Amelia slapped his face, but the man was in a panic.

"Make it stop! She's a witch!"

The entire deck was filled with the cries of terrified people. Amelia prayed beneath her breath that no one would hear this idiot. Again she slapped him. "I'm not controlling the boat, Mr. Snider."

"Make it stop!"

A sail unravelled and tumbled to the deck, crashing only just beside the pair.

"I'm not doing it, I swear to God!"

"Make it stop!" he yelled.

Amelia was suddenly desperate to make this man shut up.

"Fine! Stop." She waved her hand at the ocean.

And suddenly the boat levelled out into the waves. After a moment more of ups and downs, the boat settled into a gentle bob.

"Oh," whispered Amelia. The cries of the injured rose louder as Mr. Snider stared at Amelia with wide eyes. Amelia rose to her feet and helped pull up the shaking Mr. Snider.

"Mr. Snider, are you all right?"

The man did little more than stare and shake his head.

"Is your money all right?"

Mr. Snider blinked purposefully, and rose a hand to his coat pocket, tapping the empty material. "I've lost the pouch. I've lost the pouch! You have my money. You witch, you did this to steal my money!"

Amelia glanced around her, no one else had noticed her commandment to the boat, and yet suddenly she felt exposed. She pushed Mr Snider against the railing.

"I am not a witch, Mr. Snider. I am only a woman."

"Damn near the same thing. I have it in my mind to tell everyone about your magic."

Amelia sighed. This time, there was no scent of berries.

"It was good doing business with you, Arnold." She gripped his shoulder and pushed him back until he once again leaned out over the water. Rage was filling her head and clearing away the fear. She would have tipped him backward and dropped him off the ship (after all, in the chaos no one would notice a drowning rat off the port side), except she was stopped by a far off voice, calling to her again and again.

"Miss Stives? Miss Stives? Miss Amelia Stives! Amelia Stives you are needed!"

She hesitated, then stepped back from the quivering Mr. Snider. Turning to the caller, she was hailed by Mr. Higgins, second Mate to Captain Lyanburrner. "Miss Stives, the Captain urgently requires your attention."

Amelia sighed again. She softened her grip and looked down into Mr. Snider's glazed eyes. "Forget about this, Arnold." She straightened his suit jacket. "We'll pick it up later. But in the meanwhile, just let it all go away."

Mr. Snider nodded, and slid down onto the deck.

Amelia straightened her cape that had miraculously stayed tied to her shoulders, checked her cleavage and quickly glanced at her nails. Well, there was nothing to be done with those until she could find herself a bath.

"Aye aye, Mr. Higgins," she replied, and set off for the Captain's quarters amongst the post-panic chaos and destruction upon the Royal Sovereign Cromarty.

***

Captain Lyanburrner was in a situation that benefited Amelia. Generally known as a well-composed man, serious and steady with his upright posture that could match a king, he hailed from Littlebrook, the same small farming village where Amelia was born and raised. The Captain, as he was referred to in the village, had found a gold coin in the cow stream as a boy, and had taken it as an omen for great things to come. Having received that omen, the Captain—then known as Edward—set out on the road for London to join the British Navy and turn himself into a man. He had faded from their memories by the time he finally returned, several decades later (just after Amelia was born) in his dark naval suit with a wife on his arm.

The Captain was going to the New World. His wife was to remain in the village with the children (who were suffering from the London air). And so it was for many, many years. Until one night while docked and loading in the Quebec City port, sunk low with his tenth shot of rum, the Captain went and impregnated a woman living along the docks (there is rumour she impregnated herself as the Captain was so far gone by that point in the evening, but either way, the result was the same). And while this young woman was most certainly not his wife, she was, most certainly, the daughter of the Shipyard Master and an obligation he was unable to ignore.

Ever since that time he travelled back and forth on the Royal Sovereign Cromarty and led a double life whenever he landed. It did, in a way, tear the Captain in two. He was a soft-hearted fellow, despite his proud manners and stern orders, who melted at the sight of his children regardless of their mothers. But ultimately the duplicity destroyed his confidence and turned the Captain into a nervous sailor, seeking comfort in the soft bosom of a drunken, rum-filled haze.

Amelia had found him leaving Littlebrook on the night of her escape. She'd thrown herself barefooted, soot-covered and blood-stained, before his carriage. She'd begged that he take her far, far away.

Everyone in the village knew Amelia was different. She would never marry since her mother passed away, and she was sole female in a house full of men who needed caring. Yet she wasn't a maid in the strictest sense. Amelia swaggered as she walked; she laughed to herself; her opinions were sharp; she mixed with the gypsies; and she would fight you, they all said, if you dared call her a witch.

Captain Lyanburrner had watched her grow up from afar. His wife had told him things about the girl's family, about the men in her family and the rumours of their abuse. The Captain's own daughters had whispered about that girl, the red-headed witch of Littlebrook.

The night Amelia stopped Captain Lyanburrner, she'd burnt the family home and barn to the ground after a final beating from her father that had gone much too far; she slipped away amongst the flames as her brothers and father battled the fire on which she hoped they choked. She had thrown herself before the carriage, and sat in the cabin across from the Captain smelling of smoke and blood while looking quietly out the black reflective window. Captain Lyanburrner had tried to soothe the girl, get her to talk about the reason for her actions but she somehow worked her magic, even on that night, and instead learned about his dependence on drink and the duplicity that had broken his spirit. It was with that knowledge she struck her bargain, and the Captain agreed to sail her to the New World.

Amelia waited on the threshold as she knocked the door frame to Captain Lyanburrner's chamber. The door was open and the Captain inside, sunk in the smell of rum. She squinted in the dim lighting of the single porthole. Tiny shards of glass crunched beneath her feet. Inside the cabin, the sound of rolling shot glasses on the table gave promise of more broken glass to come.

"Captain Lyanburrner."

He took a final gulp of drink and slammed down his latest glass, then slapped both cheeks, straightened to attention, and waved in the young witch.

"Amelia," his voice boomed as he turned toward her.

"You sent for me?" Amelia was already reaching into her pocket as she stepped into the small room, pulling out her little vial of potion.

"No, not that," he replied. "I'm fine."

More than once she'd asked Captain Lyanburrner to throw away the rum. There were times when he would agree and bottles would be tossed from his small port window into the waves, yet every time he called her to his room there was another bottle on the desk and shot glasses scattered all around. It was a superstition of the Captain's never to drink twice from the same used glass.

"Come closer," he said.

She stepped forward and stood next to him. The room was small but comfortable, apart from the broken glass that must have been from the ship's drastic rocking. The bed on which he slept (a real bed, not a hammock or cot on the floor) converted to a desk in the daytime, as it was now, and was strewn with papers, ink spots and puddles of spilt liquor.

"You're a mess." Amelia smoothed back his hair and picked a loose string from his beard.

"A damn fool of a Helmsman, that Mr. Pratchett. Can you imagine? He left his post to watch a spitting contest on the deck. He'd place a fine sum on the young man contending. Nearly capsized my boat over a damn contest! She could have gone sideways if the waves had wanted it so. We were lucky to get away with such little damage to the hull. A miracle, really."

"You should tell the passengers it was a reef, otherwise they'll make up stories—sea monsters or other useless ideas."

"I have half a mind to forbid all betting on the ship, but it'd be mutiny at this point in the journey; the whole boat is going stir crazy, they're restless and bored. Not a good combination, without doubt. But no worries, my little Amelia, land is close."

Amelia picked up the half-empty bottles and reached for the port window, unhooking the latch.

"No!" bellowed the Captain, suddenly rising up and barring the window. "We are in need of those."

Even drunk, Captain Lyanburrner had an intimidating presence. But Amelia wasn't nervous around this man. He was far too flawed, despite his officer's clothing.

She kept her hand upon the window. "You, sir, have had enough."

"Miss Stives, the bottles are not for me. Or not any longer. We have a problem and you are my solution."

Amelia turned from the open port window. "Me?"

"One of my passengers, an orphan girl I took on as a favour, has gone into labour. There is already a large crowd in Dr. Howell's infirmary, no room for a girl about to birth."

Amelia sighed as she clutched the bottles and stepped back from the window. "She's not another one of yours?" she asked.

"Absolutely not! But what can I do? Leave her in a dinghy to strike out for the nearest island? Preposterous!"

He was far too soft hearted for abandoning a woman with child. That was what had gotten him into the state he now lived.

Women and babies: Amelia hated them in a way. Her mother had been the local midwife, and Amelia had naturally followed in her place after her mother was killed.

Her father hated her mother's midwife duties, so much so that Amelia's mother delivered babies in secret, waiting until Amelia's father fell into a drunken sleep before spiriting away. After what happened between them, that night her mother learnt her father had cornered young Amelia in the outhouse ... after their battle where her father had murdered her mother with his bare hands, it fell onto Amelia to continue the secret work of delivering babies. And so she found herself elbow deep in the screams, blood, piss and shit of other women, pulling children into the world.

Amelia had seen her fill of life and death.

But it was when Amelia had yet another miscarriage of her own (triggered by a hard push onto the floor due to a burnt piece of gammon) that she truly had enough of life. With tears and giggles, she traced the whisky around the walls of the family home while her brothers and father were out in the field. She happily dropped a burning candle onto the trail of alcohol. When the men reached the smoking homestead, Amelia stood before them ready to die. With rocks and fists, they attacked the proud girl, shouting "Bloody crazy witch!" before they were forced to run to the well and attempt to quell the flames. The pain of their blows filled her with the strangest sensation, something she'd not felt for a very long time: desperation. As she stood from the ground, cradling her arm and spitting out blood, she limped off into the darkness of the night. Desperate to escape. Desperate to be free.

In Captain Lyanburrner's quarters the glasses rolled gently back and forth. Amelia leaned against the dresser and looked out toward the small window, avoiding Lyanburrner's glassy eyes.

The sky was blue and clear today. There was a fresh breeze in the air. Amelia's fingers were dirty. Her nails needed to be clipped. She would need a room to birth the girl. She would need the proper instruments, and clean sheets.

"How far is she?" asked Amelia.

"How the hell should I know?" replied the Captain.

"I need to wash myself, and I'm taking your manicure set. Have Mr. Howell give me a cot and find me a room with a window, plus plenty of washed linen. Get the cook to boil some pots of water, and sterilize the paring knives, spoons and forks before bringing them to me in a fresh cloth."

"Aye," replied the Captain, sitting in his place.

She reached again in her pocket and held out the vile. "Here, take your cure."

Eyeing her hand, he motioned for it. "This has been a damn long day." He opened Amelia's vile and shot it back. He thought it was a potion to help steady his nerves; really, it was caffeine, to raise him from his drunkenness.

"Now stand up," said Amelia.

He stood.

"And get me what I need. Go on."

The captain blinked as the potion took its effect. His fingers and toes began to tingle, and his head suddenly lost its heaviness. "Right," he replied, once again slapping his cheeks and coming to attention. Putting on his stern captain's face, he stepped out and in a booming voice, began calling orders to his crew.

Amelia turned to the dresser and lifted the lid of a small dish beneath his mirror. She took out a handful of pink candies and popped one into her mouth. It tasted like strawberries.

***

Amelia stood just outside the bathing closet where the cabin boy, young Hanson Adams was holding the bucket. She was arm deep in the hot soapy water, rubbing at her skin and scratching under her nails with the potato scrubber Cook had begrudgingly lent her.

"Is she clean?" asked Amelia.

"Not at all," replied Hanson. "And she refuses to be moved from the bottom deck. We tried to move her, but she starting biting our hands and screaming bloody murder."

Pulling her arms from the water and patting them dry, Amelia reached for one of Cook's starched white aprons, another object begrudgingly given, along with the paring knife and cutlery and large tongs, and lifted it over her mess of red hair. She tied the strings around her waist.

"Hang a privacy screen around her and open the nearest window. Bring down warm water with a bar of soap. And once Cook has boiled the knives and other things, place them in a clean—*impeccably clean*—cloth, plus a kettle of boiling water and large pot, just in case. You understand me Hanson?"

Young Hanson was soaked chin to toe with the splashing of Amelia's cleaning. He'd gotten a full view of the her chest as she leaned over and bathed her arms in the bucket, splashing onto her white gown while vigorously scrubbing at her hands. His anxiety about her rumoured powers was mixed with infatuation. Hanson supposed he was under a love spell, and it felt rather good. "Yes ma'am, of course."

"Good man, Hanson." Amelia gave him a wink as she lifted her arms and tied back her escaping mane of red hair with another piece of string. "Now go on, I'll be there in a moment."

Hanson and his bucket made a quick exit.

Amelia looked at the polished metal that was mounted to the wall. Her reflection stared back in a blurred form. She looked, well, apart from the lack of long braid, she looked and stood so very much like her own mother. It was as though she had grown into the space her mother had left behind, with a few more rough edges and bad habits.

"Will you do this with me, then?" she asked the reflection.

Amelia left the bathing area and walked along the corridor, joining the stream of men, women and children walking downward toward steerage. If people weren't in the infirmary with Dr. Howell, then they were being herded by the crew to the lower steerage decks while repairs were made up top.

Suddenly, as Amelia was about to climb down the ladder to the lowest of lower-class sleeping quarters, Mr. Snider appeared by her side.

"See what you've done?" he whispered to her. "The entire ship is a mess."

Amelia shook her head, looking past Mr. Snider at the growing line of people waiting to go down the hatch.

"I've done nothing, Mr. Snider, but choose my company poorly. It was Mr. Pratchett, the helmsman, who caused the ship to tilt. He was watching *your* spitting contest, sir."

"Where are you going?"

Amelia didn't sleep in the lowest of steerage classes; if she had, she would most certainly have found this girl long before she'd needed to deliver. Instead Amelia slept one level up amongst the higher-ranking crew. (With her knife continuously on her person, should anyone try to get familiar without an invitation.)

"There's a girl gone into labour. She won't come up, so I must go down."

And down she went into the dark space that stunk of dampness and sweat.

Weak streams of daylight flooded the open hold with a dim greyness. People milled about, visiting neighbours, watching games of checkers, laying in their hammocks. It was stuffy and warm, suffocating nearly. For two months these people had sailed in the pit of the ship. No wonder they were going stir crazy. And to force them below decks on a day with so much sunshine, it was almost cruel.

Young Hanson waved at Amelia and motioned her toward the corner where large while sheets were hung across wires.

"Over here, Miss," he called. "This is where the ladies change, normally, but it's just big enough for the cot."

Through the thick warmth and whispers of the crowd, Amelia made her way to the corner.

"She's right inside, Miss."

"Thank you, Hanson. And won't you please have a word with Captain Lyanburrner? Tell him that if I can't move the girl, then these people need to be let back on deck. It's far too crowded in here for birthing. There's not enough air."

Hanson twisted the tail of his jacket and looked through the growing mass of people.

"I'll see what I can do, Miss. But it's a real mess up top."

"I know Hanson, but please ask them to be quick."

The boy ran off toward the hatch, jumping through the games and conversation, cutting through the flood of people coming downward to shimmy his way up the steps.

Amelia took a deep breath. She pulled back the curtain.

"Who are you?" snapped a young voice.

"Who am I?" replied Amelia. "I'm your salvation young miss, and don't you forget it."

***

There was a growing buzz in the dark lower hull of the ship as man, woman and child watched the sheets that hung in the corner.

"Should we intrude?"

"It's not our business."

"That poor girl."

"I hear the midwife's a witch."

"Any bets on the baby's sex?"

"Any bets if the baby lives?"

"I heard she nearly drowned the ship!"

"Amelia's no witch."

"You can't see past her bosom."

"And what about the other one? She's no picnic either."

"Oh! They're at it again!"

Marie, preferably known as Minou, had had enough of the red-headed woman. She'd been dragged from her corner, stripped of her clothes and forced—literally woman-handled between each and every contraction—to scrub with a bar of soap and wet rag in places one would never mention in polite society. It'd been over two months since Minou had last bathed and the dirt was now condensed into dark freckles across her pale French-heritage skin. And even then, two months earlier, she'd just scrubbed her arms, neck and ears and washed her dark hair with a bar of soap, hoping that the judge would take pity on her despite her biting off a piece of his ear, and not send her to prison or worse, a hanging. But of course he couldn't do that, could he? She was pregnant with his child.

Instead he forced her onto this godforsaken ship, and told her never to come back. Not to write, not to contact his wife or children, not to maintain any association of any kind to the De Bourgh family again in her life, and had shoved into her hand a parcel of money wrapped in his youngest daughter's pink rose purse before sending her on board the ship. Minou had once hoped the judge would relocate her to a happy cottage on the edge of town, visit her rarely and keep her comfortable for life. That was the entire purpose of getting pregnant by him. But when she discovered he would do nothing of the kind, the rage filled her head to toe. When he later knocked on her attic chamber door in the dead of night for the last time, she flew at him and attacked, jaws chomping hard.

Since then she'd skipped meals, jumped in place, prayed to God, but the baby inside of her insisted upon being born.

"You think I'm nothing, just some gutter rat with a baby in her stomach," Minou spat out the remains of the soap taste that lingered in her mouth. "But I'm far more than a gutter rat. I was a lady's maid, I'll have you know, and when I get back to England, there's going to be hell to pay. I'll do just fine. You judge me, but you don't know me. I'll be just fine."

"I have no doubt," replied Amelia. She was sterilizing the utensils and knives with the third pot of boiling water she'd had to order from Hanson; the first two were kicked over when she'd tried to change Minou into a clean night gown. "Lord knows that men love wild creatures."

Minou gave a bitter laugh. "Men love anything that lets them."

Amelia sighed and dropped onto the stool beside the girl, waiting for the next contraction and chorus of screams. Her white apron and the dress beneath were soaked from the effort of cleaning. This 'Minou' was more pig-headed and stubborn than Amelia herself.

And yet. Yet there was something. Something about Minou's dark eyes that occasionally, just occasionally opened wide with fear before an oncoming contraction. The way her hands clutched at that little pink purse as though it contained her entire life. Amelia had a sense Minou wasn't quite what she appeared to be, she wasn't brave, or certain, or even in control. It was a state of being Amelia knew very well.

"No," replied Amelia, sliding to the floor so she could rest her arms upon the girl's cot. "That's not true. Some women beg their men to love them, to be kind and give devotion. But no. Men will not love anything that lets them. They are quite in control of that particular emotion."

"Less controlled with others."

Amelia laughed. She looked up at Minou and the two girls, with no more than a few years between them, finally smiled at one another.

"You are having a girl," said Amelia.

"How do you know?" asked Minou.

"She feels like a girl, that's all, and I always guess right."

Minou shook her head and leaned back onto the boat hull against which her cot was aligned. "She or he, it doesn't matter. I can't keep this baby. But I hadn't planned on being on this ship either; it's not so easy to drop a child on the steps of a church when you're in the middle of an ocean."

She said it so easily, as though there was no attachment. Amelia flashed back to her most recent miscarriage in the barn. She remembered the warmth and stickiness of the blood, the pain that twisted her from the inside. Of course it wasn't an intentional pregnancy. Her father never intended to get her pregnant, though he had several times. But still, it was her baby. They had all been her babies.

"You would rather leave her to the ocean?"

Minou shook her head and stared through the window at the water. "If she were born a mermaid, I'd slip her out this porthole and hope she'd swim away."

Suddenly Minou's eyes widened in a jolt of fear. Amelia slid closer and took Minou's hand, turning her head away as Minou's moans began once more. The contractions were coming more closely together. The baby was getting nearer to delivery.

There was a knock at the curtain. Or rather, there was an 'ahem.'

"Ahem."

Minou was in the midst of a mumbled, moaning prayer, and Amelia was between the girl's legs after much protest, kicks and what was swelling into a black eye on Amelia's face, measuring the dilation. "You're not there yet, Minou," she told her patient. "But not long to go."

"But this is crazy. This is insane," said Minou, glancing down from her conference with God. "How is one woman to withstand this—" And her eyes went wide. Amelia gripped the girl's hand, and right before Minou's pain built up into screams, there came another, "Ahem" from behind the curtain.

"Not now!" shouted Amelia over the rising wails.

"Miss Stives!"

It was Mr. Snider. Slimy, sleazy, scheming Mr. Snider.

Minou burst into full-on shouting and cursing. The girl could shout, that was without doubt. She could have been opera performer with lungs like those. Suddenly, Mr. Arnold Snider jerked back the curtain with his chest puffed out and his hat tilted forward.

"What is going on in here, ladies?" he demanded.

Amelia stood from her patient and pushed Snider full-on in the chest with such force that he tripped over a loose pair of boots and fell down into the crowd of huddled women.

"I said not now, Mr. Snider!" Amelia shouted, and then she hesitated, just for an instant too long, as she noticed the ladies.

"Oh, no," she muttered.

Helping up Mr. Snider, the women nudged him back towards Amelia as they crowded inward to stop just sort of the curtain's interior with Amelia on its threshold. Mr. Snider stared at Amelia with wide eyes, most likely certain she was going to pull out her knife any moment, and cut away his purse strings.

"Well, Mr. Snider," said Martha Buckets, a round woman with six young children on board and one husband who was perpetually seasick. "Go on and ask her."

Mr. Snider cleared his throat. He opened his mouth. No words came out. He tried to clear his throat, but was still unable to speak. The speech he had prepared about "the decency of ladies and inappropriate language, and, oh, by the way, are you really a witch?" could not come out. In fact, he could hardly breathe at all.

Amelia stood there as Minou's cries settled into a quiet whimpering, and blinked at Mr. Snider.

"Augh, Augh," was all he could manage. It was as though two hands had circled his throat and were chocking away his words.

"Blimey, she has stolen his voice!" declared Martha Buckets, stamping her foot.

"She's stolen his voice," echoed the ladies. "She's a witch," they began to say.

"Don't be ridiculous," Amelia replied. "He's just had the breath knocked out of him. And what is this? Clucking together as though you've never known a birth in your lives? And how do you expect a man to react when he sees this sort of thing? It's not natural for his mind to digest." And she stamped her foot before continuing.

When all else failed, Amelia had learnt in her life, a person can depend upon the shaming of others.

"Matthew Buckets, get your wife in order. Thomas Lewis, take Mrs. Lewis away. Jefferson Hinkins, get over here and talk some sense to your woman. Gerald Bumpkin, leave off that game of chess and pay attention. Gentlemen, talk sense to your wives! And Mr. Snider," she poked the gagging man in the centre of his chest, "if I hear you taking bets on the survival of this baby or woman, I will personally see to it that you are left at the nearest and most abandoned tip of this continent that can be managed. And you can walk the remainder of your journey. Maybe the giant bears and wolves would appreciate your winnings as an appetizer to your backside?"

She turned to the women and stuck out her chin as far as it would go, stamping her foot once more.

"Ladies, leave us in peace! And Hanson..."

The cabin boy was hustling down the steerage ladder with a quarter-filled bottle of rum in his hand for Minou. He stopped mid hustle.

"Yes, Miss?"

"Tell the Captain we're stir crazy down here. He needs to let these people up immediately."

Hanson jumped with attention.

"Immediately?" he asked across the stuffy dark room filled with watching eyes.

"Just get these people out, Hanson."

"Yes ma'am," he replied, and hustled back up the hatch.

"Hanson!"

"Yes ma'am?"

"Leave the rum."

He made his way over to her with the bottle, then hurried back through the crowd and up through the hatch.

"Now, ladies," she glanced back at the huddle of women who were starting to drift further apart. "Please, let me do my job in peace. And no, I'm not a witch. But yes, your husbands would much rather sleep with me—and no wonder!"

And with that, she pulled the curtain shut.

"Well, the nerve," muttered Martha Buckets. "Let her have seven children and see how well her body fares."

And with that, Amelia could feel them all dispersing, wandering back to their men.

Minou was flat on the cot, laying back and staring up at the dark rafters of the lower deck. Her hair was scattered across the pillow, slipping over toward the floor. Sweat ran in drips across her body, and her chest rose up and down as she tried to catch her breath. And yet, Amelia was amazed to see, Minou wore the slightest trace of a smile.

"What's that then?" asked Amelia.

"Mr. Snider, he sounded like a frog." Minou giggled between her breath of recovery.

"Well, he looks like a rat. Why not sound like a frog too?"

Together they laughed softly.

"I wasn't sure it would work. I've been so off lately, and can hardly work any spells with this one inside me. I couldn't even curse the judge. Had to bite his ear off, instead."

"What do you mean?"

Amelia took a swig of rum and passed the bottle to Minou.

Minou looked at Amelia and took her in for a moment. Amelia's left eye was circled with a purple tinge from where Minou's heel had connected, but through the swelling was a look Minou had not often seen in her life. It was compassion.

"I'm a witch," Minou finally replied, releasing her lips into a wide grin that spread across her face. "Or, well, I do spells and such around the house and in my own time. They *normally* work."

"Shh, now. Don't go saying that too loudly. My great grandmother was tried and drowned for being a witch."

Minou shook her head. "We're special, Amelia. You and I are a special sort of people."

"I'm not a witch," replied Amelia.

"You feel things no one else does. And you know things too. No one expects a woman to know so many things. And me? I cast spells that normally work. That is, they did until I became pregnant. Only today I tried to sink the ship as I went into labour."

"You tried to—"

"But it didn't work, obviously." She pointed at her pregnant belly. "This one keeps stopping me. She and I aren't meant for each other, our magic doesn't mix. I can't work anything with her inside me. She's powerful too, just like us." Minou smirked. "But that Mr. Snider had it coming. I've never liked him."

Minou stopped to have a sip of rum.

"And you want to know what makes us most special?" asked Minou.

Amelia had trouble taking Minou seriously. The girl couldn't have been older than fourteen years and looked a total mess, and yet she talked so well and had ideas far beyond her age.

Amelia shrugged. "What makes us special?" she asked.

"We follow our hearts, even when it leads us to trouble. Not everyone can do that sort of thing, believe me I know. None of Judge De Bourgh's family could ever do what they pleased. Everyone just followed along."

Minou pointed to herself, lifting her head up from the pillow.

"But not me. I know how to dream. One time, I found a card in the stationary shop window that was written in this beautiful looping writing that rose up from the paper and was traced with gold paint. It read, "Follow your heart and you'll have no regrets." I bought that card and tore off the other half that was wishing happy birthday. On the back of the remaining piece, I wrote myself a letter from St. Claire herself."

Amelia removed the sheet and looked between the girl's legs, measuring her with her hand. That last contraction had been powerful. It was a wonder Minou could cast a spell between all her cramping.

It won't be long now, thought Amelia. This baby was going to come, and then what would become of it? What to do with an unwanted baby born in the hull of a ship, travelling to a place where no one has history or obligation?

Amelia folded back the sheet and sat on the ground, resting her arms once again on the cot. She lay her head down against Minou's side.

"Do you know about St. Claire?" asked Minou.

"Claire is my middle name," replied Amelia.

"Mine too," answered Minou. "We could almost be sisters, then."

Amelia thought about this girl beside her and how she'd cussed and scratched and kicked when Amelia had first entered the tent—stripping Minou of her filthy gown, scrubbing off the layers and layers of dirt from her skin, wrestling her into the white sheets and receiving a black eye in the process. Did sisters fight so ferociously?

"St. Claire was this young Italian girl," continued Minou, "who was from a very rich family. She had everything she could ever want, but you know those Italians."

No, Amelia didn't know any Italians.

"Damn it!"

Minou was struck with another wave of contractions, cursing out against the world and the inhumanity of birth, tears rolling down her cheeks. Amelia patted the young woman's forehead with a cold, wet cloth. As the contraction faded, Minou took several long pulls of rum.

"Claire was meant to be married," continued Minou. "That was her only purpose in life: to marry rich and make her family happy. But when she was about eighteen, she heard the words of St. Francis and fell passionately in love with God himself, and stole away in the night to join the priest. Francis cut her hair and she was then taken to a convent where she devoted her life to the strict practice. Her family tried to bring her back, but she refused. She chose. It was her choice. Not every woman dares to make a choice."

"True," agreed Amelia. She thought about her mother who was married to her father when she was only fourteen years old. Minou was the very same age, and they had similar long dark hair too—only her mother's was braided, always braided and tied with a ribbon. Her father had been fifteen years older and he'd never truly loved her mother. In the end he killed her with his own bare hands.

If Amelia could have strangled a person with her mind like Minou, things would have been very different.

"Not every choice leads to good things," whispered Amelia.

"Oh," gasped Minou. This time there was no screaming. Instead, Minou was biting into her own arm and trying to contain the pain.

Amelia checked beneath the sheet at the dilation. It was time. She looked up at Minou who seemed to be hunkering down instinctively, getting ready to push.

It had always seemed impossible, impossible that something like a child could squeeze through a slit in a woman's body. But here again it was about to happen. Despite the mumbled prayers that were issuing in a steady stream from Minou, begging this not to happen, she was beginning to change shape. Amelia lifted Minou forward, and helped her crouch upon the cot, stuffing a bundle of sheets beneath the girl to capture the blood and liquid.

The baby was coming. With each push, the crying Minou opened wider and wider.

"You're doing well!" cried Amelia.

"I'm not doing well!"

"You're doing very well!"

"Lord save me!"

"You're getting there."

"Take it away! Take it all away!"

"Focus, Minou. Stop your hysterics and focus. Push!"

There was a fire inside Minou, ripping her apart.

"There she is, there she is, I can see her hair!"

Minou was plain screaming now.

"Once more, Minou. Once more."

"Ahem."

"Come on, now, you can do it."

"Ahem."

"Mr. Snider!" shouted Amelia. "Disappear right now, or I'll curse your entire lineage!"

With one final prayer to God, Minou pushed. She pushed and she pushed again.

"Here now! I'm dabbing her off. Here now, here! I can see her face. Minou, I can see her little face. Just a few more pushes. You see her?" asked Amelia. "That's her head. That's your little girl's head. Now only a few more pushes."

"I'm not ready."

"This was your choice, Minou. Now you push through."

Amelia lightly tugged as the baby's arms became apparent. Bit by bit, she was able to slide the child out further. Then, as Minou gave one last push, the infant came loose into Amelia's hands and she lifted it out as the little bloodied thing took a pause, than began to cry.

"You hear her? She's out! She is out! You did it, Minou. You got her out."

Amelia was laughing as she lifted the baby towards the young witch and ex-lady's maid, resting the crying baby against Minou's chest.

"Lord, she's got lungs like you, Minou."

Minou shook her head, tears soaking her lashes, cheeks and dark sweat-matted hair. She kept shaking her head. "No. No, take her away. I cannot have her."

"Minou, she's yours."

"No. Take her off me." The young girl's pale arms grasped at the red, slippery baby and tried to pass it back to Amelia.

"Here," Amelia said, taking the baby from Minou's shaking hands and holding it against her own bosom. "I'll get her cleaned up, and then you'll see."

Minou simply shook her head. "No, I can't keep her. I won't."

Resting the baby on the edge of the cot, Amelia pulled her knife from the apron pocket—the same knife she'd carried since the night her mother had been murdered, not that she's ever in her life had the courage to use it. She couldn't raise it against her father, not when he came to her bed and had his way, not even on herself when she lost the baby, not on anyone until this moment.

Amelia blinked back the tears. Then smiled down at the loudly crying creature. "This won't hurt one bit," she whispered.

"No," squeaked a voice behind her, then louder, "No, you will not kill that child, witch!" Mr. Snider pulled back the curtain.

"Mr. Snider! This is ridiculous."

"Were you watching this entire time," asked Minou. Her blush exploded into a red bloom across her entire body.

"I saw everything," declared Mr. Snider. He stepped gingerly into the curtained area.

They were huddled in the tiny space, Amelia, Minou, the baby and Mr. Snider. The baby continued to cry, though more gently now. Amelia passed her back to Minou. "Dear, you may not want this baby, but it needs to feed. Try and help her latch on."

"Hoping to see some more, Mr. Snider?" asked Minou, as she took the child into her arms.

Minou unbuttoned the front of her nightgown, and Amelia helped her position the baby for latching. Mr. Snider turned away from the women so that his nose was against the curtain.

He cleared his throat. "Young lady, this witch is trying to kill that infant. She wants to use its heart in a spell to sink the entire ship and take away all the gold on board."

Amelia shook her head. "For all your brains, you are an idiot, Mr. Snider," she replied, remaining beside the mother and baby. Again she took out the knife, this time showing it to Minou.

Minou pulled back. "Amelia, you wouldn't hurt her, would you?"

"Miss," continued Mr. Snider, "I am certain we could sell this baby for a fine price in the New World. I have connections. There are families who cannot conceive, rich families in logging and trade. You need not kill the baby or leave it at the church. We could make a pretty sum for a healthy child."

"Mr. Snider," snapped Amelia. "If I didn't need this knife, I would use it to stab you in the leg right now."

Amelia held up the chord so that Minou could see. "In a way, you are still connected."

Minou lay back as the baby continued to suckle. She glanced at Mr. Snider, who was twisting his hat in his hands. "Thank you for your concern, Mr. Snider. But I have enough money. This baby will not be sold."

"Leave, Mr. Snider." Amelia turned and glared a him.

He didn't move. "We could make a tidy sum, young lady. Let me know if you change your mind before landing."

Amelia returned the knife to her pocket and stood up, looking him square in the eye. She gave him her warm, summer-fields smile and glowing expression (despite the purple eye). He breathed in her scent that, despite being mixed with blood and body odour, reminded him of hay fields that stretched out toward the horizon. He could feel the breeze of the land sweep down across him, pulling at his inner soul. He thought of home; he thought of England.

Mr. Snider gave a dreamy sigh.

"Go away, Mr. Snider," whispered Amelia very gently. "Go away, and don't bother with us any longer."

"Yes," he replied, nodding quite happily. "Yes, I will do that."

And away he walked, till somehow he found himself on the upper decks, and couldn't remember at all what he'd been doing just moments before. Not that it mattered one bit, another spitting contest was to be arranged, and lo and behold, there was land in sight.

With the steerage deck now empty, Amelia left the curtain open and returned to her place beside Minou, who was nursing the baby.

"So you will keep her?" she asked.

Minou shook her head. "No, I can't take care of her properly. I can't even take care of myself. But perhaps you might?"

"Me?"

"You."

"I can't keep this baby."

"She's meant for you."

"She's meant for *you*. I can't even have children. Not after what happened to me."

In the empty steerage deck, through the small open portholes, a breeze came through and brought with it the fresh sea air. It was cool against their sweat-drenched bodies, and filled their lungs.

"I love that," whispered Amelia

"Love what?"

"The wind, the air—there's so much hope." Amelia paused, looking at her finger nails, then laughed to herself. "Mostly, I like to imagine it's my mother's hand stroking my cheek like she did while alive, and we'd lay in the fields on the nights when the boys and my papa went to the pub without us. We'd spread out a blanket, and she would have me snuggle into her side while wrapping one arm around me. Then, she'd point out the stars while telling me stories about Heaven. She'd stroke my hair, and stroke my cheeks, and I'd snuggle into her when the night set in with its chill."

Minou took in a deep breath. "What was your mother's name?"

"Anne."

"She sounds like she was a very good mother. Better than I would ever be."

Amelia shrugged and picked up another clean sheet. She reached toward the baby's head and gently wiped away the remaining mucus.

"She was a very good mother."

"I never knew mine," replied Minou. "She left me with the nuns. They were kind, but they were not mothers. They named me Marie after the Virgin Mother. I changed it to Minou, because who can take that much pressure to be good?"

Amelia laughed and leaned back.

Minou kissed her daughter on the head. Then looked up at Amelia.

"I'm so tired, Amelia."

"Here." Amelia gently accepted the baby from Minou's arms, and she held the tiny child against her chest and rocked her very gently.

Minou gave a weak smile. "I'm going back to England with the next ship out. I can't take her with me. A girl will never get a position in a decent household with a baby in tow. I have no family to leave her with, either."

Minou had no connections, no assets except the scant sum of money in her velvet pink purse, and with all the possible infection on a sea voyage and dangers, it was a bad place for a new born. Amelia on the other hand knew the Captain, and she had earned a tidy sum over the past two months in her dealings with Mr. Snider.

Maybe she could take care of the baby girl for a little while, until she found the baby a proper home? But to take a child from its mother?

"Where's your sense of responsibility?" whispered Amelia.

"I have a huge sense of responsibility," replied Minou.

"It's not the way of things. I've lost my own babies; every time I lose them. The loss of a child is haunting."

"Amelia, you haven't lost this one. She's right here and she's for you. I know it in my heart. Don't you know it?"

Amelia thought that perhaps she did. Perhaps she was destined for this little girl, this little Claire who would follow her heart. She took out the knife once again, and, with the baby still in the crook of her arm, she cut the cord in a sharp pull, clamping it with a clip from her apron. Amelia wrapped the baby in a fresh sheet.

"Coo coo," she whispered.

Minou emptied her purse of coins, slipping them into her boots that were beside the cot, and then took out the card on which she'd written a letter to herself from St. Claire. She kissed it once, then showed it to Amelia, "A letter for her, when she's older, so she always remembers to follow her heart." Then, slipping it back into the small pink purse, she lay the purse beside Amelia. "Here, so she has something from her mother. Something to know that she is connected, even though we're apart."

"I'll tell her all about you, her mother the young witch who once gave me a kick in the eye."

Minou pinched her lips.

"No, don't tell her anything," she replied. "Just raise her and love her. I'm in the card, and in the writing. We can all be connected without her ever realizing."

Amelia nodded.

"I have the perfect name for you," whispered Amelia to the baby. "Marianne Claire." She looked up at Minou, whose head was on the pillow and eyes were closed. "What do you think, Minou?"

Through closed eyes, tears rolled down Minou's cheek. "It's perfect," she replied.

"Are you certain about this?" asked Amelia. She looked down at little Marianne Claire in her arms, wondering what might be in store for this tiny, delicate person. She knew she should make Minou take this child, make her raise the baby and take it back to England if necessary, but Marianne Claire was already in her arms. Amelia held the baby against her, stroking the little cheek like the breeze that passed around them.

"Really, wholly certain?" Amelia asked again.

Minou opened her eyes. The breeze continued to pour in between them, filling the space with freshness. Minou took a deep breath, then looked back at Amelia and the baby. "Not every choice leads to good things, but some of them do. It is a privilege in itself to be able to choose and Amelia, it is my privilege to choose you."

Again, Amelia nodded. She picked up the velvet pouch with the card of St. Claire and slipped it into her pocket. She was going to do this. She was going to start a new life, in a new world, with a new baby. It was her choice. Deep down inside her, resting in a place that no person could touch and time could not wither, she was surprised to feel an overwhelming sense of certainty.

"Yes," she replied quietly, "everything will be all right. You'll see. Everything is going to be okay, one way or another."

"So be it." whispered Minou.

"Amen," replied Amelia.

They sent out their prayer like a pebble from Heaven that splashes in the ocean. In a gathering circular wave, their words were carried beyond the ship, beyond the ocean, beyond the shore, beyond the ends of the earth and beyond space and time itself: rippling, swelling, and crashing from one life to another, and another, and another. Yet, at its epicentre, as the ripples spread further and further apart, were the beats of their hearts, their moment of love.

Amelia leaned into the baby and ticked her tiny nose.

"Coo, coo," whispered Amelia, kissing her little girl's head. She closed her eyes and breathed in the child's musty scent. In that moment, with a flash of recollection, she tasted strawberries, felt the pouring sunshine, and smelled with a heart-warming familiarity the warming bales of hay.

Epilogue

The beginning, middle and end, 1807

In an open strawberry field just by the cottage in Littlebrook, England, new born Amelia Claire Stives peered out from her tightly wrapped blanket with day-old eyes. She looked at sights she would eventually come to know as the long blue of the sky, the box brown of country barns, and the green lush of thriving crops. Amelia blinked against the breeze, and turned toward the warmth of her mother's chest. She heard the hum of a lullaby, and felt the stroke of a braid tip that swept across her nose.

Soon she began to slide into sleep, where she would dream of the brightest brights, and highest highs, and a southerly swish to fly her around the world and beyond. But before her dream-filled mind could take her away to new adventures that rippled with love and echoing voices of a name she did not yet understand, one voice above all stood out as it whispered near her ear. It was a voice she'd known all along, the voice that had been her world before all else existed. It was her mother.

"Hold on tight," spoke the gentleness and care, "because this moment is the beginning, middle and end of a story. You, little one, my precious Amelia Claire, are now part of a never-ending adventure."

Thank you so much for reading Claire Never-Ending. *It's been a pleasure sharing the Claires with you. As you'll see in the acknowledgements, a lot of love went into supporting this book. And speaking of book-love, this is a self-published novel, so it depends on recommendations from readers like you to help it thrive. If it's okay with you, I'd like to use this space to share a thought or two on spreading the word. Thanks so much.*

xoxo,
Catherine

A Note from the Author on Word-of-Mouthing

If done while sipping warm tea (Earl Grey is my suggestion) and eating dark chocolate, word-of-mouthing can be a pleasurable experience. It can range from conversation with friends, writing an online review, sharing in social media, or even bonding with your local bookseller as you mention *Claire Never-Ending*.

Word-of-mouthing is a great way to follow the reading experience. Another fun thing? News-lettering. That's when you sign up for my newsletter at www.CatherineBrunelle.com (scan below) so I can keep you in the loop for *Claire Never-Ending* developments, as well as other writing adventures. You can also follow along at www.facebook.com/CatherineBrunelleWrites.

Again, thank you so much for all of your support!

The Acknowledgements

Many people supported this book, even if not directly involved with *Claire Never-Ending*. Here are only a few of many.

My family—Mom, Dad, Dan, Karen, JP, and Trish—for the constant support, laughter, cups of tea, guidance, and delicious meals. As well as Anna, László, Anita, and Berci—who are masters of unconditional love and taught my husband very well in that aspect. And my extended family: from my mom's side with their support, frozen food, and years of gatherings; to my dad's side who are so far away but nevertheless remain supportive (which is really quite fantastic considering we've hardly met in person).

To my much-loved writing group—Ulrike, Kate, Carole and James—who have stuck by this book, and stuck by me during hard times, and probably deserve a page to themselves for all they have given toward this novel in terms of review.

To the library in Southampton, my point of calm in the storm with Nick, Margaret, Barbro, Marianne and Marcus.

As well as those who gave food and visits including Laura, Denise, Eric and Nadia. And also to Camille for the clarity. Not to forget my fantastic friends in the real world and online who have tweeted, commented, messaged, hugged, visited, postcarded, and cheered me forward.

To those who helped with producing this novel. Ian for the design, edits from my amazing friend Catherine (along with more tea-drinking), syntax with the talented Denise, Julie with her quick save in copy-proofing, Lou Truss for the photograph, Elizabeth for ebook guidance, the University of Southampton for my confidence, and Zsolt for his typesetting.

To those who supported my Kickstarter campaign: In so many ways (several being quite surprising), you helped this book happen. It was an overwhelming response. This book is here because of your support. You've given a gift that goes further than I can adequately express.

Lastly, and closest to my heart, to my husband, Zsolt. Thank you for believing in your wife. She believes in you too.

Catherine Brunelle is a Canadian novelist and blogger. Born in Canada, she met the love of her life in France, studied creative writing in England, swam Lake Balaton in Hungary, ate gelato in Rome, lived a summer in Jasper, and currently calls Ottawa her home. Happily married, she is busy typing on her laptop while attempting to carpe that diem with her best friend and husband, Zsolt.

If you want to read more from Catherine or get in touch, you can read her at www.CatherineBrunelle.com, like her Facebook Page, or tweet her at @bumpyboobs.

Made in the USA
Charleston, SC
31 January 2015